Clerise of Haiti

Marie-Thérèse Labossière Thomas

CLERISE OF HAITI is a work of fiction. While names of public figures may appear in the story, none of the other characters are real. They are either the product of the author's imagination or used fictitiously.

Working title: *A Haitian Experience*. Portions of this book appeared in slightly different form as *Coming of Age in Les Cayes* and *Learning the Facts of Life* on Pikliz.com, and in French and Creole as *Manman Mwen* in Haiti en Marche.

Cover art: Marie-Thérèse Labossière Thomas
Graphics: Kim Weiler

Publisher:

Trilingual Press • Près Trileng • Presse Trilingue

PO Box 391206, Cambridge, MA 02139 (USA)
Tel: 617-331-2269
E-mail: trilingualpress@tanbou.com

ISBN 13 : 978-0-9745821-8-4
ISBN 10 : 0-9745821-8-2

Library of Congress Control Number: 2010935960

Printed in the United States

First edition : October 2010

For Man'Alice, Toche, and Oscar

who nurtured my dreams

and to

all the Clerises past and present

for better tomorrows

AUTHOR'S NOTE

The word *restavèk*, which now describes young Haitian domestic workers, was considered pejorative at the time of the story, and only appears in context. Instead, the then-common expression *timoun kay* has been used in this book.

Contents

PROLOGUE

Refugee Camp, USA

1977

"What have they done to Clerise, my mother, my beautiful mother?" the girl screamed. "*Oh* Clerise, my mother, *manman mwen!*"

Cooling her face and arms on the tall metallic fence, Nicole remembered. Days had gone by on the boat across the sea and in the refugee camp, when she just went through the motions for survival, without thinking. The recent past was a blur, with sudden flashes of painful memories quickly repressed.

Now under the hot sun, feeling the coolness of the metal, she remembered. The stillness of the dark night.... The terrible car ride from the house in Port-au-Prince.... A burst of machine-gun fire when they stopped in the woods of Delmas... the moans... the pleadings... the harsh voices.... Another car ride with death toward the nearby mountains of Boutilliers.... The man's corpse propped sitting against his wife... hideous jokes... pleadings and threats.... Clerise's hand holding hers tightly.

They finally arrived in Boutilliers and were ordered out of the car. One of the armed Tonton Macoutes watched her mother and the other woman as they were forced to carry the body to the trunk. When the lid closed on her husband's corpse, the woman screamed, only to be slapped and ordered to shut up. Numb with horror and fear, only half-hearing the sadistic jokes of the machine-gun-carrying Tonton Macoute left to watch her, Nicole witnessed the two women perform the grisly task.

Now, they were herded back toward her, covered with blood in the moonlight. The Tonton Macoutes continued to plan loudly, and the one watching Nicole pushed her out to stand at the edge of a deep ditch. She faced the car with her back to the void, to be raped first, the other woman next, her mother made to watch before they would all be killed.

The moon peeked from behind the clouds as the women walked toward Nicole with blood on their hands and clothes. The younger one had tears glistening on her face and sobbed softly. Clerise, silent, seemed calm as she advanced. She only looked at Nicole, her daughter, and appeared not to hear the obscene exchanges of the Tonton Macoutes. The women were getting closer to Nicole now, almost side by side. Suddenly, Clerise lunged, pushed Nicole down the ditch. There were bursts of machine-gun fire, a scream, then another, confusion, swearing, more machine-gun fire, feet running down the ditch, other shots, the frightening impact of projectiles nearby, more swearing, now up the ditch, and all the while a desperate flight in the night, through ditches and woods, down mountains, following a stream bed toward Port-au-Prince.

Dawn came and Nicole washed quickly in the river. She heard voices coming toward her and saw country women on the way to the market place. She told them that she was lost after a fight with her boyfriend and trying get home to Carrefour. The women showed her the way.

She arrived before daybreak at her true destination in Martissant, a few miles closer than the neighborhood that she had mentioned. In the relative safety of her friends' home, she numbly told her story, too shocked to feel anything but an immense tiredness. Exhausted and spent, she fell into a deep sleep and forgot that she had become a fugitive overnight.

PART I

Clerise

CHAPTER 1

Les Cayes, Haïti

This is the story of Clerise, my mother, as I learned and tried to understand it; a story of tears and laughter, of pain and survival. This is a story of many voices.

1947

It was a typical day in Les Cayes, warm but not hot, a time to be outdoors. On the way to the pier, the many windows of the houses captured the still-bright sunlight. Here and there, palm fronds swayed in the distance, and the town's life, leisurely and slow paced, flowed with the tropical breeze.

Small groups sitting on porches and balconies conversed, enjoyed the weather, or idly watched the few passers-by. Among these, three children dressed with casual elegance approached the Kafou Orèl intersection with a woman and an adolescent girl in plain clean clothes.

"Clerise, move faster with that child! Pilou, will you stop it? I'll tell your mother when we get home!" the woman, Ermance, said.

"Pilou, let's go," pleaded Clerise, the adolescent girl, as she struggled to hold the boy's hand.

"I don't want to stop there. I don't want to kiss all the old ladies," he protested.

"If you continue," Ermance replied, "I'll tell your mother that you have been naughty again this afternoon. This time, I know your dad will spank you. Now behave. We're getting near Miss Laura's home."

Pilou dragged his feet in sullen silence as he finally managed to free his hand from Clerise's hold. He kept pulling his arm as far away from her as he could while they began to cross the street. "Miss Ermance," Clerise complained, "Pilou doesn't want to hold my hand."

The oldest child, Rose-Marie, intervened. "Pilou, just let me hold your hand. If we take more time, there'll be more people to greet."

Already eight years old, Rose-Marie could walk safely by herself. However, to go to the pier, she was still under the supervision of Ermance who, trying to speed matters at the moment, had decided to carry three-year-old Danny.

There, at the next intersection sat Miss Laura, relaxing on her rocking chair and surveying the afternoon activities. Miss Laura was the informal leader of a group made of her three sisters, her brother-in-law, and a few other ladies and gentlemen who, each afternoon by the close of business, gathered on her porch to update each other's knowledge of what had happened in town since the day before. Ranging from lower middle age to respectable maturity, they usually appeared to be involved in conversation, or just relaxing on their rockers or straight-back chairs. However, one of their main activities was to observe passers-by in great detail, greeting, waving, or nodding as appropriate, only to wait for the opportunity to exchange all applicable comments as soon as the concerned party was out of earshot.

Miss Laura's place was on the way to the pier, and when the offspring of her relatives and friends went to play there, they had to stop to greet her and her guests. The children submitted more or less reluctantly to that ritual, until they were old enough to go unescorted. Then, they made sure to walk on the other side of the street, and only waved when they passed. Such behavior was the subject of countless complaints to parents, not only from Miss Laura, but also from others who, like her, held informal gatherings on their porches.

With the attention focused at the moment on Pilou's lack of cooperation, Ermance and the children had not noticed another group coming up the street, toward them.

"*Pst, pst,* Ermance!" yelled Antoinette, the maid with the approaching group of Visel children.

Everybody turned and waved, while Pilou's mood changed immediately. He let go of Rose-Marie's hand and grabbed Clerise's, so that she could take him to meet his cousin, five-year-old Ti-Louis Visel, whom everyone called Junior.

"Let's wait here," Ermance said, motioning to Antoinette to walk faster. "Pilou, be quiet!"

Ermance and Antoinette, Pilou and Junior, Rose-Marie and her cousin Michèle Visel warmly exchanged greetings and smiles. They broke into groups and carried on private conversations, the two boys in front, the girls behind, and Antoinette with Ermance, who carried Danny, both providing general supervision.

Alone, followed Clerise, the twelve-year-old *timoun kay*, the little domestic worker, whose duty was to assist as needed in the care of the Juin children. An unassuming girl of average height and build with thick hair neatly gathered in three short braids, Clerise wore a plain blue dress and locally made *karyoka* sandals. Since she did not have anything else to do at the moment, she was happy to catch whatever she could hear of the two older maids' discreet dialogue.

"Let's hurry before more people arrive at Miss Laura's," Ermance said. "They ask so many questions, we'll never get out of there. I hope they're already busy talking. Pilou is giving me trouble."

"I just had to make that one stop up the street with the children. Thank God, they're not as bad there as they are at Miss Laura's!" Antoinette exclaimed. "Quick, let me tell you," she continued, "see the guys at the lamppost -- don't turn around now -- but, when we passed them, they were whistling at a couple of girls in TIGHT dresses. Of course, since they are Miss So-and-So, they can get away with it. Let you and me, poor maids, try something like that and you'll hear!"

Ermance chuckled, covering her mouth. "We should really get serious now," she told Antoinette. "Here we are!" Then, she quickly turned around. "Clerise! Now what are you waiting for? Go and take care of the children. Don't you see we're getting near Miss Laura's? Keep an eye on Pilou."

Miss Laura was ready and smiling. "Good afternoon! Good afternoon! What nice children! How are you? Come on, give me a kiss. Rosie, what a big girl you are! Those are pretty embroidered dresses! Who made them? I like your hairstyle, Michèle. Did you do it, Antoinette?" she continued, having the girls turn around.

Throughout Miss Laura's speech, her friends echoed her remarks with "Yes!" and "How nice!" as they scrutinized, commented upon, kissed, and complimented each of the children in turn, the boys shaking hands with the men.

These situations were the very few in which Clerise rejoiced in her low social status. While everyone ignored her except for specific requests, all she had to do to remain inconspicuous was to greet the assembly politely at a distance, and carefully hide her amusement and somewhat mischievous enjoyment of the process.

"We should be on our way to the pier, Miss Laura," Ermance said, and Clerise took the boys' hands to cross the street.

"Let's take the shortcut to the pier," Antoinette suggested. In the narrow and unpaved alley leading to the *Bureau du Port*, the Port Authority, they carefully avoided potholes and wet spots and soon arrived at the little plaza near the pier. *Le Wharf*, as it was called, did not contain any play equipment. Its central feature was a masonry platform, three or four steps above the ground, at the center of which stood a large lamppost. There, Pilou and his cousin joined their friends in a hide-and-seek game already in progress. Nearby, marble benches with the engraved names of their donors were placed semi-circularly around the bust of Simon Bolivar, a monument gratefully offered to the town's citizens by the country of Venezuela as a testimony to the hospitality and assistance that their ancestors had provided to Bolivar, who found refuge and volunteers in Les Cayes in his quest to liberate Latin America.

A little further, near almond trees, similar benches faced the beach where some older boys screamed and laughed as they approached the water and ran away as fast as they could to avoid the rush of the waves. Beyond them and out at sea, small sailing ships from various coastal localities moved eastward toward *Bòdmè*, the Seaside neighborhood, with their cargoes of food, produce, and goods.

On the plaza, Rose-Marie, Michèle, and a couple of other girls walked, sat, talked, and decided to join Pilou and his group in a hot game of tag.

"Clerise, do you want to play?" Rose-Marie asked.

"Yes, but I'm watching Danny."

"Ermance, can Clerise play? We need one more person for our team."

"Okay, she can. Danny's a little tired. I'll take care of him," Ermance answered. She had Danny sit by her, and resumed her conversation with her friends.

The game was going well. The players ran, jumped, yelled, and caught each other. Then, Danny also decided to play tag with a little girl.

"Clerise," Ermance called, "come here to watch the child."

"Oh no!" Rose-Marie exclaimed, "We're playing."

"She has to come. Danny is running, and some-one needs to watch him. If anything happens to him, what am I going to tell your mother?"

The girls debated quickly. "Can we go on the pier?" they asked the older maids. Trailing Danny around the plaza, Clerise heard some of the negotiations. "When you are over there, don't step in the water if the waves splash between the floor planks," Ermance finally said.

Soon, the girls left the plaza and began to stroll on the nearby masonry pier, which extended to some distance into the sea. At the end of the pier, near a warehouse sometimes used to store goods traded to and from the city, Clerise saw some young men in swimming trunks emerge briskly in animated conversation. Since they carried a couple of inner tubes, she assumed that they had come from the *Saint-Simon*, the old iron ship that had sunk long ago on a reef in the harbor. To her knowledge, no woman or girl had ever gone there. Still talking, the young men waved distractedly at Rose-Marie and her friends and walked further toward the street, past the armed soldier guarding the area. Meanwhile on the pier, the girls began to walk up and down the short flight of stairs that descended to sea level near the warehouse, and where local youth often sat, talked, and sometimes sang and played music when all was calm in the moonlight.

Danny was now half-asleep on Ermance's lap. Somewhat bored while keeping an eye on Pilou, Clerise wished for the days of intense activity, when foreign ships would dock at the pier. She could hardly interact with the other young servants standing nearby to watch the children play, and who also had to remain alert to prevent any mishap. A few people strolled by, selling sweets or snacks, or walking toward the beach, which extended as far as the eye could see, beyond *Dlo Reno*, the Reynaud River, now blanketed with water lilies. While some waded in the river, others crossed it over a small wooden bridge. Further away, young adults walked, stood, and conversed near a compound of two large houses that was sometimes used for outdoor fun fairs. On the beach in front of that compound, a few people, still barely visible, followed the narrow sandy pathway that led to the thatched-roof houses of *Dèyè Fò*, Behind the Fort, a small fishing neighborhood nestled among coconut and banana trees.

The older boys, who had been playing with the waves near the plaza, were now throwing rocks at the almond trees, and then eating the fallen almonds. They seemed quite absorbed in that activity until one pointed to the soldier, now advancing toward them from his post in the street. The boys stopped and turned toward the pier, pretending to watch something in the distance. Then, they started to laugh and elbow each other. Clerise glanced just in time to see the bag lady who called everyone "*zanmi*, friend" move toward the strolling girls.

Neatly dressed, the woman had her hair bound with a scarf and carried a big bundle of clothing atop her head. She took longer strides as she approached the girls who were now returning to the plaza, moving more quickly as they began to back away. Soon, Clerise heard the girls squeal and saw them scatter, as Ermance stood up clutching Danny, and yelled at her to get the soldier. Antoinette and a couple other maids ran toward the girls who continued to shriek while dodging the woman. Before Clerise could get to him, the soldier arrived at the scene, and stood between the parties. He began to argue with the bag lady, and finally escorted her from the pier after the maids led the girls back to the plaza.

Comments fused, while Rose-Marie and her friends expressed their shock and received comfort.

"That soldier isn't doing his job. How come he let her get to the children?" one of the maids said. "Their fathers should tell the colonel about that."

"The soldier was busy with the boys throwing rocks," another answered. "Besides, she's harmless. She only wants to talk to people and she argues when she can't."

"Those children don't come here to be bothered. We may all get in trouble over that thing!"

To lighten the mood, Ermance and Antoinette decided to take the children home through the *Place d'Armes*, the town square, where they could watch the military band prepare for its weekly concert. A block or so from the pier, they passed the bishop's compound and reached the square across from the cathedral. More people than usual had already gathered on the benches, as well as on surrounding porches and balconies. Children played with old canons or read the names of local heroes on the tombstones scattered on the ground, and watched the khaki-clad soldier-musicians arrive with their brass instruments gleaming in the fading light. The musicians then stepped onto the platform in the middle of the square, and tried the first notes.

"We should go home soon," Antoinette said before the band started to play. "Don't forget, we have something planned for tomorrow morning," she added quickly to quell the emerging protest.

Before they parted ways, Ermance and Antoinette decided on the course to follow in reporting the afternoon incident about the bag lady to their employers. "We can't afford to let anything like that happen again, especially not tomorrow when we're going to take the children to the marketplace," Ermance added. "We need to have a good talk with those kids." She winked, and both women laughed.

That night, as Clerise helped prepare the boys for bed, Ermance spoke gravely. "Clerise," she said, "make sure you keep an eye on the children tomorrow. Don't let anybody touch them. Pilou, you'd better behave also, or you can be in big trouble. Among all the people in the marketplace, some can be *lougawou*, werewolves. They just have to pinch you and you'll die. Rose-Marie, you and your cousin Michèle will also have to help with the boys. As older sisters, that's your job."

Later, Clerise tossed and turned on her *payas*, the pallet that she unfolded every night at the foot of Ermance's bed. Unable to fall asleep, she tried to push the warning from her mind and to forget the whispers that she had heard about one of her father's women, back in her village.

"Clerise, wake up!" Ermance said. "Wake up!" she repeated a little more loudly, careful not to wake the children in the next room.

The girl started to stir and struggled to sit up on her pallet, eyes still closed.

"Didn't you hear the Sacred Heart church bell ring five times? It's five o'clock in the morning!" Ermance continued in the same tone. "Come on, move, we have a lot to do today."

"Yes, Miss Ermance," Clerise murmured dutifully, as she blinked to keep her eyes open.

Reluctantly, she got up stumbling, confused, with nebulous feelings of resentment. Waking up as a *timoun kay* had always been difficult. She hated to be yanked out of sleep and dragged against her will to the darkness of the morning yet to come.

"What a lazy girl! What are you waiting for? We don't have all day!" Fixing her bed and getting dressed by the street light coming from the open window, Ermance had already started to lose her temper. The day was not going to be easy. "Get up, fold your bed," she continued to whisper with growing impatience. "Go get Vanè up. Don't make any noise to wake up Madam or the children. The kids' recess is ending. Soon they'll be back in school. They need their rest. Don't forget, we're taking them to the marketplace today. I need you to help me get them dressed. You'll also have to go to Mrs. Visel's to tell Antoinette when we are about ready to leave. I don't want to waste any time waiting for her over there. You understand?"

"Yes, Miss Ermance."

"Okay. I'll be downstairs in a minute to make coffee. Start preparing for that. Also, tell Vanè to be ready to go get the bread when I come down."

Still struggling to stay awake, Clerise began to drag herself out of the room while carrying her mattress downstairs to the area near the kitchen where the housekeeper slept. There, she also kept her other few possessions in a cardboard box, while she left her bedsheet and pillow in Ermance's closet. On the way downstairs, she stopped in the living room and bent down to shake Vanè, the other *timoun kay*, who was snoring on his *nat*, the thin bare straw mat where he slept without sheet or pillow. "Vanè, wake up," she said, still half asleep herself and keeping her voice low. He threw his arm up to push her away, and turned on his side, mumbling.

"Wake up," she insisted, shaking his back.

"Lemme sleep. I'm tired," he muttered.

"Me too," she said, stifling a yawn. "But don't let Miss Ermance catch you. Me, I'm gone!" On her way to the door, she saw Vanè get up and stretch a few times. He folded his *nat*, and began to rearrange the mahogany living room furniture. Pieces of straw littered the floor that he waxed every weekend on his hands and knees with a brush made of a half portion of a dried coconut. Clerise thought that Vanè would have to sleep on some rags for a couple of days if he did not get that old *nat* replaced soon. "You'd better ask for another *nat* and pick up all the straw you're dropping on the floor," she warned.

Downstairs, she quickly helped the housekeeper start the fire for the morning coffee. By the time Ermance arrived to prepare the Juins' coffee tray, Clerise was already dressed for the day, and about to set the breakfast table.

Later that morning, they left as planned for the trip to the marketplace, a much anticipated adventure, the treat of the day. As much as everyone else, Clerise had looked forward to that outing, which she expected to be different from the few instances when she had gone to the marketplace to assist the cook on tedious shopping trips. On the way, the children chatted excitedly, waved, and greeted friends and acquaintances from both sides of First Main Street. Save for a few occurrences, the salutations became more formal and distant, while still quite pleasant, the further they moved from their neighborhood.

As they made their way through the increased activities on the sidewalk near the marketplace, Ermance cautioned, "Clerise, stay between Pilou and Ti-Louis, and don't let go of their hands."

The girl ensured her hold of the children and entered the buzz of human voices and animal sounds, the aromas of richly spiced tropical food, and the deep blues, reds, earth tones, whites, yellows, and greens of the crowd, stalls, fabrics, displays, fruits, vegetables, and artifacts of the marketplace. There, under the iron-made roof built at the turn of the century, sat or milled crowds of women and men who had come from the countryside to sell their produce, along with all types of small traders, swarms of shoppers, a few beggars, and an assortment of loitering children of all ages. Across the street from the marketplace square, stood the Sacred Heart church; on the three other sides, a constant traffic of people, to and from retail businesses conducted on the ground floor of various houses, added to the bustle.

"Stay close to the children, don't let them stray at the marketplace!" had instructed Simone Juin before they left that morning, and after Ermance had already repeated her stern warning.

Consequently, they all moved in a tight and polite group, basking in vendors' and shoppers' recognition, returning greetings and smiles, gracefully accepting compliments, while Ermance and Antoinette engaged in short rounds of obligatory bargaining and light banter prior to the purchase of the smallest item. Thus, they walked amid the crowd all the way to the street facing the Sacred Heart church.

On their right, the neighborhood of *Lan Savann*, the Savannah, extended far ahead to the beach at Lilèt, a historic fort whose ruins and old cannons, as well as numerous almond trees, made for a popular place of excursion at the eastern end of the town. From where she stood, Clerise could see the stately palm trees in impeccable formation lining the road that led to the old fort. Nearby was the poorhouse where she sometimes accompanied Simone Juin and the children for brief and dutiful visits. She had not ventured, however, to the side streets of that part of Lan Savann, home of the unemployed and working poor, where many popular clubs and Vodou temples sent rumbles of drumbeat at night throughout the city. Further west, the neighborhood continued inland and along the coast, all the way to the fish market and the Seaside area near the pier.

As she glanced that way, Clerise thought, *Mezanmi!* My God! Vanè went with Miss Philomene to get the crabs and shrimps for the gumbo soup, and I forgot to give him the kids' shoes to take to the shoeshine man. *Woy!* I'm in trouble! Quickly, she bent down to rub her leg. She could almost feel the sting of old spankings.

Nervously, she looked in the opposite direction, past the children pleading for more time with Ermance and Antoinette. To her left, the town extended northward through *Kat Chemen*, The Four Roads, a neighborhood aptly named for the large intersection that marked the end of town. There, next to a huge cross, stood a small military post where a couple of bored soldiers recorded the names of passengers from any vehicle entering or leaving the city. Many who lived in Kat Chemen operated small distilleries, *gildiv*, which produced *tafya* and *kleren*, the very potent beverages of the poor, while the more well off consumed wine, rum, or imported whiskey. However, everybody used *tafya* and *kleren* in home remedies, and supplies were running low in the Juins' household.

"Miss Ermance, don't forget the *tafya* Mrs. Juin said to get," Clerise offered timidly, hoping to buy some goodwill and wondering how it would feel to follow the road to Kat Chemen and run away, as other *timoun kay* had done before.

On the way home from the marketplace, Clerise felt relieved. Nobody had been pinched by a potential werewolf, and she had not seen or recognized anyone from her village. Not that she remembered much of that time of her life, although she clearly recalled the day when her aunt, a former *timoun kay* in Mrs. Juin's family, had taken her to Les Cayes nearly four years before. A shy orphan shuffled among maternal relatives, Clerise had departed with advice and blessings from family and friends. They expected her to walk in the footsteps of her aunt, now managing the household of Mrs. Juin's sister in Port-au-Prince.

Lost in thought, Clerise kept her usual place behind everyone else in their mostly silent and tired little group. They were returning home through Second Main Street which ran parallel to First Main Street all the way across town, and she recalled that she had forgotten to send Vanè on the shoeshine errand. She also realized that she had failed in her other duty to provide pages of the old newspapers, magazines, or notebooks needed to wrap the seafood — including conch, lobster, crab, shrimp, and especially the long slim red *babaren* fish — to the cook, for transportation from the fish market. The cook usually went there alone or with a low-status *timoun kay* such as Vanè.

That day, the latter had been assigned to help in the shopping and preparation for the *tomtom ak kalalou*, the breadfruit and plantain paste served with gumbo soup. Clerise hoped that, with luck, she would still be able to catch him for the needed errand to the shoeshine man.

Upon their arrival home, they found Vanè vigorously pounding the *tomtom* in a pestle. Clerise approached him discreetly as soon as she could. "Did you take the kids' shoes to be cleaned?" she whispered.

"I didn't know which ones to take. It's not my fault," he replied, still pounding.

"When can you go?"

"I don't know. I'm working with Ms. Philomene."

"Then, I'll have to take them myself, or clean them the best I can."

"You still have time to take them to the shoeshine man before he goes home, but Miss Ermance is going to be mad. You're going to get it!" Vanè said.

On her way to bring an item to the seamstress making Rose-Marie's school uniforms, Clerise took the shoes to the shoeshine man in Kafou Orèl and told him of her predicament. She was able to pick up the cleaned shoes right before he left for the day, which saved her from the looming threat of Ermance's punishment.

School opened a little while later, and that is when the matter of the missing book began to unfold. By then, Clerise had returned to the one-room school that she attended regularly three times a week, from two to three thirty in the afternoon, after escorting the Juin children to and from their own schools and to various errands during their midday recess.

It all started with Rose-Marie's search for the story that she had written at the end of the summer, her first attempt at literary production outside her school assignments. She had shown the work to her proud parents who had always encouraged her passion for reading, and provided the books and magazines that had inspired her to write her story.

On that day, Rose-Marie had planned to take the manuscript to her piano lesson, to show it to her teacher and to the other girls who also came to practice during the schools' midday recess. Unable to find her text, she arrived late at her teacher's home, remained preoccupied throughout the lesson, and was scolded for doing poorly. On the way home, she shared her concern with Clerise, who still escorted her for short distances.

"Clerise, where do you think my book can be? I looked everywhere! I wrote the story in a blue school notebook, one with the multiplication table in the back."

"I haven't seen it, Miss Rosie. I looked also. I don't know where it can be."

"Pilou can't remember anything about it. My mother doesn't know either. I showed it to dad, and he gave it back to me right away. Ermance has helped me search upstairs, and we haven't found it. Where can it be? Do you think that Danny...? Oh, no!"

"It's not Danny. All he did was look at the pictures in the old papers that your mom gave him. Those are the ones he tears. Your mom says to let him do it because he's going to want to know what the writing says. Maybe we should look downstairs, and ask Ms. Philomene, Ms. Louise, and Vanè if they saw your notebook. You never know."

"Ok! I may have left it in the playroom, and Louise could have put it somewhere. I'll ask her as soon as I get home."

That was a lucky guess. Clerise later heard that Louise, the housekeeper, recalled that while cleaning the playroom a few days before, she had found a notebook folded in the middle, on top of newspapers that Pilou had discarded after some failed attempts at making sailboats. She had placed the whole pile on the bottom shelf of the large hutch used for storage of reading material, in the corner of the room adjacent to the kitchen. Full of hope, Rose-Marie rushed there only to be disappointed. "Where can it be?" she asked, her voice strained, as she continued to search. "Vanè, have you seen the notebook that was here?"

"Isn't that a school notebook with some writing on it? That's the one Ms. Philomene used to go to the fish market, to wrap the fish."

Rose-Marie closed her eyes, shook her head in disbelief, and brought her hands to her face. "Clerise," she screamed, "you are the one who should give the paper for that! How could you do such a thing? I thought you said you didn't know where my story was!"

"I didn't give your notebook to Ms. Philomene, Miss Rosie," Clerise protested. "Vanè, remember yesterday afternoon I went out to get those catalogues for Mrs. Juin. When I came back, Ms. Philomene had already left for the fish market. I don't know anything about that, honest!"

"She took some of the notebook too, the day you went to the marketplace," Vanè said.

"Where's Philomene now?" Rose-Marie urged. "Maybe she hasn't used the story pages."

"She went out for a moment. She said she'd be right back."

Alas! Philomene appeared to suffer from selective amnesia. She could not remember at all what she had used on any preceding day to wrap any type of seafood, beyond what Clerise had provided for that purpose. Desperately crying and sobbing, Rose-Marie asked her mother to fire the cook. Mrs. Juin only promised that she would provide strong directions as to who had access to the storage hutch, and for what reasons, in the future.

Thus, Rose-Marie decided to take matters in her own hands and, for that purpose, enlisted Clerise and Vanè's reluctant assistance. Then she started to plot her revenge, vowing to make Philomene pay dearly for the fateful shopping trip.

Philomene's granddaughter, Elvire, had recently been the Juins' housekeeper. Both women, who lived nearby in an area of town called Anba Komedi, usually came to work early in the morning and left in the evening after dinner was served. A few months after Elvire had left the household, a beaming Philomene arrived at work one morning, and told Mrs. Juin, "Madam, Elvire had a boy last night at the hospital."

"Oh! Is she well?"

"She's fine, and the baby too."

"What did she name him?"

"She named him Luc. The baby looks just like his dad!"

"Is he going to take care of the child?"

"I think so. He's crazy about his son."

"What about Elvire?"

"She's all right. Mr. Mirot says he'll also take care of her."

"Is the baby big?"

"A big, healthy boy, Madam! Now I'd better go to the kitchen and do my work. We are all so very happy!"

"Tell Elvire that I wish her the best," Mrs. Juin said.

Nearby, Clerise paused a little to listen, then pretended not to have heard. Rose-Marie frowned and turned to her mother. "Mr. Mirot?" she asked. "He is not married to Elvire. He is old, too. How can he have a baby?"

"That's all true," Mrs. Juin said quickly. "But obviously Mr. Mirot is not too old to have a child. By the way, isn't it time for you to go and study?"

Later, Clerise was able to learn more, through Ermance's eagerness to share the juicy tidbit with Antoinette. "…she started to get sick a few times. She either left work early or didn't come at all. Mrs. Juin became suspicious and talked to Philomene. I guess that's when she knew the full story, and she let Elvire go quietly."

"That was when Philomene got angry and left, wasn't it? Mrs. Juin had to talk her into coming back."

"Yeah, that's right. But, isn't that something? Mr. Mirot's daughter is way older than Elvire, and she's the only child that has his name. I heard Mrs. Mirot died very young, but the man has plenty of other kids."

"You can bet that his daughter isn't going to give up any of Mirot's money, if anything happens."

"If Elvire has any brains, she'll take advantage of a good thing while it lasts and start a small business. You know he's not going to take care of her forever."

"She'd better play it smart, or before you know it she'll be back where she started from. Even if Mirot takes care of the child, she'll have to work if he stops supporting her."

"*Woy, woy, woy!* After going with that old goat! Some things can be very hard. Such a young girl! I don't think she's more than seventeen."

"Mrs. Juin told me to stay away from Mirot and from a couple more of those old single men," Ermance chuckled. "Good advice!"

In any case, now openly "kept" by Mr. Mirot, Elvire had moved somewhat closer to the Juins' residence. She lived in the Anba Lopital neighborhood, practically at the western end of town, not too far from the pier, behind the Post Office and the Department of Public Works, and close to the municipal slaughterhouse.

Still beaming with pride after several months, and cutting corners to supplement Elvire's finances, Philomene had a vendor deliver little Luc's milk every day at her workplace. There, she boiled it, using the Juins' charcoal. She was blissfully unaware of her vulnerability.

"You see that baby's milk…," a scheming Rose-Marie whispered to Clerise and Vanè, her co-conspirators.

Part of Rose-Marie's plan had to do with the area of Pon Gonbo, near the Juins' residence. There, working and middle-class families lived side by side, and operated all types of conveniently located small businesses. Philomene, who had lived for a while in Pon Gonbo, always sought to keep abreast of new developments in the neighborhood. At least every day, she tried to go there before she began to cook lunch, often under the guise of getting some absolutely essential ingredient like tomato paste or any similar item. Those errands followed her shopping trips to the market place and the boiling of milk for baby Luc.

Rose-Marie seized that opportunity to execute her plan. While Clerise hid the covered pan of the baby's milk under the long kitchen masonry range where the ash from the charcoal fell during cooking time, Vanè kept watch as agreed, as Rose-Marie supervised the operation. When Vanè notified them of Philomene's arrival, the two girls ran upstairs to the room above the kitchen to watch the result of their handiwork through a crack in the wooden floor.

The next step in Philomene's routine was to take the milk, now cooled, to Elvire's home a couple of blocks away. Then, she would return to conclude the preparation of lunch, her major task of the day, since the rice, beans, meat, vegetables, plantains, and sweet potatoes were already in place or pretty much on the way.

Smiling and relaxed, Philomene arrived in the kitchen after her last-minute errands. Quite naturally, she went to get the baby's milk. Surprised not to find it, she briefly looked around, then stopped, thought for a while, scratched her head, and searched again. Then she checked everywhere, opening cabinet doors, looking on shelves, tiptoeing and bending, up and down, right and left, getting more and more frantic. Upstairs, Rose-Marie and Clerise, sprawled on the floor on each side of the crack, took turns looking at the action below, chuckling and motioning to each other to remain silent.

Then, Louise stepped into the kitchen. "Have you seen my milk pan?" Philomene asked. "I left it here for a moment to go out, and now I can't find it."

"I remember seeing it on the range some time this morning. Where can it be?"

"I don't know. I can't understand. Maybe Ermance has an idea."

"I'll get her for you, Philomene. I'll be right back too. What happened to that milk?"

Ermance did not know either, and the girls upstairs were taking turns watching, covering their mouths to stifle laughter, and reminding each other to keep quiet. They sobered when Mrs. Juin, notified, went to the kitchen.

While everyone conjectured, Philomene continued to look around, and move in all directions.

"What could have happened?" they mused.

"I saw Vanè around here this morning, when Philomene was out," Ermance said. "He looked kind of sneaky."

In the yard not too far away, Vanè tried to appear busy while watching the situation unfold.

"Vanè, come here!" Mrs. Juin called.

"Yes, Madam!"

"Where is Ms. Philomene's milk pan?"

"What milk pan? I don't know Madam!" he answered, fidgeting and casting glances sideways toward the floor.

"Did you drink the milk?"

"No, Madam! I did not," he protested.

"I saw you here this morning," intervened Ermance. "What were you trying to hide when Philomene was out?"

"Nothing."

"What were you doing around here, then?"

Keeping his eyes downcast, Vanè remained silent.

"You'd better tell."

"Yes," he stammered. "…Clerise…Yes…… "

"Clerise what? Come on, hurry up! What did Clerise do?"

"She hid Ms. Philomene's milk pan," he blurted.

"Where?"

The crowd was pressing.

"Here," Vanè began to point.

"Where? Go get it!"

He looked at the ceiling and appeared ready to bolt. Upstairs, the girls grew cautious. Still taking turns watching, they saw the women follow Vanè closely as he took a few steps in the kitchen, then gasp in surprise when he pulled the milk from its hiding place. Philomene grabbed her pan and lifted the cover to check for damage.

"What an idea!"

"Look at that!"

"Clerise! Come here! Where are you?" Mrs. Juin called.

"Yes Ma'm!" She rushed downstairs, Rose-Marie in tow.

"Mom," Rose-Marie volunteered, "I told Clerise to hide the milk."

"And why was that?"

"Because Philomene had destroyed my story."

"What! What an idea! Those children! I am sorry Philomene. That was really bad what you did! Clerise and Vanè, if I catch you at something like that again, you will be in big trouble! Rose-Marie, come with me, I want to talk to you. Philomene, you should be on your way now with that milk. And you kids, apologize to Philomene."

"Sorry, Philomene. Sorry, Ms. Philomene," they muttered.

After Mrs. Juin and Rose-Marie had left, Ermance and Louise, also on their way out of the kitchen, turned to Clerise and Vanè. "Look at you! What do you think!" they sneered. "I wish for your sake that you never try something like that on me!"

"And that goes for me too!"

Although in a hurry, Philomene was too upset to leave without giving Vanè a *zoklo*, a sharp hit with one knuckle on the side of his head. For good measure, she also pinched Clerise hard on the arm and warned them both against future mischief.

No one there mentioned Rose-Marie, who, by that time, had left with her mother. From what Clerise later heard, Mrs. Juin, who tried hard not to laugh, warned her daughter and advised her that although she understood the motive, she could not condone the behavior.

Clerise held her sore arm, winced, and did not dare to make a noise. She realized that nothing had happened to Rose-Marie, but did not want to think about it. For the following days, she was at her best behavior and hoped to have the whole matter forgotten.

Unlike Clerise, Vanè became rebellious. He started to grumble when unhappy about assignments. Then he began to question orders, expressing disagreement or open annoyance, and no longer bothered to hide his feelings. He neglected his work, causing chain reactions and numerous complaints to Mrs. Juin from nearly everyone, and took quite a long time to return from errands. Clerise often caught him playing or talking in the streets with other *timoun kay* boys, and suspected that sometimes he also ran all the way to the market-place to see his mother.

Herself a former maid, Vanè's mother barely eked a living as a vendor. She walked barefoot long distances trying to resell produce along roads and in market places. Vanè also went barefoot everywhere, except on special occasions, although the other servants in the Juin household always wore shoes or sandals, unless inside the house or on quick errands in the neighborhood. Ermance, however, never went barefoot.

Now thirteen, Vanè was a year older than Clerise. She remembered his arrival in the household three years earlier, after she had already been there for nearly a year. That day, he and his mom were both crying as they hugged and clung to each other in the entrance hallway, before they parted. Then, Ermance had given him a cardboard box in which to store his few belongings, and showed him a space near the trash-collecting area behind the kitchen where he would dress every day.

At first, Clerise and Rose-Marie had occasionally played with him, but then, Ermance told them that they should stop and let Vanè do his work. In addition, he had to address Rose-Marie as "Miss" and Clerise also began to call her that from time to time. After Ermance notified Vanè of the new rules, he kept to himself, became progressively sullen and, after a while, began to cut corners in his work. Unlike Clerise who assisted in the care of the Juin children and the light housekeeping, and ran the "clean" errands, Vanè took care of the waste disposal, ran the early morning errands, was sometimes dispatched late at night, and did anything else that involved getting dirty or carrying loads. Although enrolled in school, he attended only as his duties allowed, sometimes in the afternoons.

As Vanè's behavior worsened after the baby's milk episode, Ermance, Louise, and Philomene did not spare *zoklo, kalòt*, slaps on the head, and shoves, all to no avail. Then, Mrs. Juin meted more formal punishment. In several instances, Vanè had to kneel in a corner, with arms folded and head down, for extended periods of time. Mrs. Juin also hit him a few times on the behind and legs with a belt.

Then, Mrs. Juin summoned Vanè's mother concerning her son's misdeeds, and an air of expectation permeated the household. The woman arrived one Saturday. Barefoot as usual, she wore a straw hat and a faded gray dress. After brief salutations to all present, she went to stand with Mrs. Juin in a corner of the yard. Clerise heard words such as "*l ap fè move timoun*, he is acting badly. . . *move zanmi*, bad friends. . . *p ap fè travay li*, not doing his work. . . *reponn,* talk back. . . *radi,* sassy. . ." upon which Vanè's mother appeared indignant.

"Madam," she said. "I don't tolerate disrespect to adults. I didn't raise Vanè to be that way. I don't know what's wrong with him, but it's going to stop."

"Come here, Vanè," Mrs. Juin said. "You heard your mom. What do you have to say for yourself?"

Vanè took his time to approach. "Walk faster," his mother snapped. "You don't make adults wait. Madam asked you what you have to say for yourself. I'm waiting."

Vanè looked from one to the other. "I don't know, Madam," he muttered.

"Don't look at adults in the eye. Keep your head down. If you don't know what's going on with you, I'll make you know," his mother said before turning to Mrs. Juin. "Madam, I'm going to give him a spanking he'll remember."

"That should help," Mrs. Juin agreed. "Ermance," she said, "bring a belt."

Vanè did not move or make a sound as his mother hit him. Clerise, the Juin children, and the servants watched in surprise because, in similar situation with Mrs. Juin, even before the first blow, Vanè would scream, cry, and beg so much that Mrs. Juin would give up almost as soon as she began. This time, when his mother struck, he just stood up, taking it.

"Mrs. Juin doesn't know how to spank children. But this! It's just shooing flies," Philomene said dismissively as she turned back and went to the kitchen.

Vanè's mother hit harder. The blows landed on his short pants and legs, and still he didn't move.

"I think that's enough," Mrs. Juin said. "Vanè, you understand now what you are doing?"

"Yes, Madam," he whispered.

"Do your work, respect your elders, and don't make me come back for more," his mother said, apparently still fuming.

"See what happens when people misbehave," Mrs. Juin warned Clerise and the children. "Don't let that happen to you."

After Mrs. Juin and the children left the yard, Ermance and Louise went to their chores while Vanè's mother took him to the entrance hallway for a talk. Clerise, who had stayed in the yard to do some washing, observed them from time to time, though they could hardly see her. She remembered that, when Vanè had first arrived in the household, Mrs. Juin had to ask his mother not to come as often as she did to see him, since such visits did not help his adjustment. At the time, Clerise had watched them interact. "*Ti Vann*, Little Vann..." the mother would say with a caress to her son's close-cropped head. Then, Clerise had missed her own mother and longed for her love.

Now, Vanè stood facing his mother in the hallway, head down. She put her hand to his face and lifted his chin. "*Ti Vann mwen*, my little Vann," she said, "don't make me have to do that to you again. Those people feed you, clothe you, give you a place to sleep, and send you to school. You know I can't do that for you. You'll be hungry if they send you home. Whatever happens, do your work, respect your elders. You'll grow up to be a strong man." Clerise saw her wipe a tear from Vanè's eye and put an arm around his shoulder. Both seemed to be crying.

Clerise could not bear to see more and did not know what to think. She felt that Vanè needed to be punished, and decided to continue to be angry at him for his behavior, which only brought her trouble and added work. She noticed that, following the spanking from his mother, Vanè did show some improvement. However, he soon reverted to his new ways, flaunting his defiant self. Then, Mr. Juin was brought to the picture to give him a couple of good spankings with a *rigwaz*, the local short cowhide whip. Finally, Mrs. Juin decided to send him back home.

To that effect, she contacted the woman who helped her recruit domestic workers from the countryside, then announced the imminent arrival of another boy to replace Vanè. Summoned once more, Vanè's mother arrived the following Saturday. She pleaded with Mrs. Juin to give her son another chance and tried to make Vanè promise to behave. He remained sullen and spoke with extreme reluctance. After Mrs. Juin checked his belongings to insure that nothing would be missing from the household, he barely said goodbye, while his mother appeared on the verge of tears. Clerise watched him go and noted that he never looked back.

CHAPTER 2

Facts of Life

"Why couldn't you understand that Vanè was happy to leave the Juins', after the way they treated you both?" I asked my mother with a touch of scorn.

Clerise paused for a moment and briefly closed her eyes. "Nicole," she said, "I knew that what happened to us wasn't fair, but Vanè had somewhere to go, and I didn't. I never saw him again." Then, she leaned slightly forward, rested her chin on her fingers and looked far past me. "I wish my mother had lived," she added.

I felt somewhat guilty. "Tell me more about your parents," I asked, to make amends.

1950

From the back of the rehearsal room, Clerise watched Danny's teacher and another adult volunteer enact a communion scene with appropriate devotion. It was Danny's turn to prepare for his first communion, and the process had started with an oral test that the local parish priest administered in various schools. Those who passed received a lollipop and could proceed further. As she took Danny to his first communion rehearsals, Clerise, now fifteen, often felt an old build-up of anxiety. Again, she heard the horror stories repeated to each generation of new communicants during the countless practice sessions involving non-consecrated wafers.

"Make sure that you don't bite the wafer. Swallow it right away," the teacher urged, while gingerly posing the practice wafer on the extended tongue of his kneeling assistant. "Even if a small part of it gets stuck on your palate," he pointed to his mouth with his finger, "never touch it with your hands. Instead, use the tip of your tongue, like this..." With mouth wide open, he continued the demonstration for his rapt audience.

A little boy raised his hand. "What happens if you bite the wafer?" he asked in a small voice.

"They say that the wafer will bleed in your mouth and fill it with blood," the teacher answered gravely. The audience shuddered.

Clerise struggled to suppress a smile. While the tales were losing their edge, she still felt the full impact of the most terrible stories, those related to Vodou practitioners who, when pretending to take communion in good faith, furtively used a handkerchief to hide the wafer, which they later fed to snakes for magic purposes. The children listened in horror, as the teacher emphasized the grievous consequences of such a mortal sin, guaranteed to lead straight to hell if one died suddenly before going to confession. After receiving more dire warnings and appropriate demonstrations, the future communicants began to move forward for their individual practice.

Watching them, Clerise recalled that, for a long time, she had also feared to die in her sleep and wake up in hell because of the mortal sin of not confessing her occasional feelings of resentment toward her employers, especially since Vanè's departure. The night that he left, she had fought back tears, thinking of the unfairness that they had both experienced as a result of Rose-Marie's revenge plot against Philomene. At the time, she had felt that Vanè chose to behave as he did because he knew that he could go home. Thus, she had decided to forget him. A few days later, under Ermance's supervision, she had begun to train the new boy who had come from the countryside to join the household as a *timoun kay*.

More than the remote possibility of damnation however, she worried that the priest would find a way to warn Mrs. Juin of her resentment. Consequently, she decided to categorize both her grudge and omission as venial sins which could, at the most, cost her some time in purgatory. However, she always made sure to recite an "Act of Contrition" before going to sleep, just in case.

Meanwhile, in the household, the early preparation for the first communion started with the making of Danny's new suit and selection of appropriate clothing for all family members. Between fittings, confession rehearsals, and other activities, Mrs. Juin dispatched everyone, Ermance, Clerise, Louise, Rose-Marie, Pilou, and the new *timoun kay*, to countless errands. Commemorative communion images were ordered to be mailed out of town and also passed around on the day of the event.

Mrs. Juin's mother, Mrs. Visel, came from Port-au-Prince with Clerise's aunt, Elia, to help with the last touches. They arrived one evening, tired from a long road trip, with gifts for everyone, as well as cans and boxes of imported food. Then, Elia took immediate charge of the household. The day after her arrival, she began to carry a set of keys, that Mrs. Juin had given her, for all the locked *armoires*, hutches, sideboards, and closets in the house, both for practical reasons and as a symbol of her authority.

"My sister is so lucky!" Simone Juin said to one of her childhood friends, who had come to pay her respects, as they waited for Mrs. Visel. "You know how I felt when my mom decided to go and live in Port-au-Prince after my dad died so that she and Elia could help take care of the children there. I wish Elia had stayed with me."

"I can understand that," the friend answered. "But when your mom moved to Port-au-Prince, she left you Philomene as a cook."

"Philomene is Philomene. Mother raised Elia, who is part of the family. Elia has style and can take care of anything; that's why my sister can rely on her completely. I was just married when Mother moved, and Philomene had been with her for several years. So, Mother decided that she would leave her with me. I can't complain, though! But it's certainly not the same."

Mrs. Visel continued to see her visitors for a couple of days, then decided to go for some errands in town, taking Clerise along to help carry the bags. Their first stop was to get the commemorative images already ordered. The printer, who also served as the town's registrar, had his office on the ground floor of his house, and his equipment in the back. From the front porch, Clerise heard Mrs. Visel exclaim about the excellence of the work.

"Clerise, look at this!" Mrs. Visel said as she walked out the door. She held a traditional, European-imported stock image of a boy's first communion, now gold dusted and custom engraved in gold letters. Beaming, the printer and his wife followed her outside.

"Oh! That is very pretty!" Clerise agreed from afar.

"This is Clerise, Elia's niece," Mrs. Visel offered casually.

"We see her with Simone's kids," the printer's wife said. "She seems to be very responsible."

Clerise nodded, exchanging greetings with the couple.

"I'll tell Elia what I heard about her niece today," Mrs. Visel mentioned, taking her leave. "She'll be pleased."

The compliments about Clerise's behavior continued, as they shopped for small gifts of rosaries and religious trinkets to be given to visiting first communicants, and also when they later left a commemorative communion image with the pale and quietly aging sisters of the newspaper owner for an announcement in the society column.

On the sidewalk in front of *La Glacière*, a bar with a steady, faithful, exclusively male upper-class clientele, Mrs. Visel shook hands with a couple of older men who had stood from their chairs to greet her as she passed.

At that time of the day, only the most hard-core patrons were already sitting inside at the tables and open bar. Later, in the brightly lit courtyard, bored middle-age hard drinkers would meet as they did every day after work, to gossip, exchange stories, and occasionally, as a favor to a friend or relative, initiate a younger counterpart into one of the basics of machismo: the art of keeping steady while under the influence.

The fact that Mrs. Visel had left her standing on the side and chosen to ignore her presence at that stop did not surprise Clerise, in light of the advice that she had often heard Simone Juin give the older maids. This time, it was her turn. "You are getting to be a young woman now; be careful with men," Mrs. Visel told her as they resumed their walk.

When they returned home, Elia heard all the compliments about her niece. She smiled and patted Clerise's shoulder. The girl stood still, her eyes to the floor, and smiled a little, not knowing how else to react.

"I'll count on you to help!" Elia said.

Now, the final first communion activities were about to begin.

The day of Danny's first confession, Clerise picked him from school for the midday recess, at the *Frères de l'Instruction Chrétienne*, the Brothers for Christian Education. She stayed a few steps behind as he walked with a friend.

Danny appeared preoccupied. "They said we would feel light after confession. I was happy after I finished. But now, I don't feel any different than before," he said.

"Well, I do," The other boy answered smugly. "Bye, I'll see you later," he waved before entering his house.

Rose-Marie and Michèle Visel came down the street, before Clerise could inquire about the matter. "What's going on, Danny?" his sister asked. "Aren't you glad you went to confession?" she continued as he kept on walking. He did not answer.

"Can I tell them?" Clerise offered. He nodded yes, and did not look at them. Still walking, the girls questioned him in turn. "Did you tell the priest all your sins?" Again, a nod, yes. "Are you sure you didn't forget any?"

"I told him everything that I practiced with mom. I even practiced this morning," Danny said.

"What was the penance?"

"One Our Father and three Hail Mary's."

"That seems to be right for the first time," Rose-Marie said.

"You can always talk to your mom about it," Michèle added before leaving them to go home.

"I think you must be tired," Clerise told him. "Now that we're home, just go talk to your mom."

"Those kids are funny," Rose-Marie laughed after he left. "Remember that little girl, last year, who forgot her sins at confession. She walked right out to where the priest sat, so she could hand him the list of her sins that she couldn't read."

Clerise giggled. "What about that other little girl who saw the priest bend his head toward her side of the confessional to hear what she wanted to say and she thought he wanted her to kiss him? So, she walked out to him and kissed his cheek."

"That's a new one," Rose-Marie laughed. "I bet you heard it this morning."

Reassured after the talk with his mom, Danny spent the rest of the day in quiet sanctity. He went to bed early after a light dinner and, strictly following the required fast, did not even take a sip of water before his first communion.

In the well-decorated Cathedral filled with the communicants and their entourage, the ceremony unfolded with due solemnity. Later, after a special family breakfast, Clerise escorted Danny to have his picture taken at the Pharmacy and Photo-Studio near the marketplace, and to the mandatory visits to friends, relatives, acquaintances, present and former teachers, as well as members of the clergy. All over town, they met other first communicants coming in and out of homes, businesses, and institutions. While most wore their school uniform or more or less elaborate special cloth-ing, a few girls had embroidered ankle-length white dresses with matching purse and gloves, and sometimes a long lace veil under a crown of flowers. Accompanied or not by a responsible adult, with or without a couple of brothers and sisters, or a few friends, the communi-cants and their escorts had refreshments at various stops, where they also received religious pictures or trinkets, and in some instances distributed commemorative images.

After she took Danny around, Clerise thought of her own first communion. She had not gone for any visits afterwards, and the preparations for the event had involved only the very basics. With not enough school hours to study religion, she had to attend *Katechis*, the catechism sessions that women and teenage volunteers from religious lay organizations offered to young domestic workers on Sunday afternoons, to prepare for their first communion. Because of the time required, few succeeded in reaching that goal.

On the memorable day, clad in a new dress and hat, Clerise had attended her special Mass along with other participants from her *Katechis* group. The ceremony took place without fanfare in one of the lateral chapels of the nearly empty Cathedral. One of the few employers present, Mrs. Juin attended along with Ermance, Rose-Marie, and Pilou. Beaming, Clerise left the church in their midst and returned home to a breakfast of patties and kola, her favorite drink, all set on a table and prepared especially for her. It was a milestone that she never forgot, and for that she was grateful to the Juins.

The following Sunday, Mrs. Visel and the Juins met for lunch at the home of Jules Visel, Mrs. Juin's brother, the father of Michèle and Ti-Louis. A first communion party for Danny and his friend, who lived next door to the Visels, was planned there for the afternoon. Smaller than the grandiose reception that the Juins had offered for their first child, Rose-Marie, the celebrations for Pilou, and now Danny, involved some of their friends, the maids escorting them, and a few parents.

While Elia stayed home to prepare some of her specialties, Simone Juin; her sister-in-law, Adeline Visel; and their close friend, the mother of the other communicant, the very pregnant Solange Jobert, organized the activities at the Visel house. Clerise's assignment was to work with her aunt and run errands as needed between the two residences.

"Here, beat the egg whites for the *soupirs*," Elia said. "They need to be real stiff before we even start putting in the sugar. Mrs. Visel told me that they are called *meringues* abroad, tsk..." she added dismissively, sucking her teeth.

As she worked, Clerise observed her short, stout, dark-skinned, and middle-aged aunt, whose sternness toward her contrasted with an otherwise flashing smile. Beating her own eggs for the *crème renversée*, Elia sat not too far. "We have to make a lot of those *soupirs*," she said. "So, you should work hard and pay attention to what you do."

"*Wi, Matant,* Yes, Auntie," Clerise answered.

"You see," Elia continued. "The reason why I am in charge of everything in the house of Mrs. Juin's sister in Port-au-Prince, is because I'm serious about my work. Without me, she wouldn't have been able to go and help her husband in his business, with four children at home. Mrs. Visel is getting old and I've always been with her. I was engaged once, but my fiancé died. I never got married. You hear that?"

Clerise stole a glance at her. "Yes, Auntie," she answered quickly, keeping an eye on her eggs.

Elia got up from her chair and continued to speak as she added some ingredients to her bowl. "The fact that I do a good job is what allows me to help my family as I do. You remember your cousin Simone, the one they called Tita in this house, because she had the same first name as Mrs. Juin?"

"I think so, yes Matant," Clerise hesitated, recalling that she last saw her cousin in her village when she was about six years old, the first time that she had met her aunt. Then, she lived with another one of her mother's sisters, who had several children of her own.

"Philomene, you remember Tita?" Elia yelled toward the kitchen.

"Yes, your niece," Philomene answered with her back turned, activating the charcoal.

"I brought her here, but look at what she did! It only took her two years, to leave her job to run off with a *sanzave*, a good-for-nothing man! Just two years! That's when Mrs. Juin needed a *timoun kay*. You got that chance, Clerise. Don't you blow it!" she stressed, as she continued to work.

When everything was finally ready, Clerise and the boy *timoun kay* made a couple of trips to transport the homemade bread and various desserts to the Visel's home, returning with the portions of entrées and other dishes set aside for Elia and her helpers at the Juins' residence. On the way back, Clerise lingered, reluctant to face her aunt.

By the time Clerise arrived home on her last trip from the Visels', Elia and Philomene had already settled for lunch.

"Here you are," Elia said. "I was just now telling Philomene about your mom. If she had come to work for Mrs. Visel, she would still be alive. Instead, she chose to go with your father! Now, don't get me started on him!"

Clerise busied herself with the dishes that she had brought.

"I remember there was something about her father," Philomene mused. "What was it again?"

"He has children all over the place. That's why he could hardly take care of Clerise. He sets some of his *manman pitit*, the mothers of his children, on some small piece of land so they can sell whatever they make. That's what happened to my sister. But, the real deal is his *fanm kay*, the woman with whom he shares his house."

Clerise felt her heart beat faster. She dreaded the old tale, yet wanted to hear it once more. Silently she continued to place trays and dish covers in nearby cabinets, with the other *timoun kay*, then began to put food on their plates.

"Isn't that the woman they said was a *lougawou*, a werewolf?" Philomene asked.

"That very one. After Clerise was born, each time my sister started to get pregnant, she lost the baby. People say the woman was doing it because she was jealous, and that she poisoned my sister," Elia answered. She shook her head and closed her eyes.

"Alatraka!" Philomene exclaimed. "And what did Clerise's father do?"

"Nothing. He didn't believe it. She controls him totally. That *lougawou!*"

Clerise no longer felt hungry. She put her plate down and began to sort the utensils to wash.

"Aren't you eating, Clerise?" Elia asked. "Those things happened long ago. There's nothing we can do about it now. But you should know what happened, to be on guard. Has your father come to see you?"

"Long time ago," Clerise said.

Philomene got up to clean the pans. "Go, sit down, and eat," she told Clerise. "I remember her dad visiting her a couple of times after she came here," she continued. "He would bring some plantains or things like that to Mrs. Juin, and never stay long. He stopped coming after he tried to take Clerise to his village for a visit. He had to bring her back almost right away. 'She was so sad! She was crying so much, because she missed you,' he said to Mrs. Juin. As far as I know, he hasn't been back since."

"That's no great loss," Elia said as she handed her plate to Philomene to wash, then went upstairs to take a nap.

After Philomene went home and the boy *timoun kay* began to prepare to go to *Katechis*, Elia yelled for Clerise to come and join her. "I want to tell you something. Just keep that to yourself," she said. "Before your mother was buried, her body was poisoned, so no one would turn her into a zombie."

"I heard that when I was little," Clerise said.

"There was a knife put in your mother's coffin, for her to defend herself, if she had to."

"I also heard that. Who did it?"

"I don't even know; and that's for the protection of those who did it as well as mine. You don't need to know, either." Elia paused. "Don't forget," she said, "better not tell anyone about having been *benyen*, either. That was for your protection too. I was not there, then. I left all of those things behind. And you should too."

"Yes, Auntie. You told me that when you brought me here, when I was eight," Clerise answered, vaguely remembering those baths full of leaves, and the little bracelets and charms that she wore in her village against evil influences.

"The people we work for don't mix at all with that kind of stuff. They have to trust us with their kids," Elia continued. "The children are like my own. I know I spoil them sometimes, but I make sure they do their school work and behave properly. That's what you'll need to do too. You hear?"

"*Wi, Matant*, Yes, Auntie." Clerise answered, feeling her eyes about to close. All she wanted was to go downstairs, lean a chair against a wall, and sleep. She felt relieved when Elia again laid down to rest on the cot in Mrs. Visel's room, and finally dismissed her.

A few days after the first communion, Simone Juin and her mother sat on lounge chairs in the backyard, sorting and mending washed clothes to be ironed. Nearby, on a small stool, Elia removed debris and hulls from the white rice spread in a round woven grass tray, a *bichèt*, set on her lap. The women conversed as they worked, and Clerise noted that the only times she had seen her aunt sitting with her employers was in the kitchen or in the back yard, and never with visitors present.

"Before you two return to Port-au-Prince, and since we are all tired after those first communion activities, I could send for Manman Dada to come and give us massages. What do you think?" Simone Juin said, as she fixed the hem of one of Rose-Marie's dresses.

Mrs. Visel held up a shirt. "I would really love that. What about you Elia?"

"Sounds great!" Elia flashed a smile and started to get up. "Should I tell Philomene to pass the word to Manman Dada?"

"Okay, but no need to rush. When you finish with the rice."

"People from the countryside really know a lot," Mrs. Visel said. "Take your friend Emma, for example," she told her daughter, "she could never get pregnant until that old man from the countryside gave her some remedy."

"He's the one who also healed one of the priests who had gotten very ill at the bishop's compound, after doctors had given up on him," Mrs. Juin added.

"That's true, I remember when it happened," Elia said.

Simone Juin paused. "Most of the medicine that we take comes from natural ingredients. People from the countryside have passed that knowledge from generation to generation. That's why I think the Catholic campaign of *rejete* against Vodou went too far. So much knowledge possibly lost!"

"Well, we still have to be careful. Evil exists," her mother replied.

"Hum ...hum," Elia agreed. She got up and stepped aside to fan the rice, tossing it into the air and catching it on the tray several times.

Simone Juin chuckled. "Good thing we have Manman Dada. No worry with her!"

A couple of days later, the old woman arrived from the countryside. She began her work immediately, starting with Mrs. Visel, her daughter, and the three Juin children. When Clerise's turn finally came after Elia, Ermance, and Louise, she laid down on Ermance's bed, whose mattress had been covered with a rubber sheet for protection. Manman Dada massaged her vigorously from head to toe with warm palma-christi oil, pulling on extremities, stretching, pressing, and kneading. *"Biskèt ou te tonbe* – your sternum popped," she said at the end. "But I took care of it." Before she collected her fee and left, she conferred with Mrs. Juin, Mrs. Visel, and Elia, providing recommendations for rest and herbal teas.

"Pitit mwen, my child," she said touching Clerise's shoulder when she met her on the way out, "you have

really grown. Keep on doing well. God will bless you and give you strength."

Later, for the first time since the conversation with her aunt about her mother, Clerise allowed herself to remember her life of long ago, and to think of her father. She recalled not wanting to go with him to the village, a fact that the Juins had interpreted as an expression of her attachment to their family, and which had made them consider her a permanent member of their household. At the time, she had been terrified of her stepmother and felt safe in Les Cayes. Now, she noticed that her aunt and employers seemed to look at her often when they conversed, and to pay more attention to her than usual. And she wondered why.

A familiar sound from the street caught her attention. *"Men Manni an! Men Manni an! MAN...NICOTA CA...LIENTE!"* the street vendor yelled from the top of her lungs, adding Spanish words to her Creole advertisement of warm roasted peanuts. Her use of the foreign language never failed to attract potential clients in the neighborhood.

As usual, by mid-morning the woman crossed Kafou Orèl, a large wooden tray with high edges, a *bak*, full of peanuts sitting in perfect equilibrium atop her head, over a *tiyon*, a coiled rag cushion. With a scarf around her hair and another tightly wrapped around her hips, she took leisurely strides and carried a small stool, all the while advertising her ware, *"MAN... NICOTA CA... LIENTE!"*

"*Madanm*, come sell some peanuts!" Clerise called. "Ms. Ermance, Ms. Philomene, here comes the peanut vendor."

"Rosy, Pilou, Danny, the peanut vendor's coming!" Ermance called.

"Watch out for her," Philomene said, "she's been giving very small portions lately. She may be cheating and using a measuring cup with double bottom."

Everyone was present by the time the peanut vendor arrived on the front porch, under the balcony. Quickly, she sat on her stool, placed the *bak* on her lap, and the *tiyon* on the ground. Then, she started to take orders, unaware that she was under scrutiny.

"That's very small," Philomene remarked. "And why do you have to stick your thumb at the edge of the measuring cup? That way you use some of the space without filling it with peanuts!"

"Also, why do you give smaller portions to the children? Don't they pay the same as everyone else? Look at Danny's portion, that's robbery!" Ermance added.

"I'll arrange that. Come child, I'll give you some more," the peanut vendor said very quickly.

"What about me?" Clerise asked. "Ms. Philomene, see how small mine is."

The vendor looked at her sideways and cut her eyes. "You girl! You've already started to eat yours," she said. "There, I'll only give you a few more." Then, she swiftly dropped in her bosom the cloth bag filled with the pennies already collected.

"His portion was even smaller than mine," Clerise said, pointing to Antoine, the boy *timoun kay*. "You should give him some more."

The woman looked her up and down and sucked her teeth as she complied. Then, she gathered her stool, *tiyon*, *bak*, and promptly fled resuming her siren song. *"MAN... NICOTA CAL...IENTE!"*

"Thieving woman! *Manman Volèz!*" Ermance proffered indignantly.

"Maybe she didn't even go to Cuba," Philomene added. "She must've learned how to say those things in Spanish."

"Yeah! She doesn't have money to travel," Danny said.

"That doesn't mean anything," Philomene retorted. "In years past, people didn't need to have money to go to Cuba. Lots of people from the countryside went there to cut sugarcane. That's when the Americans, the *blan meriken*, had taken over the country. Many of those who went, stayed in Cuba and didn't return. Those who came back, are called '*viejo*.' My daughter, Elvire's mother, went and didn't return. Some of the big people in town made lots of money in that business."

"The kids in my school say that one of the beggars near the Cathedral is a *viejo*," Rose-Marie added.

"I heard some of my relatives went too," Clerise said. She felt a hand on her arm and turned. She had not noticed her aunt's arrival.

"You're right. And we never heard anything from them, either," Elia agreed. Then, she turned to Antoine, the *timoun kay*. "You forgot to thank Miss Clerise," she said.

Everyone stopped to look at her and then at Clerise.

"Who? Me?" Clerise asked.

"Yes," Elia continued casually. "Antoine, you should always thank people who help you, and Miss Clerise did."

The boy seemed amused. "Thank you, *Miss* Clerise," he said. Clerise mumbled in embarrassment.

Later, as she did her chores, Elia bestowed upon her one of her large smiles. "You did very well today with that peanut vendor," she said. "Now, you are ready to move forward."

When the time came for her aunt to return to Port-au-Prince, Clerise began to feel that she would miss her. Still stern, Elia had however started to display some affection toward her, occasionally putting an arm around her shoulders, or making a comment related to their family. Clerise felt that she had passed some kind of test. She noticed that Mrs. Juin, Mrs. Visel, and Elia no longer stopped talking when she approached. Instead, they often smiled and directed her to help Ermance in some new chore, such as making laundry and grocery lists in conjunction with Mrs. Juin or Philomene.

Following the first communion, Clerise also noted that Elia increased the time she spent in or near the kitchen, cleaning the adjacent room, reorganizing cabinets, and having Antoine scrub the bottom of pans.

Consequently, Philomene decreased her "errands" in the neighborhood. The day she stopped preparing side meals for her family at the Juins' home, Elia had asked Clerise to follow her into the kitchen. There, she paused, closed her eyes with a contented smile and breathed deeply. "This all smells so good!" she said.

Philomene turned sharply to look at her. "I try my best, to cook as they like," she answered.

"What do we have here?" Elia continued, moving to uncover pans and chatting about each dish.

Philomene answered briefly as she stood in one place, busily fanning the charcoal under what Clerise knew was her personal cooking.

Elia came nearer. "What is this?" she said, lifting the lid.

"Oh, that!" Philomene chuckled. "That's just a little thing I'm doing for my granddaughter, Elvire."

"*Mezanmi!* My God!" Elia shook her head, "I wouldn't think that, busy as you are, you'd have time for that. Come Clerise," she added, still shaking her head in disbelief, "I want you to help me fix something in the next room."

After a while, she returned to the kitchen and began to perform small chores, directing Clerise to do this and that, as she chatted with Philomene about life in Port-au-Prince. "I don't know what I'll find there when I return," she said at one point. "I know every trick in the book. I don't let anything pass, under my watch."

Clerise glanced at Philomene who deftly turned the conversation to other matters. "Yes, that's true,"

Philomene agreed, and continued immediately. "You really miss the people in Port-au-Prince, don't you? Especially the children. How're they doing?" And that started Elia on another round of conversation.

Before she left the kitchen however, she sighed, addressing no one in particular. "After all my work here, I hope everything will be all right when I leave." Clerise felt that her aunt was speaking for her benefit.

Later, she caught part of a conversation between Mrs. Juin and Mrs. Visel. "Well, I think the situation will resume as usual after Elia's departure. Philomene will behave for a while, and then she'll return to her old ways. I don't mind, as long as the job is done, but she needs a jolt from time to time, to keep her from going too far." Clerise made a mental note to remember that comment and think more about it.

Ever since the episode with the peanut vendor, everyone in the household had started to refer to her as "Miss Clerise" when speaking to Antoine, the *timoun kay*. Although still technically a *timoun kay* herself, she was about to outgrow her one-room school and looked forward to the sewing and embroidery lessons which she knew would come next.

Elia kissed her on both cheeks before she left. "I'm proud of you," she said. "Keep up the good work. I'm counting on you."

Clerise felt tears come to her eyes, and kept her head down. "*Orevwa Matant*, Goodbye, Auntie."

It was the first time someone had kissed her since she had left her village as a little girl, so many years ago. She promised herself not to let her aunt down.

To be called "*Mademoiselle*, Miss," had potentially placed her above her aunt's social status. Elia's incontestable prestige among her peers translated in the title of "*Manzè*, Ms.," a compromise between "Mrs." and "Miss," the latter reserved for single and childless women of higher social standing. However, in the Juins circle, even the youngest children called Elia by her given name. Following their parents' example, the youngsters otherwise treated her with respect and deference, while aware of social nuances and behaving accordingly.

Clerise decided to follow in her aunt's footsteps. Determined not to repeat her mother's experience in the village, she also knew that she wanted, someday, to have a home and a family of her own. The talk of an imminent change in the household had also contributed to that dream.

Ermance was getting married. For a while now, the Juins had officially authorized her fiancé, Merilus Altenor, to come to their home and visit in the evening. Then, the couple would sit and talk in the courtyard, just outside the kitchen door.

Meanwhile, in the kitchen, the lively conversation would involve items of special interest. There, the servants ate after clearing the dining room table upstairs, following the Juins' meal. Without a formal table of their own, they kept their plate on their lap and only used a spoon. While the adults set their straight back chairs to lean against the wall for relaxation, the children sat on low chairs or benches, by order of status. As a result, Antoine, the *timoun kay* who had replaced Vanè, often had to sit on the floor.

The younger Juin children also chose to sit on the floor for fun, as they found more urgent interests worth pursuing in the kitchen than in family conversations at the table upstairs after their own meal. Their timely arrival downstairs insured that they would get some of the food stuck at the bottom of pans, which they thought to be more of a delicacy than what was served in the dining room. Also, the kitchen provided freedom from constant attention to good manners and the use of correct French grammar and pronunciation.

There, everyone spoke Creole, with or without the mouth full, while making sure to keep the noise level low. In addition, and as a matter of considerable entertainment in the evening, folk tales and traditional riddles called *kont* were told, or *tire*. Then, Philomene also returned from her home, bringing along her great-grandson Luc and sometimes his mother Elvire. Friends of the Juins' employees, who worked in various households in the neighborhood, often dropped by for conversation and gossip. That way, everyone remained constantly informed of noteworthy items.

The most interesting facts found their way upstairs via the children, the top echelon of the household staff during occasional small talks with Mrs. Juin, or the *timoun kay* assigned to assist older children. In the past, Rose-Marie had participated in the gatherings downstairs, but as she grew older, she gradually limited her socializing with the servants. Meanwhile, for Pilou, and especially Danny, those times were still one of the highlights of their day.

The kitchen was also a good place to learn of the town's lore, as transmitted from one generation to another. In that case, Philomene provided the link, and once in a while, according to circumstances, she described or mentioned past events of particular impact such as fires, floods, or hurricanes, with only a vague reference to their time frame.

Shortly after nine o'clock, Ermance walked outside, as usual, with her fiancé for some more conversation and passionate good-byes in the darkness of the porch-sidewalk. Then, she reentered the house. "Clerise, come here for a minute," she said, "Pay attention to what I'm going to show you. We need to close the doors well at night so thieves don't come in the house." While Clerise observed, Ermance closed the front door, and locked it with a large iron key. "Tomorrow, that will become part of your job," she stated.

By six o'clock the next morning, Clerise assumed the responsibility of opening the front door, under the watchful eyes of the older maid, who showed her how to verify that no tampering with security precautions had taken place overnight. Later, the house became alive and sunny through its many doors and windows that remained open to the sea breeze during the day and for most of the evening.

Everyone felt that Ermance would be sorely missed. Her fiancé, Merilus, a construction worker, had already ordered some of their furniture from a small shop in Lan Savann, as Ermance busily embroidered their combined initials on the sheets, tablecloths, and other items of her *trousseau*. Her plan was to start a small business of sewing or retailing, once married.

After Ermance had accepted his proposal, Merilus formally requested her hand in marriage, by letter to her mother. Mrs. Juin had helped in the matter, since the aspirant had also declared to her his honorable intentions. Ermance's mother responded favorably, and her grandiose letter, prepared by a learned individual from her village, welcomed Merilus in a mixture of French, Creole, and a few Latin phrases thrown here and there. Now also considered somewhat part of the Juin household, Merilus took care to observe proper forms and limit his visits to decent hours of the evening. As a result, he was well liked and made to feel welcome.

Thus, Mrs. Juin constantly referred to Ermance's engagement and imminent marriage as one of her personal achievements. She often reminded the future bride to keep all necessary restraints upon passionate feelings, and even possible pressure from Merilus, until the wedding day. As she put it, such was not only a matter of self and mutual respect, but more importantly a sure way to sustain the future groom's interest and eagerness. She never failed to mention cases of abandoned and ruined women, sometimes left with unwanted children, because of a fatal and untimely "moment of weakness." Ermance became a shining example to other domestic workers, and particularly to Clerise who was also expected to walk in her footsteps.

"I remember when Moustik, the cripple in Kafou Orèl, was trying to be fresh with Miss Ermance," Clerise said in the kitchen, as she joined the chorus of praise. "She didn't pay any attention to him."

"Ermance never looked at any man who would not be serious with her," Louise added. "She knew she wanted to get married and not play around."

"Remember the lottery vendor who liked her?"

"Ha!… What could he do, just selling lottery! That's not stable at all!"

"What about the *fresko* vendor!" Philomene added, while everyone started to laugh. "I never saw Ermance so upset in my life!"

In that case, the *fresko* vendor was not different from the other small entrepreneurs or hired help who, like him, sold shaved ice covered with fruit syrup. Clad in tattered clothes and barefoot, the man advertised his much-appreciated and inexpensive treat, as he pushed through the streets his barely painted cart. Then, he gradually improved his appearance and arrived one day in new shoes, shirt, and pants. While pouring syrup on Ermance's shaved-ice that he had made extra large, he murmured shyly: "Miss, I love you…"

"How dare you?" Ermance yelled, backing a few steps, with a hand on her hip. "What do you think? You must be out of your mind! Keep your *fresko*, I don't want it. Don't you ever dare to come back here! You bold, disrespectful, *Frekan!*"

After that incident, the man lost his clientele in the neighborhood, as everyone knew that he was fresh, a *frekan*. He stopped coming in the area, and instead conducted his business in other parts of town.

Everyone in the household had shared Ermance's outrage at the *fresko* vendor's violation of established social boundaries. Under her verbal assault, the man left in such shame and ridicule that Clerise could not help but feel a flicker of pity, albeit quickly suppressed. Although the *fresko* vendor had not dared to create a scandal and thereby cause embarrassment to Ermance, the very assertive market women who came from the countryside to sell their meat and produce did not have such restraints.

As they crossed town early in the morning, they advertised their wares with utmost energy on the way to the market place, while making scheduled stops at the residences of their regular customers, their *pratik*, with whom they maintained a complex relationship. Since the Juins steady income allowed for an orderly shopping schedule, they purchased a substantial portion of their food in their home. Thus, Mrs. Juin and Ermance also undertook to educate Clerise in the traditional intricacies of serious bargaining.

"Here comes the hen vendor. Call Philomene, Ermance!" said Mrs. Juin, from her seat in the backyard. "Clerise, make sure to watch carefully."

Tied by their feet in groups of two and hanging upside down from the arms of the vendor, the birds' indignant chuckles punctuated her shouts of *"Bèl poul, bèl poul!* Beautiful hens, beautiful hens!" as she moved toward the Juins residence. The woman managed to keep her balance with a basketful of produce atop her head, as she maintained order among her struggling charges. With a morning cacophony of roosters' calls, dogs' barking, lottery vendors' solicitations, casual car honking, hails to sellers from various residences, and other sounds incipient to the setting, the vendor entered the Juin's yard from the street outside.

"Good morning *Pra!* Good morning ladies!" she offered cheerfully, using to call Mrs. Juin and Philomene the affectionate abbreviation of *Pratik,* to mark their steady business relationship. After a brief exchange of pleasantries, the vendor continued. "Look at these beautiful hens! Help me get them off my arm while I put my basket down. I also have some eggs here."

As she complied with the request, Philomene also weighed the birds at arm's length. "I want this one, and that one over there," she said.

Visibly annoyed at having to modify the arrangement of her birds, the vendor still managed to keep her cool. "Whatever you want *Pra,*" she told Philomene. "But these two that are here together, I've kept them especially for you. They're the best of the lot," she added, handing over the hens in question.

"I can look at them both, but I still like to see that other one. I'm going to check each one of them separately."

While assessing the situation, Mrs. Juin also evaluated Philomene's performance. Under the vendor's watchful eyes, Philomene carefully inspected the selected birds, which she held one by one by the legs, upside down, and shook a little to test for weight and reflexes. Then, she opened the beak to check the breath, looked under the tongue, in the eyes, lifted the wings under which she blew, and finally pulled a feather, checking for such undesirable illnesses as *tyak* and *lapipi*. Finally, she tested for age, by assessing the bone structure.

"*Poul sa a rèk!* That hen is old!" she declared contemptuously, as she handed to the vendor her very first reject.

"*Rèk?* Old? That young chick? You don't know what you're talking about!"

"Yes, it is old. The bones are hard."

Now ignoring Philomene, the vendor turned toward Mrs. Juin with an indignation that she seemed barely able to contain. "Madam, I don't come here to play. Let me know if you are serious about buying from me?"

"But *Pratik*, she is only choosing," Mrs. Juin said soothingly. "Philomene, what do you think of the two other birds?"

From there, began a mutually satisfactory round of bargaining at the end of which Mrs. Juin took the opportunity to inform the vendor of Clerise's future role.

As she spoke, a new seller entered the yard. With a singsong, she advertised the wares set on a *bak* atop her head. *"Men bèl pwa, bèl diri, bèl mayi moulen!* Beautiful rice, beautiful beans, beautiful corn meal." Meanwhile, shouts of *"Men chabon, men chabon!* Charcoal, charcoal!" resonated down the street, followed by sounds of increasingly animated voices. "I need to go get some charcoal," Philomene announced, as an excuse to move closer to the action.

"Clerise, why don't you go with Ms. Philomene and see what is going on too," Simone Juin suggested.

In the middle of the street, a donkey, loaded with two full bags of charcoal, stubbornly resisted a woman's efforts to move forward. As vendor and beast tugged in opposite directions, they remained at a standstill, in the midst of conflicting advice from people on the side-walk. Then, with some assistance from passers-by, the woman began to push, pull, and shove, while shouting insults and encouragements to the reluctant animal, all to no avail. Then, with growing exasperation, she ap-plied a few blows with a twig on the donkey's rear end, and directed a rich repertoire of choice epithets to various onlookers who showed amusement or curiosity at her predicament. Immobilized at the scene, a truck driver stuck his head out of his vehicle. "Lady, what are the two of you doing, standing like that in the middle of the street?" he yelled, as he furiously blared his horn. At that, the donkey bolted so fast that it nearly knocked

Clerise down, while the clamoring vendor followed in hot pursuit, amid the general brouhaha. Thus, ended Clerise's first formal shopping lesson.

As she learned to interact with older vendors, Clerise continued to join the Juin children in buying sweets and candies from *timoun kay* selling in the streets. One of their regular suppliers, a girl vendor, taught her and Rose-Marie to speak *jagon*, the Creole pig Latin.

Now allowed to go out free of supervision, the nearly twelve year-old Rose-Marie found that situation a mixed blessing. "Everywhere I go, I always have to take Pilou and Danny with me," she complained. "Why can't they go by themselves with Clerise, if she has to be there too?"

Mrs. Juin spoke with calculated patience. "Clerise is there to help you keep an eye on the boys," she said.

"Good thing that Pilou is about to go by himself. I can't wait for that! Then, I hope he takes Danny along, and Clerise can go help him!"

Rose-Marie's major problem was that the boys, especially Danny, could not wait to get home to tell Mrs. Juin of any remotely suspicious conversation between their sister and her friends, especially when romance was possibly involved. Thus, she more than welcomed the chance to learn to speak *jagon*. As she practiced with the sweets vendor, she immediately shared her knowledge with her friends, and pretty soon the frustrated boys were left in the dark. Clerise, who was also fluent in the language, could not help but overhearing all the secrets, without being included in the conversation. Although Clerise's responsibilities had increased, Rose-Marie was in charge, as Ermance no longer accompanied the children to the pier. It was a delicate situation for Clerise: supervising without appropriate authority — a balancing act of tact and diplomacy.

While she served in the Juins' dining room, Clerise also learned to remain inconspicuous at appropriate times. There, she gained exposure to the values and manners of the *elite*, which she was expected to help instill in future generations. She learned of the background and behavior of many of the town's families, and of local, national, and international events. She heard stories involving personal and mutually shared experiences of the Juins and their acquaintances and, as the years went by, became quite cognizant in those matters.

Ermance's imminent departure gave her the responsibility of setting the dining table. With Antoine's assistance, she would place the everyday china, dinnerware, assorted napkins, and drinking glasses — with a larger one at Mr. Juin's seat, as a symbol of his authority — on a clean tablecloth. A centerpiece in the middle of the table completed the preparations. Then, the food, sent by Philomene, would arrive at the pantry adjacent to the dining room.

With the Juins sitting at the table, Clerise, Louise, or Antoine, would pass the dishes and stand almost at attention a few steps away, ready to comply with any request. Meanwhile, Ermance stayed nearby to insure the liaison between the pantry and the kitchen, and summon help as needed for trips up and down the stairs to replenish plates. Conversations at the table were not to be of the servants' concern. However to them, these talks were as entertaining and informative as those in the kitchen were to the Juin children.

"Rosie and her friends speak Spanish, and I can't understand what they say," Danny complained.

"That's not Spanish, that's *jagon!*" Pilou interjected somewhat contemptuously.

"*Jargon!* With an R," their mother intervened. "That is the proper way to say it in French."

"Rosie, where did you learn to speak *jargon*," Edmond Juin asked with a touch of amusement.

"One of the girls who comes here to sell sweets in the afternoon taught me."

"I feel sorry for some of those children. I have seen little girls as young as eight or ten years old selling sweets, candies, pastries, or roasted coffee early in the morning or late at night. There should be a law against that," her father replied.

"The one who taught me only sells in the afternoon," Rose-Marie protested, "and she always wears clean clothes and shoes."

"It depends upon where they live," Simone Juin said. "Some of these children sometimes cry in the streets at night. They are too afraid to return to their employers' home, to be beaten because they have not sold enough."

As they continued to speak, Clerise felt happy that she did not have to go and sell anything in the streets. She remembered herself as an excited eight-year-old on her way to town and to a bright future hopefully similar to that of her aunt. At first, she had not understood much of the French that her employers spoke, and had even experienced some difficulty with their urban Creole; but she gradually adopted their mannerisms and patterns of speech. In her seven years in Les Cayes, she took pride in her increased ability to speak French to the younger children, according to their parents' wishes.

"Clerise, some water, please," Rose-Marie said.

When Ermance left to get married in her village, Clerise had already assumed a large share of her responsibilities. As she was crossing Kafou Orèl one morning, she saw Miss Laura, the town's gossip, motioning to her from her side gate. Pretending not to see, Clerise was about to engage down the street toward the Juin residence, when Miss Laura's *timoun kay* reached her at full speed.

"Miss Clerise," the girl said, "Miss Laura wants to talk to you."

"What for?"

"I think it's about Ms. Ermance," the girl answered as they walked, and with what Clerise saw as a slightly mischievous grin.

Half-hidden behind her fence, Miss Laura waved her closer. "Clerise, come here," she said, and then proceeded with some small talk. By the time they broached the subject of interest, Clerise was surprised that Miss Laura not only knew her name, but was also familiar with details of her personal history.

"Ermance got married right on time," Miss Laura said. "With the children growing up now, she wouldn't have been needed much longer. I know Simone would have helped find another job."

"Yes, that's true," Miss Laura's sister agreed from behind the fence.

Ignoring the comment, Miss Laura continued. "But, Clerise, it's not the same for you. They took you since you were little, and you're Elia's niece. You're part of the family. They'll always find something for you to do."

When Clerise left, she thought of the complications that could potentially arise from the emerging relationship with her new pal, Miss Laura. She hurried home, preparing to explain her lateness to Mrs. Juin, and wondered whether or not she should seek advice from her, Philomene, or both, concerning Miss Laura's future inquiries. She felt vulnerable as she prepared to face new challenges.

CHAPTER 3

Class and Color

That afternoon in Port-au-Prince, Clerise and I stood on the side-walk, trying to catch a cab. In the slow rush-hour traffic, the driver of a car glanced at us with a flicker of recognition. Quickly, he turned toward his companion, a young cafe-au-lait woman in sophisticated makeup. They shared a few words, started to laugh, and kept on conversing as their car inched away. The young man then adjusted his rear-view mirror and looked in our direction.

"That guy seems familiar. Do you know him, Nicole?" my mother asked.

"Yes," I said, and mentioned who he was.

"The one who wouldn't learn, and was kicked out of school?" she asked, and I agreed. "The guy who used to like you?" Clerise continued.

"Yes, and I heard that his family sent him here to Port-au-Prince because of that. I don't know what they thought! He was just pestering me and my friends, and I didn't even like him!"

"I also heard some of those whispers. Things have not changed much in Les Cayes," Clerise said. "Like father, like son," she added, and something in her tone evoked painful memories.

1951

When she arrived in Les Cayes, one of the choice times for Clerise to explore the mores of her new environment was at formal dinner parties at the Juins' residence. To begin the preparations, Simone Juin would pull her French cookbooks and plan an elaborate menu, with the advice and cooperation of various family women who stopped by, or were available when summoned.

Always present to assist in these special occasions was Marie, an elderly woman who, raised as a *timoun kay* by the Juin children's great-grandmother, had remained in the family. She lived with Edmond Juin's father and his two single daughters. In matters of etiquette, Marie was the supreme authority among the Juins. She was the repository of knowledge of at least three generations, and only made concessions when convinced that changes had officially taken place in the established tradition. When Mrs. Visel decided to move to Port-au-Prince, she felt confident that her daughter, the young and inexperienced Mrs. Edmond Juin, would have no problem training her staff for special occasions, since Marie was there to help.

Marie knew exactly what to do, and when. She trained and supervised the staff in practicing ahead of time how to fill glasses with the different wines that Edmond Juin had selected, and emphasized which wine went in which glass, and at what time during the course of the meal.

During the event itself, Marie stayed in the pantry for overall coordination, as the adult maids, Ermance and Louise, attended to the guests. Meanwhile, Clerise and the other current *timoun kay* remained available and out of sight, ran up and down the stairs to and from the kitchen, and carried back and forth dishes and messages, as well as specific and precise instructions from Marie to Philomene. However, since Ermance's departure, Clerise had started to serve in the dining room while Elvire, Philomene's daughter, came to provide additional help between the kitchen and the pantry.

Before the guests' arrival, Clerise often felt lost in admiration of the table, then set with the Juins' good linen, china, crystal, and silverware. To her, the Juins and their friends were models of savoir-faire, sophistication, and good taste. Marie's presence was to insure that all went well, and to free Simone Juin to entertain her guests. Therefore, the old woman did not hesitate to step in the dining room to assist anyone who had trouble with the elaborate ritual, and tactfully help to sidestep a few social disasters. As she had trained Ermance, Marie was now ready to complete Clerise's instruction.

Thanks to that special coaching, any high status domestic leaving the Juins' service after a reasonable length of time and with proper references, was almost sure to find similar work in town at more than the average salary. Sometimes, Simone Juin also "loaned" her skilled employees to a friend in need, for a large or small reception, or for very special occasions, including weddings, baptisms, or official functions.

"Marie told us all kinds of things about what used to happen in old times here," Rose-Marie said to her mother. "There are very juicy items about some people."

"Learning about past stories is fine, but there are things best left unsaid."

"You need to know about these things," Marie interjected as soon as Simone Juin was out of the room. "You need to know whom to marry or not to marry, how to defend yourself if people try to insult you, and also whom you are dealing with.... Clerise, you'd better listen to what I am saying. If any of those kids turn out all soft like Mrs. Juin, you're the one who will have to tell their children what they need to know."

In fact, the sins against "impeccable" *elite* credentials were so numerous and wide ranging, that one never knew what a potential opponent could use in an argument. Those transgressions included having been poor, or having lived in a less than desirable neighborhood – if not in the countryside – at some time within the past two or three generations, on either side of the family. The same time span applied to bankruptcies, extra marital affairs of grandmothers, aunts, or other female relatives. Other long-term offenses also included: illicit love relationships of family spinsters with foreign priests, habitual and public drunkenness, inability by any member of the family to speak proper French without a strong Creole accent or *bouch su*, exercise of a less than socially acceptable profession by a forebear, traceable roots in the countryside, "illegitimacy," fraud, profiteering from migrations of braceros or sugar-cane cutters to Cuba, political corruption, cowardice, vulgarity, greed, sudden and mysterious enrichment usually attributed to the suspicion of being a *lougawou* or werewolf. To that latter category could be added whispered accusations of keeping zombies for forced labor in some secret corner of one's residence or countryside landholding; of having *bakas* or black dogs associated with evil practices; of secretly practicing Vodou and having *pwen* or special magical powers; of partaking in suspicious occult behavior, such as doing ritual cartwheels at midnight at street corners, either naked or dressed in white.

Since the *elite* took pride in its European values and lifestyle, any serious deviation from that pattern amounted to a capital offense. Social *faux-pas* generated a lifetime of ridicule to be passed to future generations. Although African traditions permeated all aspects of the national life, they were not officially acknowledged or openly accepted by the tiny and self-described *elite*. However, no dance music could rival the national meringue for sheer fun, although the older generation held in more formal regard the waltz, tango, and other foreign rhythms. Those who came from abroad set the tone for their fellow citizens, and advised them of the latest dances and fashions which, in the past, had included the U.S.-originated Charleston and the Lambeth Rock, then the rage in Paris. Later, as travel

abroad markedly declined, those who arrived from Port-
au-Prince brought to town such exotica as the cha-cha-
cha, the bolero, and later the twist, and the French ye-ye
music. The more one knew of foreign mores and used
imported items, the better was her or his social standing.

On that matter, no other area in Les Cayes surpassed
the affluent neighborhood of Lan Gabyon, at the north-
western end of town. There, in small, modern villas,
lived most of the truly economically successful
members of the traditional *elite*, as well as some middle-
class entrepreneurs who had not quite yet been accepted
in that circle, but did not seem to care. With the short
distances in town, few people owned private automo-
biles, and only a handful of women drove. Most of the
car owners, including several of the Juin's acquaintances,
lived in Lan Gabyon.

The street leading there crossed the entire length of
the town, from the beach in Lan Savann, straight
through Kafou Orèl and Pon Gonbo, and passed *La
Salle Saint Louis*, a movie theater built by the local
bishop. Nearby, lived Madan Dejan the woman who
took care of the Juins' laundry on a weekly basis.

Now responsible for keeping track of minor accounts
and insuring liaison with Madan Dejan, Clerise arrived at
her home to finalize arrangements for a special ironing
in conjunction with the Juins' imminent dinner party.

"Miss Clerise, my mother went to the river. She's
washing clothes at *La Ravin*," a young girl volunteered.

Clerise patted a little boy's head, and continued further down the street, aware of her growing prestige as she exchanged greetings along the way. On the inside road past the soccer field where crowds gathered from all over town to watch the national pastime, she heard the usual songs and chatter before she reached the bank of *La Ravin*. Madan Dejan was not among the women, many naked to the waist, who washed and dried piles of clothes in the river and on nearby rocks. A few children waded and splashed happily in the water.

"*Bonjou*, Miss Clerise! Good morning!" the women answered her greeting. "Madan Dejan went further down the river today."

Clerise thanked them, returned to the main street, and continued straight past Lan Gabyon and the site of what was to become a simple and modern complex of small one-story houses for military families, at the outskirt of town. No high ranking military officer was expected to live there, since the Army provided a spacious house to the colonel in charge of the department in Lan Gabyon, almost across the street from the military headquarters.

After she had made the necessary arrangements with Madan Dejan, Clerise returned to town, leaving behind the road to De Mapou and Charpentier, the semirural areas where a few of the city's families either owned second homes, or chose to live for various reasons. Somewhere beyond, was the road to the village of her birth.

On the way to the Juins' home, she stopped for brief chats and felt a sense of belonging, of being truly part of Les Cayes.

"I'm a little tired. I walked so far under the hot sun," she told Louise, after reporting to Mrs. Juin about her unexpectedly long errand. "I'm going to take a quick rest in my room. If I'm not up at two, can you come and get me?"

Still, after all those years of sleeping on a pallet on the floor, she found somewhat difficult to believe that the bed she had inherited from Ermance was now hers. With her clothes on, she laid down gingerly and closed her eyes for a short nap.

That night, the Juins held a dinner party for Mr. and Mrs. Maurice Brijan who were in town for a brief visit. The brother of Miss Jeanne Brijan who had recently opened the only full bookstore in town, Maurice had returned from Europe to settle in Haiti, with his French wife. They planned to live in Port-au-Prince. Attending to the guests, who included various Juin and Visel relatives as well as Mrs. Juin's best friend Solange Jobert and her husband, Clerise tried not to miss a word of the conversation.

"When are you going to move to Port-au-Prince, Edmond?" Maurice Brijan asked. "You'll do well there. We can all see that the province is dying. There is not much future here for the kids."

"I like my life in Les Cayes. It's quiet, peaceful. We are still able to live decently. The kids are safe and feel loved. We have simple pleasures. The beach is only a few blocks away. The rivers are nearby."

"Those rivers, ha! Don't forget to say that sometimes they flood a whole area, and cause everybody except the victims to come out and socialize while taking a good look at, and commenting upon, the event!" Solange Jobert, Mrs. Juin's best friend, quipped.

Eugene Juin, Edmond's father, replied philosophically, "As everything else in town, the rivers go back quickly to their normal routine, and life picks up pretty much where it had left off."

"I find it easy to enjoy the natural beauty of the city, the sea breeze, the lush vegetation, and the mountains far in the horizon," Monique Brijan commented.

Her sister-in-law, Jeanne, the bookstore owner, responded enthusiastically, "Then, we should take you to L'Ile-à-Vaches and Cayes-à-l'Eau, the islands that you have probably seen at some distance in the sea. They are visible on clear days from the pier."

"Like green jewels in the ocean, they provide unforgettable sights and Eden-like beaches, not only to their residents, but also to the few city dwellers who can afford an excursion by private motor boat, and to those less fortunate who travel there by sailboat for business," Simone Juin declaimed with mock seriousness.

"Unfortunately, they are not large enough to protect the city from hurricanes, which at times, can strike, destroy, and devastate with incredible violence," Louis Visel, her brother, added. "But what I find remarkable is that each time such a disaster happens, the people of

Les Cayes rebuild, sometimes from scratch, in their respective areas."

"Well, most people have lived all their life in Les Cayes, and so have their parents and their parents' parents, way back in time," Andre Juin joined. "Newcomers are fast absorbed by the population, and adjust quickly. We have a nationwide reputation for our hospitality and traditions. At times of national need, citizens from Les Cayes have provided leadership in the name of democratic ideals."

"Still, our city is also one of gossip, and that can become annoying sometimes," Adeline Visel commented. "Fortunately, the kids are dynamic, *une belle jeunesse*, and they have quite a bit of fun."

"By the way," Solange Jobert mentioned, "do you know that Paul Frimère recently told Laura a scary movie plot that he made appear like a real story. Two hours later, he heard at least four different variations of his tale as he walked up Main Street."

"When Laura found out that she had been tricked," Adeline Visel chuckled, "she summoned Paul to her porch, shook her finger at him and said, 'Young man, don't you ever do anything like that to me again!'"

"Those kids are terrible!" Simone Juin said, echoing everyone's laughter.

"Perhaps a little too much," her husband added.

Amid the amusement, Clerise could barely suppress a chuckle while she served at the table. She remembered the day Miss Laura had asked her if she had heard about a huge beast devouring lots of people in Port-au-Prince.

"The kids are also really excited about Jocelyne Nerville's wedding. I think that they are preparing a party at their club," Edmond Juin's brother, Andre, said.

Miss Jeanne Brijan pursed her lips, "Well, I think that Jocelyne is rather young to be married. I have questions about her judgment, and I told her mother how I feel. All I have ever seen her read are romance magazines. Once she came to the store and went straight to the racy French novels. I had to tell her in no uncertain terms that those were not for proper young ladies, and that if I ever saw one of those in her hands, I would notify her parents. Considering the circumstances, the marriage may not be ideal, but it may be the right thing to do at this time."

"Jocelyne is the young cousin that I have mentioned to you," Maurice explained to his wife Monique.

Monique Brijan was, to say the least, quite a curiosity to Clerise, the Juin children, the rest of the household, and the town in general. Although not the first white foreigner seen in town, she appeared different from the priests, brothers, and nuns, as well as from the American missionary families who kept to themselves in their establishment in a nearby village. Those families occasionally came to town in pick up trucks for brief forays to the stores with stringy blond-haired, frightened-looking children hanging close to their parents, and the adults gathering their brood and walking purposefully with inscrutable expressions. In their establishment, they ministered to the local villagers through a church and dispensary, and in later years opened a radio station. The American missionaries generated little interest in town, although those who happened to see them during their shopping trips commented upon their behavior with some amusement.

Other Caucasians in town included members of a Catholic order of prosperous looking Canadian-American priests, to which belonged one of the city's long-tenured bishops. His arrival in the city ended the traditional prominence of the French clergy. The new *Monseigneur* progressively replaced the religious orders of French Breton nuns with energetic Canadian Sisters who spread beyond the town into the countryside. However, in most parishes, the French held their ground and had little to do with the Canadian priests, who lived in a comfortable and modern mansion a little past the neighborhood of Lan Gabyon, and, for the most part, had minimal contact with the local population. They usually traveled in a van from their house to the bishop's compound, smoking enormous cigars and laughing heartily at some private joke.

Thus, for the *elite*, Monique Brijan represented a direct link to the France to which they were attached by language and culture, although always keenly aware and proud that their ancestors had forged their country by defeating the powerful armies of Napoleon Bonaparte.

"When our ancestors fought in the French Army against the British and the Spaniards during the colonial period," Solange Jobert's husband commented, "France was the country of the 1789 Revolution, of 'Liberty, Equality, Fraternity.'"

"If I remember well," Monique Brijan interjected, "at the time, the then colony of Saint-Domingue was France's richest overseas possession."

"Well, the European demand for sugar had led to the development of large plantations. As a result, the opulence of the *elites* — white, mulatto, and black — was built upon the kidnapping and enslavement of masses of Africans, who became the largest segment of the population," one of Edmond Juin's sisters pointedly answered.

Motioning to Clerise to refill the glasses, Simone Juin intervened. "Monique, you seem quite interested in Haitian history. Is that what brought you two together?"

"My interest started after we met. However, I find your history fascinating, especially since now it is also mine. In addition, I happen to be among those who think that Bonaparte betrayed many of the ideals of the French Revolution," the French woman replied tactfully.

"She keeps bombarding me with questions about Haiti," her husband echoed good-naturedly. "Quick! I need help!" he pleaded, throwing his hands in a gesture of mock despair.

"Come on! You have been doing okay so far. I just want to be a competent mother in every way, for our children to be," Monique laughed.

"You can also find some excellent information through various books and publications here. In fact,

Jeanne is our resident expert on the matter," Edmond Juin suggested.

Later, in the kitchen, Elvire remarked, "That woman is so pale, she must be sickly."

"She'll look better, once she stays a little in the sun," Philomene offered.

"With all the beautiful women around here…" Louise began. And she added, "Pilou, when you are ready to get married, you should get a beautiful woman like your mom. Madam has such nice long straight hair and beautiful brown skin!"

"Rosie may not have straight hair like her mother. But, she is a pretty girl with lots of hair. I remember the pretty curls that Ermance used to make for her on Sundays. All she had to do was to roll the hair the day before in those little *papiyòt*, and curl them with the wet comb around that round stick on Sunday morning," Clerise replied.

"Remember how Madam was upset when the Mother Superior said Rosie needed to press her hair to play the angel?" Louise remarked.

More interested in the leftovers than in the conversation, Pilou mentioned distractedly, "Mom said that Rosie's curls were pretty enough without that pressing."

"Rosie wanted to do it, because she wanted to have bangs like Michèle, and mom let her," Danny declared between two mouthfuls.

On her way upstairs with a plate for Marie who had remained available there to attend to the guests, Clerise added, "Even if the children here don't have their mother's hair, they all look beautiful."

"And they'll also have beautiful children, as long as they don't marry somebody ugly like me," Louise joked.

"Pilou and Danny, you'd better listen to that. But, that Brijan guy, he must have really wanted to put a lot of milk in his coffee!" Philomene said.

While Clerise found the subject of the Brijans fascinating, she had little time to devote much thought to the matter. Among her many new duties, she also had to assist Pilou and Danny in their studies since Simone Juin had, the year before, become immersed in Rose-Marie's preparation for the very comprehensive Primary Studies Certificate examination, the *Certificat d'Etudes Primaires*. Therefore, every afternoon after school, Clerise made sure that the boys had a snack, changed into play clothes, and returned home after a brief recreation outside. Then, she drilled them in memorizing the textbook passages assigned from school before they made a final recitation to their mother. Thus, her exposure to Simone Juin's coaching of Rose-Marie, and her work with the boys, allowed Clerise to become somewhat versed in the subjects covered. That knowledge often applied to her everyday life or interests.

However, the Brijans did not cease to intrigue her. On that matter, she knew that the mixture of races had started in Haiti in 1492, in the early days of contact between Columbus' Spaniards and the indigenous population that the Europeans had called Indians. As the latter were rapidly decimated by illness and forced labor in the local gold mines, they were replaced by enslaved Africans. Thus began the infamous triangular trade where a live population of *bois d'ébène*, ebony wood, was abducted from Africa to be sold in the Americas, from where riches were then transported to Europe. Soon after their arrival in the then Spanish colony of Hispaniola, Africans started to revolt, and took to the mountains with remaining "Indians." Thus they formed Maroon communities, from the Spanish word *cimarron*, or untamed. Those settlements became a refuge to freedom seekers, and fanned the flames of resistance throughout the history of the island.

For Clerise as well as the Juin children, the stories of the freedom fighters were sources of endless pride. However, in the context of his studies, Danny had some questions which required his mother's expertise.

"My history book mentions 'those poor wretches' who were taken from Africa and put in slave ships. Are those people also my ancestors who fought the French? Or, are they only the ancestors of people from the countryside?" he asked, as he arrived with Clerise in Simone Juin's room one early evening for his final recitation.

"It is a little complicated to explain," his mother answered. "I think you are asking that question because you are at the beginning of your history manual, while you hear what your brother and sister study further in the book. Come here," she added motioning to him, "you see that picture of slaves and *affranchis*, the free people of color. See how they are dressed differently," she said pointing at the history book. "I am going to say a lot of what you probably know already, but that may help you understand better."

Listening to her explanation, Clerise gained a clearer perspective of Haitian history. She realized that, during nearly three tumultuous centuries of inter-European rivalries, a group of *affranchis*, including the mixed-blood gens de couleur and free blacks had emerged in the land. Often wealthy since the days of piracy, when the survival of the early French buccaneers depended on their alliance with other segments of the population against Spanish settlers, many *affranchis* owned properties, including enslaved Africans. In the then French colony of Saint-Domingue, their freedom and tacit equality with whites was recognized by the Black Code of 1685.

"Okay, Danny. Do you follow me so far?" Simone Juin asked. Engrossed in the story, he nodded affirmatively, while looking at various illustrations in the book.

Clerise also continued to listen to Simone Juin, as she marked pages of assigned lessons in the remaining textbooks. She realized that, with an increasing European demand for sugar, plantations developed and the slave trade grew to the point where racial discrimination had to be enforced to insure the stability of the system. Then, as they tried to regain their civil and political rights during the French Revolution, the *affranchis* entered in shifting alliances with their African brethren against the white colonists. In a particularly painful episode, a group of *affranchis* shamefully abandoned to the revenge of enraged whites the enslaved Africans whose assistance had insured their victory in battle. Sealed by the infamous *Concordat de Damiens*, the Treaty of Damiens, that betrayal had profound historical repercussions.

"Are the *affranchis* my ancestors?" Danny asked, not looking at his mother.

"From that time, I would say mostly yes. But all *affranchis* either arrived here in slave ships, or descended from Africans who had come in those ships. Also, some of the Africans who were in slavery during that period became prominent later, and joined the *affranchis* who were already property owners," Simone Juin explained, still flipping through the history book. "Clerise you can stay," she continued as the young woman neared the door. "Since you help the children study, it is good that you listen to this."

"Yes, Madam," Clerise answered, as she thought, *Now I know who my ancestors really were!* Then, she stood by the door to hear the rest of the story.

The Africans took advantage of the struggle between *affranchis* and white colonists, and rose in a massive uprising. Their alliance with the internationally embattled representatives of the French Revolution insured official recognition of their freedom. As they won political power in the North of the country under Toussaint Louverture, a former slave who by then had become a general in the French army, they began to challenge the former *affranchis* for political and economic prominence. Ultimately, the Northern forces of former slaves faced Southern armies led from Les Cayes by the mulatto general Andre Rigaud, the leader of the *affran-chis*, in a pre-Independence and bloody civil war whose flames had been fanned by the French. The Northern troops won, leaving deep and long-lasting scars. Many wealthy Southerners left for exile to France, Louisiana, other French territories, and nearby islands.

"Then, when Bonaparte sent his troops to destroy the freedom and equality that had been so dearly won, the former slaves and *affranchis* united. Under Dessalines' leadership, they fought and proclaimed Haiti's independence on January 1, 1804," Simone Juin concluded, closing the history book. "Now, Danny, do you understand a little more about your ancestors?"

He kept his eyes on the book. "I think so," he replied.

Rose-Marie, who had arrived in the room and listened quietly while she sat on her mother's bed, had a question. "How come we, and many families that we know, have other kinds of foreign ancestors?" she asked.

"In addition to our common African roots, many of the people that we know also include various mixtures of French, Jewish, German, British, or Italian ancestry. That's because young men from Europe who came to do business in the country often married Haitian women. One of the reasons may have been that laws dating from the time of Independence, and later repealed during the 1915 American occupation, forbade ownership of land by white foreigners, the former 'masters.' However, the Poles and Germans who had defected from the French army and joined the Haitian cause during the Independence war were exempted from those laws, and given automatic citizenship. Those same early Haitian laws also offered freedom and citizenship to any runaway slave who set foot in the country," Simone Juin explained.

"Did any of them come to Haiti?" Rose-Marie inquired.

"Yes. Descendants of blacks from the U.S. whose ancestors were invited by various governments to settle in Haiti, as well as of Jamaicans, Guadeloupeans, and other islanders have integrated very well here, at all social levels. That's why, most of the time, we don't even know any more who their ancestors were," she concluded.

In that context, the news of Jocelyne Nerville's wedding quickly spread by word-of-mouth. A *grimelle très aguichante* — a light-skinned sexy girl — Jocelyne had been the object of countless critical, albeit muted, comments by many in town, including her cousin the bookstore owner. Her most important assets were, by order of importance, her family name, her skin color, her voluptuous body, sensuous walk, and pretty face.

Her family had been prominent in town for several generations. Now rather impoverished, her branch of the Nervilles had managed — in spite of various near "plunges" into the middle class — to retain a tenuous hold on the fringes of the *elite*. Jocelyne's parents were both said to be of "good, but poor families," and counted various relatives, friends, and associates deeply entrenched within the national and local *elite*. Although Mr. Nerville had worked only sporadically for years, he had never missed a day at La Glacière where he socialized with his friends over drinks, for which they discreetly paid the tab. Consequently, Mr. Nerville always maintained an appropriate level of dignity and prestige when dealing with his peers, and a measure of hauteur toward those he considered social "inferiors."

A long-suffering and saintly woman, Mrs. Nerville visited her many relatives with great consistency, and was always ready to assist in their various business and social activities. As a result, the Nervilles were well liked in their social circle, *leur monde*, and able to maintain a modicum of pretense as legitimate members of the bourgeoisie. However, because of that precarious position, they were most careful to maintain social distances, proudly claiming that "in our family, we do not have color prejudice, but we have class prejudice." The goal was to secure a good marriage for Jocelyne and some education for her brothers, so as to restore the family's fortunes.

Some of the Nerville's relatives had not been so lucky. One or two generations of genteel poverty coupled with "bad" marriages or *plasay*, common-law unions with working class or country women, had contributed to sever their ties with the *elite*. Having thus "plunged," they were no longer considered to be of the same clan as the "good" Nervilles; so, they joined other kin of

104 – Marie-Thérèse Labossière Thomas

prominent families who were said to be "just of the same name, but not otherwise related."

On her father's side, Jocelyne was a distant cousin of Adeline Visel, who was thus able to provide some privileged information to her sister-in-law Simone Juin.

"They made the decision rather suddenly. I had no idea they were going to be married that soon."

"I am really glad for the Nervilles," Simone answered diplomatically. "By the way, would you like something to drink?"

"Only some water. I am trying not to get too big, although Louis keeps protesting that the more curves, the better!"

"Oh yes, we need to have some flesh on our bones. That's healthy and pleasant to see. That's what men like anyway," Simone Juin laughed. "Are you sure you only want the water?"

"It will do for now."

"Clerise!" Simone called from the second floor.

"Yes Madam!" the girl answered, not in any hurry to return upstairs. Dragging her feet, she reluctantly started to move. She had just arrived from bringing the morning snack to the children at school and from running other errands. About to change into her work clothes, she felt eager to begin some chores in the kitchen. Helping Philomene was one of her favorite activities, and she loved to watch each step of the complicated ritual of food preparation. Rose-Marie also liked to join sometimes, asking endless questions. While often grouchy and impatient, Philomene tolerated Rose-Marie's inquiries as well as Clerise assistance.

"Clerise! Where are you?" Mrs. Juin yelled.

"Yes Ma'm! Here I am!" Clerise answered, rushing upstairs.

"Where were you? Bring a glass of water to Mrs. Louis. Make it very cool and bring it quickly. "

"Yes Ma'm."

Clerise went to the next room and returned promptly with the requested item that she had placed over a doily on a tray. Her task completed, she waited to be dismissed.

"Thank you Clerise. Oh, that's good! I was awfully thirsty! I may want some more, so don't go away yet!" exclaimed Adeline Visel, as she joined her sister-in-law in browsing through thick hand-made volumes of fabric samples that Clerise had brought earlier from a store on Main Street. The two women sat next to each other at the dining room table, exchanging comments.

"By the way, Clerise, why don't you dust that side of the room and fix things a little, while you wait." Mrs. Juin said. Turning to her sister-in law, she added, "I was going to ask you…. Where is Jocelyne's fiancé from?"

"I don't know exactly… somewhere from the North I think. I haven't heard much about that. I don't know anything about his family, but he is a young engineer with a future, and seems to be suitable. He is also totally in love with Jocelyne!"

"Well, she is pretty, and quite young. How old is she now? About seventeen?"

"Yes, in a couple of months. But you know, it's a good thing for her parents to get her married now. Her mind was not on school at all. I don't think she has completed primary school, and I'm sure that she has not passed her *Certificat d'Etudes Primaires*. The sooner they marry her off, the better for all concerned. The fiancé is being transferred out of town. That's why he didn't want to wait to get married."

"What's the man's exact name?"

Adeline paused for a moment and frowned a little. "It's something like Bopin or something close," she answered. "I have never heard that name before. Anyway, he says that he is going to tutor her and help her continue her education."

"If he loves Jocelyne that much, he will probably help her family too. Poor Germaine, she needs that now. She has already suffered so much. Such a saint!"

"You see," continued Adeline, her arms resting on the fabric book, "I heard that there are quite a few negative comments in town about that marriage. Some people here are so prejudiced! But I can assure you that the young man has excellent manners, from what I have heard. I saw him a couple of times. He isn't what I would call handsome, but he presents well. He'll benefit from the Nervilles' connections in Port-au-Prince. Besides, Jocelyne's father has always said that he did not plan for a daughter to sit long at his house 'warming chairs.' With a girl like Jocelyne, who knows what could happen? She is so flirtatious. But to be fair, she is also nice and affectionate."

"I heard that, at first, her dad was not quite happy with the situation."

"True. It took some convincing. But he had to submit to reason."

"The wedding is going to take place in Port-au-Prince, isn't it? Are you going?"

"No, there won't be many guests. They are going to keep things simple."

"It may be the best thing for them to do. I hope that Jocelyne will be very happy."

"He saw her, fell in love, and she went along. They may not end up having great looking children, but the man speaks excellent French, and seems very positive toward the whole family. As we know, theirs is certainly not the first such union. Black power, *le Noirisme*, has again recently ruled the country with Estimé, and can return at any time. We'll see!"

"Well, that's part of our national history," Simone Juin replied. She flipped the catalog pages and glanced at the fabric samples. "As they say, 'Nobody is out of the thigh of Jupiter.' The mulattos were pretty arrogant under the previous government, and I can understand the reaction that brought the change. But the bitterness sometimes scares me!" she mused. "It's funny though, because look at our family. We have all shades of skin color, and so do most of the people we know." She shook her head in dismay, and then pointed at a piece of fabric. "Do you like this one?" she asked.

Adeline glanced at the fabric. "Not bad," she said. "But I think that we should also look at some other material, to compare. Clerise, bring us that catalog from the chair over there."

"In a way, things are also changing here," Simone Juin continued, while Clerise complied with the request. "In their club, our kids are more open then we are. They also do fun fairs where the public is invited, and it doesn't cost much to get in.... Clerise," she asked, "do you remember who won that big antique doll last time at the fun fair?"

"I'm not sure, Madam," she began, as the women resumed their conversation

"Wake up dear," Adeline Visel said, "color prejudice may not show that much here, but when people move to Port-au-Prince, they change. I heard that sometimes they pretend not to see or even know their relatives or friends. In Port-au-Prince, most people don't care who you are. What counts is what you look like — the lighter, the better. — and how much money you have."

"Don't forget name and connections; they also count. The difference is that here, in Les Cayes, most people have known each other for generations," Simone Juin said.

"Look," her sister-in-law chimed in, "who can be more of a mulatto than Virginia, our former maid? Her father was apparently an American marine, and her mother is one of those light-skin peasants from that area near Saint-Jean du Sud. Can you imagine Virginia at one of the clubs?"

"What about our friends Michel Comart and Claude Lemieux who are having all these mulatto children in

Lan Savann and in the outskirts of town in Charpentier. They have cut contact with practically everyone they knew. But in contrast look at the Baimonts and the Lumiens, for example. Those are very dark, fine, upstanding people, pillars of our society, founding members of all our clubs."

"Yes, and I understand that some of them are also invited to the *Noiriste* club. I also find interesting that many light-skinned people, who are not in our social group, have embraced that so-called black power movement. As they say: 'a poor mulatto is a black man, and a rich black man is a mulatto.'"

"Mostly true," Simone Juin nodded in agreement. "My father told me that, in the past, the old *Noiriste* families had a lot of influence in the countryside. They could levy armies and make alliances. Color helped them connect with 'the masses,'" she quoted with her fingers. "That's why they mainly married dark-skinned people from the upper classes."

"Well, that balance of power ended with the American occupation, and the Port-au-Prince mulattos took control. The *Noiriste* movement of '46 has raised so many negative feelings, though," Adeline sighed. "Fortunately, things are more quiet now!"

Simone shot her a warning glance and briefly tilted her head toward Clerise who, by then, had resumed her cleaning. "For all I know," she said, "politicians have always used poor people to their own ends. They promise a lot and forget everything as soon as they get what they want. Look at those who took power in '46. Most of them have married mulatto women. Their children are going to be full-fledged members of the *elite*. That's how it always happens. By the way Adeline, do you still want your water?"

"No, not really... I think I'm okay now."

There was a brief silence. Then, Simone Juin asked, "Clerise, you heard what we just discussed. What do you think?"

The question took Clerise by surprise. It was clearly a test of her trustworthiness and loyalty to the Juins. Her future was at stake.

Over the years, she had practiced the art of having her presence forgotten when she heard of sensitive subjects involving class, color, and politics. That had been quite an education. She was also aware of appropriate occasions to smile discreetly, or suppress laughter, so as not to appear distant, hypocritical, or otherwise too bold. In intimate circles, she was sometimes briefly included in conversations as she did her work, and participated with the expected mix of cooperation and reserve befitting her position.

She allowed herself a few seconds to think. "Madam, your people are those who treat you well," she answered.

"Quite true, Clerise! I know that you have good judgment and *bon santiman*, true positive feelings. You are really Elia's niece, and she will be proud of you. Continue to do a good job!"

Again, she had passed a test.

The political struggles in the larger society found a subtle echo in the Juin's household, with the kitchen as the main stage. The context was food distribution. Once Philomene had prepared the meal and put it in plates, the servants took turns to carry dishes for each course from the ground floor to the dining room upstairs. After the Juins ate, the leftovers were returned to the kitchen and apportioned to the household staff. Initially, Ermance had performed that duty. After her departure, Philomene began to distribute the food, until such time as Clerise would be fully able to assume that new responsibility. When favorite items were prepared however, the Juins so thoroughly enjoyed the treat that, to the dismay of the attending servants, little remained in the dishes at the table upstairs.

That night at dinner time, Clerise made a special trip to the kitchen. "Ms. Philomene," she said, handing her a nearly empty dish, "that silverfish you made is going real fast. I need to bring some more upstairs."

Philomene took a wooden ladder and dug in a pan. She took a large piece of fish to place in the dish, only to have it fall back in the pan a couple of times. "That fish keeps breaking! I can't even put a decent piece in the plate. *Alatraka!* Isn't that too bad!" Philomene exclaimed, as she placed the now smaller portion in the dish. Then, she pointed to what was left in the pan, raised her eyebrows, made a face, and tilted her head. "Do you think I should send those little pieces upstairs?"

Clerise suppressed a giggle. "I don't really think so," she said. "What you have left in the pan should stay here. You can't send that in a dish."

Later, after clearing the table upstairs, Clerise returned to the kitchen with a nearly empty fish plate. "Madam gave me some money to get us some food from the outside, since there is not enough fish left," she announced.

Antoine, the current *timoun kay* was then dispatched to buy some *fritay*, the very renowned fried food, from Philomene's friend Mama in Pon Gonbo. Grumbling, he left for that unwelcome errand with the assurance that, upon his return, he would find his part of the choice dish that had remained in the pan, thanks to Philomene's ingenuity. As they joined the domestic staff, the Juin children also happily consumed their allotted portion.

Then, Clerise said, "The lady who just moved down the street, and has that little *boutik* where I get things for Ms. Philomene, chopped the hair of the girl who works for her."

"Why did she do that?" Rose-Marie asked.

"The girl is a light skinned *grimèl*. Her hair was chopped because it was longer than the woman's daughters. That's why the girl always wears a dirty beret and some old clothes."

Elvire, who had stopped to visit with her son Luc, was indignant. *"Ki kalite moun sa yo?* What kind of people are these? I see that girl sometimes. She doesn't look well treated."

"People say she's hungry most of the time. I heard they beat her often too," Clerise added.

"It may even be worse," Philomene said. "Antoine, you are lucky to live here, and Clerise can tell you that too."

Thus, Antoine, the thirteen-year-old boy who had replaced Vanè, felt sufficiently encouraged to share the sensational news that, for that night, made him almost a star. As he was of the lowest status within the group assembled in the kitchen, he usually spoke little, so as not to be called *frekan*, bold or forward. But then, he just had to tell the story of Giliane Milset.

Giliane, who was about sixteen years old at the time, lived in a large house several blocks away in another part of town, with her parents and many younger siblings. The Milset family was very colorful indeed, and somewhat unique among the *elite*. Relative newcomers to that group, Mr. and Mrs. Milset had the combined advantage of their light skin color, a steady income from business ventures, and more or less official connections with established members of the bourgeoisie. As they were fun loving, likable, and enjoyed entertaining, their social ascension was swift.

In contrast to their attitude toward their social peers, the Milsets had no close associates among the other classes. Their politeness, care, and concern vanished in their interaction with their servants, and many in their neighborhood said that a lot was demanded from the *timoun kay*, who seemed to attend to the children's personal needs in manners unknown in most other households. Often, neighbors would hear a teenaged boy yell to a young servant, "Girl, come and wash my feet!" Consequently, their domestic workers did not miss an occasion to safely disparage them or complain about problems real or imagined.

In the Juins' kitchen, the gossip often focused upon the Milsets. The latest episode of their saga was of such nature that Antoine, the lowly *timoun kay*, cast his customary reserve and felt that he could at least try to share the story. "Debien, the boy who works at Mrs. Milset, he ran away."

"Why?" everyone asked.

Emboldened, Antoine began to warm up, and after much prodding, recounted the rest of the story. "The water is not working at Mrs. Milset's. It's Debien who carries the water buckets upstairs for the people to wash. He put crushed hot pepper seeds in Miss Giliane's *bidet* water."

Exclamations fused from all corners. "What happened after that?"

"She must not have seen it. It was late in the evening. Debien started running when he heard the first howl. That's how they know he did it."

There was an explosion of laughter.

"Have they found him?" someone managed to ask.

"No. But they've looked for him everywhere."

"How did you hear about this?"

"The Milset people don't want anyone to know. But another boy who works near their house told me. And I haven't seen Debien for a while," Antoine said with the glee that he could no longer contain.

In the kitchen, the laughter could not subside, and soon, everyone in the Juin household knew of Giliane's misadventure.

"Mom said that we should all learn from this," Rose-Marie told her cousin Gisèle who had arrived from Port-au-Prince for a vacation.

"Ouch! That must have hurt," Gisèle commiserated. "Is she okay?"

Seventeen and popular, Gisèle Mussain, Simone Juin's niece and goddaughter, was a year older than Clerise. The fact that she came from the capital gave her a special aura of sophistication in her local circle of friends. About to leave for Jamaica to attend secretarial school, Gisèle was enjoying her final stay in town. Constantly on the go, she had lots of buddies, including some of Miss Laura's nieces, with whom she traded fresh tidbits of information. Presently, she was quite interested in Paul Frimère, the young man who had played a trick on Miss Laura. He also pursued her assiduously. Nurtured by their friends, the budding romance remained shrouded in proper discretion. However, the Juins appeared less than pleased, since Mr. Juin considered Paul a good-for-nothing, lazy bum without a future. Mrs. Juin only hoped that the whole matter would disappear during her niece's stay abroad. Thus, she feigned ignorance, or responded evasively to any joke or passing comment from relatives or friends.

To complicate matters, Clerise also found herself day-dreaming about the dashing, funny, and handsome Paul, whose romantic appeal to many young women was well known in town. The situation was most uncomfortable during his frequent visits to the Juin's residence. Ashamed of her secret crush, Clerise took care not to betray any of her feelings to anyone, at any time. Because of the existing social taboos, she knew that her romantic dreams would never be reciprocated, and that it would take little to expose her to shame, humiliation, and ridicule. Tradition had insured that she could only be an object of lust for upper class males. Thus, she was aware that foolish thoughts would only make her lose her standing in town, a standing gained through her position in the respectable Juin household, but which was still precarious.

Because Gisèle and Paul were both related to the bride-to-be, Jocelyne Nerville, through various levels of intricate alliances, they seized upon the occasion of her wedding to organize a party at the youth club near the pier. Busily running together all over town, they elicited indulgent smiles from friends and acquaintances, while the Juins continued their policy of polite ignorance.

One afternoon, Clerise was ironing in the little room adjacent to the study downstairs. Deep in thought, she heard a babble of talk and laughter that almost made her jump in surprise. Gisèle and Paul, who had arrived from an errand, continued to chatter.

"I want to show you that book," Gisèle said, leading Paul to the study. "Hi, Clerise," she continued. "Can you fix Paul a lemonade?"

"I would like it to come from you," Paul answered. He took Gisèle's hand and looked deeply into her eyes.

They lingered for a moment. "I'll be right back," she said, and left for the pantry upstairs.

"Can Clerise help me find that book in the study? That will help us save time," Paul asked.

"Clerise, why don't you help Mr. Paul find that book. You know where everything is. I am sure that you'll find it faster than I can anyway."

"Yes, Miss Gisèle," Clerise answered, nearly in shock.

As she reached the bookshelves toward the back of the room, Paul came close.

"Good afternoon, Clerise."

"Good afternoon, Mr. Paul," she answered without looking.

"Clerise, do you know how beautiful you have become?"

Those were the very words of her dreams. She turned toward him with a book in her hand, and froze. Quickly, he grabbed her shoulders, "Clerise, beautiful Clerise!"

The book fell. She took hold of her senses, and stepped back. "Mr. Paul, don't do that!"

He moved toward her, with an eye to the door. "Clerise, beautiful girl! *Mwen damou pou ou*. I am falling in love with you."

Suddenly disgusted by his duplicity, she regained her composure and said firmly, "Mr. Paul, if you don't stop, I will have to tell Mrs. Juin."

"Here's your lemonade, Paul. I hope you'll like it!" Gisèle called joyfully from the other room, as she returned from her trip upstairs.

He rushed to meet her and answered in his most suave voice, "I know that I will love it Gisèle! Doesn't it come from you?"

Clerise quietly left the room.

"Madam, Mr. Paul was disrespectful toward me, *li fè frekan avè m*," Clerise said to Mrs. Juin.

Simone Juin was alarmed. "When did it happen? What took place?"

"When Miss Gisèle was here," Clerise started, and tears began to pour down her face. She proceeded to recount what had happened in the study. "Also, yesterday," she continued, "when I was passing in Kafou Orèl, Mr. Paul and his friends were under the lamppost. Someone whistled at me. Mr. Paul started laughing loudly, and then he yelled 'Robert, I didn't know you were into chambermaids now!' I didn't turn. I just kept on walking straight home."

"I saw her crying downstairs," said Rose-Marie who had escorted Clerise to Mrs. Juin. "At first, she wouldn't tell me what was going on. She was afraid to cause trouble. I didn't want to tell you anything in front of dad, because I didn't know how he would react."

"Well, you were right. Your dad and I feel strongly that we have an obligation to protect the children who live here. Their families entrusted them to our care. Edmond is a principled man, and he is not particularly fond of Paul. Better not tell him anything right now! I'll take care of the matter. This afternoon, I will send Antoine to ask Paul to come and see me. We'll have a talk, and he will know that I mean business. I am sure that you will not have to worry about anything like that any more Clerise. What a bum!"

Right then, a commotion outside, in the street below, made everyone rush to the window facing Kafou Orèl. Mr. Juin, who had just arrived home for the midday break, also came to look.

People poured from nearby houses and businesses. They stood in the street, on porches, on balconies, talking and pointing excitedly. A prisoner, trying to escape from the line of inmates routinely escorted to court by a rifle-carrying gendarme, was running up the street. Slightly built, and close to middle age, the man wore a cheap brown suit and an old imported hat. It was a rare sight, since most prisoners were young men from the countryside who went to their arraignment in tattered rags. Often, they had to carry on their shoulders the evidence of their crime, such as a goat, or a bunch of plantains. However, the escapee appeared to be a minor country official or business employee.

In the midst of the commotion, a military jeep arrived at normal speed. The driver, a beefy lieutenant with high political connections, had developed a reputation for rudeness and brutality. Those standing in the street quickly moved to the sidewalk. The jeep slowed down. The lieutenant looked around and appeared to assess the situation. Then he stopped the vehicle, jumped out, and rushed in pursuit. The escapee had nearly reached the top of a fairly high wall. The lieutenant came close, and drew his gun. From the street, one could almost hear a collective gasp. The man had already pulled halfway over the wall, one leg almost on top, the other further down. He looked back and seemed to panic. The officer reached him, grabbed his foot, yanked him down, and began to hit him ferociously over the head with the butt of his pistol. Blood gushed from the man's forehead.

"*Assassin! Assassin!* Murderer!" Simone Juin screamed as her husband pulled her from the window.

That night, she had a miscarriage and lost her twin babies.

PART II

Rose-Marie

CHAPTER 4

Life Cycle

When Nicole asked me to help her fill some gaps in her mother's life story, I felt deeply moved. It was a mixture of surprise and joy, along with the old blend of guilt and sadness which resurfaced when I thought of Clerise. Her daughter and I were finally communicating after so many years, and that in itself was another story. As I spoke to Nicole on the phone, I heard faintly in the background the beat of the most popular and contentious tune of the past Carnival season in Haiti.

1952

Mardi Gras, the Carnival was the one time in Les Cayes when everybody expected surprise, entertainment, and fun. It started slowly on the Sunday following Three Kings Day, gradually picked a tempo during the following Sundays, and culminated in colorful and noisy bloom during Fat Sunday, Monday, and Tuesday, the three days before Ash Wednesday. In later years, the preceding Saturday was added as a special day of fun for students, but by no means limited to them alone. The whole period officially ended on Mardi Gras, Fat Tuesday, although the name was also applied to the entire season.

Everybody in town looked forward to Mardi Gras; everyone, that is, except the Catholic clergy. Right after the *premye gratis*, the first Sunday of Mardi Gras, in churches and religious schools all over town, priests, nuns, and brothers eagerly tried to ward their charges off the dangers of Carnival, threatening hell, fire, and brimstone for any transgression committed then, and particularly — horror of horror! — for the sin of impurity. Since the talks were usually veiled and kept within the absolute limit of discretion, the subject often remained abstract or puzzling to the noninitiate. For those in the know, however, two choices remained available: either to do nothing of the sort, or at least not necessarily as a result of Carnival; or else, if ready and willing to fall into temptation, to obtain forgiveness by doing penance after the fact. That, of course, would not take place until the end of the festivities, on Ash Wednesday, or shortly thereafter, when confession became a must for everyone of the faith.

Nevertheless, starting by mid-morning on the first Sunday, the *premye gratis* of Mardi Gras, a few boys in masks and scary costumes were the first ones out. They had great fun any time some little kid ran away from them screaming with fear. By afternoon, small and amateurish costumed groups from one of the outlining neighborhoods of Dèyè Fò or Lan Savann toured the major streets with drums and maybe one or two other homemade instruments. They would stop at houses of the notability, or anywhere else when requested, to sing a catchy tune in praise of an actual or potentially generous benefactor, or to dance for a few pennies.

On the following Sunday mornings, teenage boys of all social backgrounds, also in spooky costumes, joined the masked younger boys in the streets to scare them, as well as other children, until the early hours of the afternoon. By midday, several unemployed and low-income adult males in more or less elaborate makeshift disguises strolled around town, sometimes just for fun, often to earn some money. Their short comic acts, wooden puppet shows, or assorted tricks never failed to attract small crowds.

One of their con games was *Lamayòt*, a name whose obscure meaning never came into question, since it was a constant of the Carnival season, and as far as anyone knew, would always take place at that time.

By mid-morning, on that second Sunday of Carnival, the shouts of *"Men Lamayòt!* Here comes Lamayòt!" made everyone rush to the street. Excitement and anticipation filled the air.

Disguised just barely enough to conceal his identity and add a little drama to the proceedings, a man arrived slowly, holding tightly under his arm a shoe box more or less crudely decorated. After a small and impatient crowd had gathered, he started his pitch about the wonders hidden in his box. With curiosity mounting in the audience, Pilou asked: "How much you charge to let us see what's in there?"

"Give me *venn senk kòb*, and for those twenty five cents I'll let you see all the extraordinary things that are in this wonderful box."

"You can't give him twenty five cents," said one of Pilou's friends. "Then, we won't have anything left for the other Mardi Gras people."

While the boys continued to debate, an assortment of maids, *timoun kay*, and younger children also engaged in the bargaining.

"Here, I have five cents," a little girl volunteered.

"Rose-Marie, do you have five cents?" Danny asked.

By then, the other boys had come with their share of the negotiated reduced fee. As those who had contributed funds worked their way to the front row amid protest and discussion, the remainder of the crowd continued to push, shove, stand on tiptoes to look over shoulders, and try to be at the best vantage point. Then, the performer backed a few steps and, in good theatrical fashion, brought in full view his mysterious box. Quick as lightning, he opened and closed the lid, allowing only the people nearest him to have a peek. Thus, no one knew for sure what was shown. Since the box contained either an old rag doll, a wooden puppet, a dried lizard or snake, or anything else in that order, the guesswork was endless.

"You didn't let us see enough. You should let us see what's in that box again," someone said.

"Well, you only paid fifteen cents. *Mezi lajan-w, mezi wanga-w*, You only get what you paid for," replied the con man, with the box tightly secured again under his arm. Then, deaf to any protestation or request, short of a repeat paid performance, he proceeded to the next blocks followed by a small and still curious crowd, as a testimony to his popularity and an asset to his business.

Only boys of all social conditions and low status domestic workers could escort *Lamayòt* up the street. Bound by rules of respectability, those who remained behind relentlessly questioned the fortunate ones who were able to see the most.

Then, Rose-Marie noticed a man across the street, staring at Clerise. He looked intently and did not try to hide his interest. Clerise ignored him and entered the house.

"Do you know what was in the box?" Rose-Marie asked. She had to watch from the balcony, because she was already thirteen years old.

"I don't think anyone saw anything."

"Who was that man who kept looking at you?"

"I don't know," Clerise mused, "but I've seen him somewhere before."

As Sundays passed and Carnival progressed, more and more elaborate and structured groups started to emerge, including *Lavni* and *Tirayè*, the latter with sugarcane leaves that its members waved rhythmically to the beat of songs and drums. At first, those groups remained in their working-class neighborhoods of Lan Savann, Lilèt, and other areas near the market place, as well as Kat Chemen at the outskirt of town. Then, they ventured more on the main streets beginning late in the evening, then increasingly earlier, and finally in the afternoon at the end of the season.

At different times in the life of the city, other groups followed the same pattern simultaneously or in succession, and performed their numbers at major street corners: the *Wa Djab*, in rich costumes, holding an elaborately made diamond-shaped tower, by strings, on top of their heads; the group *Bese-Pise*, whose very down-to-earth name and accompanying gesture did not deter much from the spectacle of its eye-catching dances, gracefully performed by adults and children in bright *madras* turbans and flowing robes; the group *Trese-Riban*, whose maypole dance routine included the use of ribbons of various length; all uniquely original in an array of colors and sounds.

In subsequent years, by mid-season, the main event of the Carnival started to unfold with the appearance of the two major organized groups in town, *Lajenès* and *Tato*, who competed fiercely for the hearts and minds of their fellow citizens. For maximum effect, they combined theme costumes for the regular members, an occasional float, a well-equipped musical band moving slowly in a big open truck and blazing its latest creation, usually insulting to the competition or poking fun at someone else in town, with a chorus repeated by the wildly dancing and shouting crowd of followers stretching for blocks at a time. Nevertheless, in spite of the hotly contested debates among fans, no clear winner had ever emerged.

With passions running high in an atmosphere of free flowing alcohol and lust, local authorities were careful not to let the two groups meet, especially at the end of the season. Previous accidental encounters had resulted in a few bloody fights, and even in some limited battles, with conch shells used as projectiles.

The core membership of *Tato* and *Lajenès* also included low-income people, prostitutes, plus some middle class men in the leadership. The latter did not participate in the wild dancing, shouting, and other deportments. Rather, at least in the daytime, they walked at the front of the crowd, somewhat on the side, to make sure that all was in order. Such policing, with the assistance of a few ever-present *gendarmes*, was especially important when formally announced visits were paid to leading citizens chosen as sponsors.

Aside from such occurrences, the *elite*, its female household employees, and the middle classes enjoyed everything having to do with organized crowds during Carnival from the safe distance of porches, balconies, or cars. Exempt from that rule were older teenage boys and young men, whose direct involvement in the festivities was tolerated, or at least politely ignored, provided that they kept a certain decorum while passing through respectable neighborhoods during daytime hours.

That year, one of the leading Mardi Gras groups had announced a visit to the Visels. With friends and relatives gathered on the hosts' balcony, Rose-Marie waited. Near her, Clerise peered at the crowd coming from blocks away as waves of revelers moved and pulsated toward them. The air vibrated with the pounding of drums and the chorus of songs, while the Juins, Visels, and their friends graciously nodded, waved, and smiled at the crowd below.

The dancing and noise gradually subsided. The band began its theme song. The crowd joined and waived various flags in an official salute to the honored host. On behalf of his family, Louis Visel briefly thanked the group for the visit and the distinction, and invited the leaders, the band, and a few selected others to his home for a couple of drinks. There, he also offered several bottles of rum which were passed from hand to hand to the crowd outside, while everyone took a well-deserved break. With shouts of thanks and renewed energy, the revelers departed in a tumult of music and songs.

From her end of the balcony, Rose-Marie saw the mystery man directly across the street, looking at Clerise. He nodded, and in the heat of the moment, Clerise smiled and slightly nodded in turn.

Toward the end of Mardi Gras, the local authorities and the business community organized a general parade that included all the groups. On one of the richly decorated floats, Rose-Marie, Pilou, Danny, and their friends, all in exotic costumes, singing cute French songs and throwing kisses around, participated more directly, albeit not too closely, in the exuberant festivities.

That evening, Clerise, "on loan" to the Joberts for the children's ball at the Military Club, was about to enter the door as Rose-Marie and her friends arrived. Again, Clerise's now customary suitor stood nearby. He smiled at her and nodded. Rose-Marie saw her flush with embarrassment and respond discreetly. Later, to Rose-Marie's teasing, Clerise responded that she had seen the man before while on an errand near the marketplace; she also appeared secretly pleased.

The *Cercle Militaire* catered to an exclusive clientele, including the *elite* and the half-dozen or so military officers in town. The Army provided the facilities, support services, administrative staff, and band, while the membership dues covered additional costs. High government officials whether *Noiristes*, or middle class intellectuals, who did not usually associate with the traditional *elite*, sometimes attended official functions at the club, upon invitation. However, only members and their guests participated in social events such as children's balls.

While the children danced on the floor, chatted at their various tables, or sipped sodas at the bar, Rose-Marie saw the colonel, currently in charge of the department, join Edmond Juin who stood nearby.

"How is Mrs. Juin doing? I hope that she is okay now."

"She has been pretty shaken. But now she is fine, thank you. How about you?"

"As you know, things are sometimes tough. I wanted to tell you that the lieutenant involved in the recent incident has been reprimanded for his behavior. His reaction was excessive. By the way, your son Pilou is growing into a fine young man. He will make a good officer."

"Well… I was thinking more of sending him to study abroad, so that he would come back and take over the business."

"Come on, you also have Danny! Maybe one of them will want to join us in the military."

Edmond Juin laughed. "There is plenty of time before either one of them is ready for that. May I offer you a drink?"

Moments later, as children paraded for the best costume contest, a panel of judges presided by the colonel named Pilou "King for the Day." He chose as his queen one of the colonel's daughter. For days, Clerise and Rose-Marie did not miss a chance to supply all the details of the event to the rest of the household.

After Mardi Gras came the *Rara* season. That evening, Clerise and the children ran from the kitchen to the balcony as they heard the approaching Vodou drums. Those who had remained downstairs, as well as others in the neighborhood, huddled on front porches, close to house doors. In the semidarkness of the street, the *Raras* advanced behind their flag in a small, raucous group. Except for a few dignitaries completely dressed in red, the members, who had probably come from one of the poorest sections of town or surrounding areas, did not wear any disguise. At the center of the group, one of the dignitaries, the *Majò Jon*, performed astounding feats of baton twirling to the accompaniment of drums, bamboo-tube *vaksin*, and salacious tunes. He appeared particularly impressive in the diffuse light of the *lamp tèt gridap*, the kerosene lamps made of tin cans that women street vendors, young and old, carried to provide lighting while they distributed for a fee some homemade beverages. Everyone knew that, as in Carnival, alcohol and sex played their part among the *Rara*. For some reason, however, the young pleasure seekers of the upper classes did not venture past the outer fringes of these groups, and did not stay there too late in the evening. The *Rara* season ended with the last week of Lent.

On her way home with Philomene and her son, after the last stragglers from the *Rara* group had moved up the street, Elvire lingered behind and waved cheerfully to Clerise and the children still in the balcony.

"What's the matter with her?" Rose-Marie wondered. "She never does that."

Clerise shrugged. "She must be happy for some reason.... Danny, it's past bedtime," she continued, taking him inside.

What happened next, Rose-Marie only learned much later.

The following day, Elvire returned to the house. She approached Clerise and whispered: "I see that you have an admirer."

"I don't know what you're talking about."

"Meet me on the porch after I see my grandmother, and I'll tell you more about it."

A short while later, Clerise followed Elvire outside.

"This guy is crazy about you. You know who I'm talking about. He said that you know who he is."

"What do you mean?"

"Come on Clerise, you two have already been exchanging signals. Don't tell me you don't like him too, even a little bit."

"I have merely responded to polite greetings from a stranger. And that's all."

"That's not all, and you know it. The guy has a good job. He says he loves you. That's your chance, girl! At least, let him talk to you."

"How can I do that? Is he going to come and talk to Mrs. Juin?"

"No, no, no, not yet. First, you have to talk to him so he can know where he stands. I can arrange that for you."

"How are you going to do it without getting me in trouble?"

"Trust me, everything will be fine."

All did not go well, however, as Simone Juin happened to notice the unusual conversation taking place on her porch.

"What were you discussing with Elvire?" she asked Clerise.

"Nothing much, Madam. Just a little conversation."

"Listen Clerise, you are a growing young woman, and I want to warn you to stay away from Elvire. She is not good company for you. I won't repeat rumors, but suffice to say that for her to be kept by an older man is already bad enough. You don't want to turn out like her, do you?"

"No, Madam."

Thus, Clerise managed to communicate to Elvire the need to delay their plan, at least for a while. Except for brief greetings hastily arranged with Elvire's help on her way to various errands, she saw less of her suitor, felt resentment toward Simone Juin, and often appeared sullen.

"Clerise," Simone Juin said sometime later, "Laura mentioned to me that she sees you often running errands with Elvire. I want that to stop immediately. I can't keep you from talking to her when she comes to visit in the evening, but that should be all."

You must really think the guy is too good for me! Clerise thought.

Rose-Marie started to detect a change in her mood. "Are you okay?" she asked.

"What makes you think I have something? I'm fine," Clerise answered.

At the end of the Lent period, from the day before Good Friday until Easter Sunday, all official and commercial business stopped in town, and church activities took precedence. As a result, on Thursday, Friday, and Saturday, almost everyone ate only light meals of seafood, including such delicacies as imported canned salmon, when affordable; this was not only as a

way to do penance in compliance with Church requirements, but also, and if applicable, in order to allow the
household help some time for the necessary devotions.
By three in the afternoon on Friday, young people used
stones or any object capable of causing a resounding
noise, to bang repeatedly on the metallic lampposts
standing in the middle of the major streets throughout
the city. Shortly thereafter, the population crowded into
various churches for lengthy devotions.

While nearly everyone in the Juin household left for
church on the afternoon of that Good Friday, Clerise
managed to remain behind, ostensibly to complete some
chores. Later, as arranged, she met with Elvire in one of
the alleys leading to the pier, near the Seaside
neighborhood, a couple of blocks from the Cathedral.
By then, the area was nearly deserted.

"Let's hurry, Elvire," she said. "I can't really stay. You
know Madam is going to ask questions if I get to
church too late."

"It'll only take a minute. Come on! He's dying to see
you!"

"I don't really know if I should. I never did anything
like that before."

"Do you want to remain a maid all your life? How can
he get to know you, if he never talks to you?"

"All I want is to get married some day, and have my
own family."

"He knows what kind of girl you are. Anyway, here he
is. I'll let you talk. I'll stand guard for you. If anybody
comes, I'll cough real loud."

The man hastened to meet Clerise as soon as he saw her. "*Mademoiselle*," he said, bowing slightly, "every time I see you, I love you even more."

"Thank you, *Monsieur*," she answered. "But I really have to go."

As she left, he took her hand. "When can I see you again?"

"I don't know. Check with Elvire," she said, rushing away with confused emotions.

"He just has to talk to you again," Elvire said, while Clerise watched the children on the beach.

Easter had passed and the warm weather called for a good swim. With his peer group, Pilou had completed the informal rite of passage for local boys. They had swum from the end of the pier to the *Saint Simon*, the remnant of the ship that had sunk long ago on a reef in the harbor, and thus gained admittance to that male youth enclave. However, Danny and his friends still stayed with the girls, past Dlo Reno, on the beach south of the pier.

There, the children of the *elite* in imported bathing suits, and sometimes middle class boys in cut-off pants, learned to swim using inflated rubber tire hoses as flotation devices with guidance from parents, siblings, or friends. Maids and *timoun kay* participated in the beach outings to free their employers and older siblings from the burden of routine child care. Sometimes, Clerise, or another trusted older maid, supervised the activities.

That day, she had stayed near the shore, wading in shallow waters with the younger children. As she warned the older girls not to go too far, she thought that she really never had the choice of learning to swim. She looked at the full cotton slip that she wore, briefly imagined herself in a bathing suit, and shook her head to dispel the impossible idea. In addition to the prohibitive cost of the item, she also knew that such a daring act would be considered a blatant sexual display to *elite* males and make her an object of gossip and ridicule in the community. Then, she would lose her job without any chance of finding similar employment in town. She shuddered, thinking of possible alternatives.

Thus, she kept herself busy with the children. They fished for the clams abundantly found on the shore, just by washing off fistful of sand and dropping the tightly closed shells in any container available.

"Let's take as many clams as we can, so we can have enough to make a lot of soup later when we get home," she told the children.

Then, she saw Elvire arriving from a distance with her now five year-old son, Luc, in tow. As they arrived, Clerise stepped away from the children for a quick chat.

"I've something to tell you," Elvire said.

"You know you can't stay," Clerise replied. She bent down and pretended to look for something on the sand.

"What is it now? Can't I take my child further down the beach to Dèyè Fò, if I want to?" Elvire replied, with a hand on her hip.

"What is it then?"

"He saw you right here, at the beach, a couple of days ago. He didn't want to get close to you, so you wouldn't get in trouble. He told me that since that time he can't eat, he can't sleep. He just has to talk to you again."

"I really don't know if I should do that."

"Then, how would you like for Mrs. Juin to find out that you went to a secret rendezvous with a man? Girl, for your own good, you'd better make sure that whatever is going on between you two gets serious real quick."

"Okay, I'll let you know what I can do."

"Just stop at my house the first chance you get. There's something I'd like to show you, too."

They arranged for a meeting on May First, the national holiday of Agriculture and Labor. That day, Edmond Juin was to receive an official decoration and become a Knight of the National Order of Labor, an honor usually bestowed upon "deserving" citizens of the upper classes for their work in the community. Then a high-ranking city official, acting in the name of the President of the Republic, would confer the title on the current recipients and deliver the accompanying certificate, duly signed by the highest authorities of the country. Clerise had planned to sneak out that day to Elvire's house, under the guise of running an errand, while the Juins were at City Hall for the award ceremony.

As usual, the festivities began early in the morning with a military parade which started from the barracks in Lan Gabyon. At the lead, and on each side, two soldiers waved at leg level a short whip, the *rigwaz*, as a warning to those who would step out of the sidewalk and venture into the street, too close to the center of the action. There, playing various types of martial music, the Army brass band preceded two contingents of troops, including their officers, all in resplendent uniforms. A small group of young onlookers, held at a respectful distance by rigwaz-bearing gendarmes, trailed the parade all the way to *La Place d'Armes*, across the street from the Cathedral.

"Clerise," Rose-Marie said when she returned from the ceremonies in the afternoon, after a lengthy stay at the Visels', "you should have seen! First, there was the *Te Deum* Mass at the Cathedral. Dad, the other men who were going to be decorated with him, and the Union leaders, all went to sit with the government officials in the front...."

Although Clerise only appeared to be half-listening, Rose-Marie continued to recount the events of the day. After the Mass, the Union members, singing *Let's make our bosses happy, under our Union's flag...* and other customary songs, staged their own parade to City Hall where they remained outside, while their leaders entered the premises for the official ceremonies. Meanwhile, the Army, with its music, returned to the barracks. Later, the Union members disbanded in order to prepare for more celebrations.

A slight change in Clerise's demeanor alerted Rose-Marie. "What's the matter? Are you okay?" she inquired.

"I just feel a little tired. After I finish to set your school uniform for tomorrow, I'm going to sit down and take a rest."

Later that evening, Clerise did not come to the balcony, as usual, to watch the customary *Retraite aux Flambeaux*. A spectacular event held each year, that traditional May Day torchlight walk was much larger than the goings on of a *Rara* group, albeit somewhat similar, with the same type of membership, music, and street vendors. Instead of the *Rara's* red costumes and the banners, the participants carried lit torches, which they waved up and down to the rhythm of the music. Uncharacteristically that night, Clerise sat quietly by the kitchen door and continued to claim fatigue when questioned. The next day, she carried an aura of sadness when she resumed her household chores.

That somber mood continued through the festivities of the Eighteenth of May which was not only Flag Day, a national holiday, but also the Day of Youth and University. Again, in that circumstance, Clerise showed no interest in the customary military parade followed by the *Te Deum* at the Cathedral in the morning, nor in the special student performances held in the afternoon at the soccer field in Lan Gabyon, which she had never failed to attend. She did not even sing for days the traditional song *C'est nous jeunesse étudiante*, We are the Student Youth, that elementary school children practiced all over town during that period, while they heard over and over the story of the creation of the flag.

Although Clerise never learned the song at her own school, she had continuously practiced it with the Juin children. The year before, when she had turned sixteen, she had stopped going to her one-room afternoon school. Then, she started to learn the basics of sewing and embroidery, twice a week, with one of the many seamstresses in town. Simone Juin provided the small instructional fee. With the children growing and fewer chores to do at home, Clerise also began to assist occasionally at Edmond Juin's store, as a form of on-the-job training. Now she received a modest stipend and was no longer considered to be a *timoun kay*, although not quite an official adult maid.

While keeping her busy, those activities still left some time for leisure. However, unlike the past years, she did not attend any of the soccer games played in Lan Gabyon during that period. She also paid little attention to the accounts of passionate excitement, debates, and occasional fist fights among fans of competing teams, while gendarmes with *rigwaz* restored order.

"Remember that guy who was looking at you during Mardi Gras?" Rose-Marie asked during one of those conversations.

Clerise continued to arrange the boys' clothes in the tall closet in their bedroom. She appeared to stiffen and did not respond.

"Clerise did you hear me?"

"Uh huh..."

"I saw him a few times at the soccer games. Doesn't he work with the people who fix the streets?"

Apparently absorbed in her work, Clerise continued to remain silent.

Rose-Marie continued, "I think he does. Anyway, I also saw him a few times at the soccer games. He didn't seem to make the connection between you and me. But guess what?"

"What?" Clerise answered almost in a whisper, her back still to Rose-Marie.

"I saw him the other day in one of the trucks leaving for Port-au-Prince. The truck was already full of passengers. They stopped up the street to pick up someone. He was sitting at the end of a row. Then he got down to let the other passenger in, and... guess what?"

"What?" Rose-Marie could barely hear. Clerise had stopped her work. She stood still and did not turn.

"He looked toward this house, as if he wanted to see you," Rose-Marie giggled.

Clerise did not answer or move.

"What's the matter with you? Don't you think it's funny? Are you crying?" Rose-Marie asked as she moved closer.

Clerise shook her head and brought a hand to her face. She appeared to wipe away tears. "No," she said. "Something got in my eye. I'm going to take care of it."

"You seem to be upset," Rose-Marie insisted.

Clerise did not speak. She shook her head in denial, averted her face, and left the room.

In June, when the summer vacation began, Clerise escorted the children to excursions to Gelée, the beach area at the outskirts of town, named after a river which ended there in a superb, cool, crisp, natural green pond, overflowing in a clear stream into the blue sea. With her customary competence and a measure of detachment, she also supervised as needed, or watched the children ride their bikes to the nearby village of Charpentier to swim in the rivers.

When it came time to leave for Ducis where some of the town's families owned or rented second homes, she went along with the women, children, teenagers, and majority of household staff, while the husbands joined on weekends. Soon, Gisèle Mussain — now suitably married and who had also come for a short vacation with her new baby — Simone Juin, Matant Elia, and old Mrs. Visel started to have long private conversations with Clerise.

At the end of September, Rose-Marie left to attend boarding school in Port-au-Prince. The depth of Clerise's sorrow at her departure surprised her. "Don't cry, Clerise. I'll be back for Christmas vacation," she said, hiding her own pain. "It won't take that long. I'll write often."

Shortly thereafter, Rose-Marie received a letter from her mother. "As you know," Simone Juin said, "Clerise had not been feeling well lately. She went back to her village a few days ago and will return to us whenever possible." Rose-Marie found the news disturbing. From her experience of life in Les Cayes, she knew that live-in servants had to be healthy in order to keep their jobs. Should they be ill, but apparently soon able to resume their duties, the employer would decide either to allow treatment at home, or in the common ward at the hospital. Home care was generally reserved for the most senior domestic workers, the very few who had served families for at least ten years or more. Others, when affected with long-term conditions, were summarily dismissed and had to carry the cost and burden of health care either personally or through their family. Clerise's situation fell between those two alternatives.

In her answer to her mother, Rose-Marie asked: "Why couldn't Clerise go to the hospital?" In her mind, she envisioned the situation at home, and still wondered about what might have happened. She could see the hospital, a block or so from First Main Street. It was the only one in the entire region, and the source of support for all health facilities in the area. More or less adequately staffed depending upon political fortunes, the original hospital compound also included a Catholic chapel, commonly called *L'Hospice*. Later, a nursing school, one of the two or three in existence in the whole country at the time, was added in some of the unused space.

The hospital mainly served middle and low-income in-patients. For the upper classes, cases requiring hospitalization generally involved a trip to the better equipped facilities in Port-au-Prince, or even abroad, unless the use of local resources appeared more practical for a variety of reasons. In those instances, only private accommodations would do. Women of the bourgeoisie usually had their babies at home, delivered by private physicians who also took care of the family's minor illnesses. The household help was not so lucky.

From past experience, Rose-Marie knew that only in rare instances had a maid gone home, and then returned to resume her duties with the same family. She thought with sadness that with Clerise's departure, a part of her childhood had perhaps ended.

"I understand your concerns," Simone Juin replied. "But before Clerise went home, we made sure that she would be okay. We expect her back with us when she is ready." Somewhat reassured, Rose-Marie still had doubts. She wondered whether or not the man from Mardi Gras had something to do with Clerise's absence. However, she decided not to seek clarification from her mother so as not to aggravate, perhaps needlessly, an already difficult situation.

When Rose-Marie went home for Christmas recess, she remembered how Clerise loved the carols that filled the air from the beginning of December. Those songs, all in French, either related to the religious significance of the holiday; addressed such traditional symbols as Santa Claus, the Christmas tree, or gift giving; or evoked winter, snow, and a fire in the hearth. Although generally irrelevant in the tropical context, the latter topics had meaning for the exceptional few who had previously traveled abroad, and for those exposed to such exotic concepts through books and magazines. However, aside from the words, Clerise loved the music and the atmosphere that it created.

She also enjoyed the traditional pictures of Santa Claus, pink faced, white bearded and haired, fat and jolly, appearing in stores, along with decorations and toys of all sorts. Then, she encouraged the young children to be at their best behavior, reinforcing their parents' admonition that they would only receive a short *rigwaz* whip, as a present, if they acted otherwise.

Thus, year after year, Clerise helped the adults shop in great mystery, for a variety of imported luxury toys such as cars, trucks, wagons, bicycles, guns, books, dolls as well as related houses, appliances and furniture, from the two or three major — but modestly sized — variety stores in town, and from Miss Brijan's bookstore. For gifts to those of more modest means, she purchased the same items in decreasing sizes and proportions, from smaller stores and storefront establishments. The *timoun kay* usually received locally made rag dolls, bamboo doll houses, *fanal* — lanterns made of cardboard and colored paper — or other low-priced toy in that category.

That year, Rose-Marie felt more like an adult as she replaced Clerise for some of the last minute Christmas shopping. With her cousin, Michèle Visel, she carefully made her way home amid blasts of firecrackers. All over town, boys on school recess ran through and across streets to confer, set firecrackers, and rush for cover. Near Kafou Orèl, the girls saw Pilou, Danny, Ti-Louis

Visel, and their friends, cheering at particularly loud explosions. Among the boys, they spotted a couple of *timoun kay* particularly appreciated for their boldness with firecrackers who, they assumed, participated in the activities between errands. As she passed the group, Rose-Marie proceeded with caution.

"Those boys will throw a firecracker behind your feet as you walk, just to scare you. Then, they laugh like idiots if you scream," she told Michèle when they arrived at a safe distance.

"Not if they like you," her cousin answered. "Have they ever done anything like that to you?"

"No, but sometimes they do it to other girls," Rose-Marie said as she turned for a glance in the boys' direction. "You remember how fearless Clerise was," she continued, "and how she encouraged you to set the firecrackers with the boys?"

"Yes," Michèle laughed. "She told me that I was one of the few girls who were not afraid, and that I should go and have fun."

As the season progressed, Rose-Marie felt Clerise's absence even more, while everyone in town continued to prepare for the festivities to come.

On the afternoon of Christmas Eve, the Juin children helped set and decorate the Christmas tree in their living-room. Assembled and arranged from pine branches brought from villages far away in the mountains, their tree reached up to their high ceiling and was said to be one of the tallest in town. Visible from the street, it elicited admiration from passers-by. Each year, the Juins purchased the pine branches from the one or two truckloads available to a limited clientele. Then, they set their Christmas tree in a family tradition complete with imported ornaments, stars, angels, shiny garlands, balloons, and multicolored lights, old and new.

"How is Clerise? When is she coming home?" Rose-Marie asked as she handed an ornament to her mother.

"Yes, when is she coming back?" echoed Pilou and Danny untangling a garland.

"In a little while," Simone Juin answered.

"What's the matter with her?"

"The doctor thinks that she needs a rest. She'll be back soon."

"I thought she didn't want to go home."

"Well, it was hard for her. But she is doing okay. She keeps in touch."

"I hope she is also having a good time. I miss her! She really liked to help put that tree together."

The last balloons placed on the tree, Pilou and Danny joined neighborhood children playing outside with fireworks, sparklers, balloons, and noisemakers. Later that evening, the Juins once more remembered Clerise when it became time to take Danny to his grandfather's home to spend the night under Marie's supervision, while everyone else went to church for Midnight Mass. Still engaged in the festivities, older children filled the streets, while raucous groups of young men sang, laughed, joked, and enjoyed a few drinks as they passed through various neighborhoods either on foot or in trucks.

"After Midnight Mass, we'll eat the *reveyon* at Grandpa Eugene's, and then we'll take you home to see what *Papa Noël* has brought you." Simone Juin said to Danny.

"When will I be able to go to Midnight Mass?"

"When you are ten. That's when I started going," Pilou answered.

"Me too," Rose-Marie added. "And you'd better try to sleep as soon as you get to Grandpa's, because *Papa Noël* will also make a stop there for you."

On the way back, she inquired, "Mom, how old was Clerise when she came to stay with us."

"About eight years old, I think."

"About Danny's age, then."

"Probably."

Why?"

"Because, I was just thinking of all those *timoun kay* helping to put gifts under the tree. Have they ever believed in *Papa Noël?*"

"I don't know. Life in the countryside is very different. When everybody gets so busy on Christmas Eve, their services are needed. But we have always given a gift, however small, to everyone in the household. It is the humane thing to do."

"You have also told those children not to let us know that there was no *Papa Noël*. A girl told me about that when I was seven, and Clerise who was only eleven at the time, protested so hard to deny it! She didn't want you to think that she was the one who told me. She thought that you would send her back home."

Simone Juin laughed, then shook her head. "Clerise is a good girl! Too bad life is the way it is."

The following week, old Mrs. Visel and Elia arrived with gifts from the Port-au-Prince relatives, while fireworks, sparklers, and celebrations continued everywhere in town, toward New Year's Eve. Happy to see them both, Rose-Marie was, however, more interested in going for bike rides all over town with her friends and to enjoy her vacation. Although no longer in full force, the North Wind still had enough gusts to push the bikes once in a while through the streets.

When Elia, who usually made the trip to visit her relatives later during the year, prepared to leave for Fonfrède the next day, Rose-Marie added a box of candies to the package that her mother was sending to Clerise.

"Tell her that I miss her. Is she going to come back with you?"

"Give her some time," Simone Juin said. "She'll be back soon."

Reassured about her mother's true intent, Rose-Marie fully enjoyed the New Year's Eve celebrations, which included the usual fireworks, singing, carousing, and social events at the various clubs.

January First, Independence Day, started with the customary military parade, followed by the *Te Deum*, early in the morning. A little later, people in their finery filled the streets. Adults and children, escorted or not by maids and *timoun kay*, went out to visit relatives and friends. Getting shorter as the day progressed, the visits included an offer of candies and refreshment, and sometimes of *zetrenn*, a modest gift of money for the escort, by the host or hostess.

For the past few years, it had been Clerise's job to take the children to see the Juins' relatives and friends. Because of her absence, Rose-Marie had to assume that duty, while she managed to hide her satisfaction of being in charge under a display of great annoyance. With her cousin Michèle, she led the reluctant children through the ritual in which the two girls had adamantly refused to participate the year before. Then, getting on their bikes the next day, they had only made the absolutely necessary visits to the closest relatives. Now, going through town with the children, they entered various houses where those of the *elite*, young and old, sat with their peers as they conversed and sipped refreshments, while the escorting employees were either admitted to the privileged circle, or given seats somewhat away from the main group, or else left standing. On that matter, Clerise's status had varied according to the household.

By midday, as the visits ended, the children went to their respective homes for the traditional and rather formal New Year's feast, prepared and served by the domestic workers. On that occasion, as well as on her birthday, Marie was invited to sit at the table with Eugene Juin's family. So was Elia, in Port-au-Prince. Although the older maids had often demurred and privately said that they would gladly dispense from the honor, they were always coaxed to comply with what the Juin-Visel–Mussain clan considered to be a part of their enlightened tradition. Sadly, Rose-Marie thought that it would have been Clerise's first year to sit with them at the table on that New Year's Day.

The meal over, and everything put in place, the big moment came for those live-in household employees who had yet had a chance to go out for the day, as they prepared to take to the streets while everyone else rested or relaxed. With hair hastily straightened with a hot comb, locally made inexpensive new clothes or hand-me-downs stiffly starched, and tight squeaking new shoes, maids, *garçons*, and *timoun kay* tried to look their best to tour their employers' friends and acquaintances.

"*Bonn Ane!* - Happy New Year!" an early group of *timoun kay* said to Rose-Marie who was substituting for her mother in the living room. The younger girls advanced timidly to kiss her, and a couple of adolescent boys and girls remained at a distance.

"*Mèsi, parèyman,* Thank you, the same to you," she answered while handing a few coins, the expected *zetrenn*, to each of the visitors and setting aside small bills for older well-wishers to come.

She watched them leave and thought that if lucky, persevering, and tenacious, domestic workers could do pretty well in *zetrenn*, considering their meager resources. As a result, at the end of the day, some were often seen limping on tired feet constricted by new shoes, or nearly falling at every step when not used to wearing high heels, still trying to reach a few households.

Later that afternoon, Rose-Marie watched from the balcony the flow of *ti jou dlan*, the little New Year's Day people, as they were called, and remembered the time when Clerise was part of that crowd after assisting in the morning visits. In subsequent years, she and Clerise had stood side by side on the balcony and exchanged comments on passers-by. She also thought of her anger at the remarks that one of her mother's acquaintances had casually made in front of Clerise. "It's funny," the woman said, "when they trail through your house and expect you to kiss their forehead where grease from the hair straightening, combined with the sweat from walking under the afternoon sun, with remnants of pink powder here and there, has made an uneven and shiny mixture. Sometimes they even walk straight to you, and kiss you as if it were the most natural thing in the world. To prevent that, I usually extend my hand quickly to keep them at a distance. If that doesn't work, I blow the kiss in the air, far enough to avoid any contact." Clerise had remained impassive while Simone Juin quickly changed the subject.

"I got word from Elia," announced old Mrs. Visel, who had her own crowd of visitors when she was in town. "She arrived well in Fonfrède, and she is fine. Clerise was happy to see her and says thanks for the gifts."

Pleased to hear the news, the children prepared to attend the festivities of January Second, the Day of the Ancestors, again a national holiday. Then, afternoon speeches on the *Place d'Armes* led to all kinds of races and other activities, at the end of which local authorities rewarded the winners. Onlookers who came from everywhere in town, crowded balconies and porches of the houses around La Place d'Armes, as well as the plaza itself, to watch the events to their culmination: the climbing of the greased pole, the *Ma Swife*.

Standing in one corner of La Place d'Armes, with the coveted prize of money or imported ham tied at the top, the very tall *Ma Swife* offered a challenge to the many who failed and to the one who succeeded, to the encouragements of the crowd. When a young man clad in barely more than a loincloth took the prize, then quickly slid down the pole, the audience erupted in cheers. After the official congratulations, the winner was led right away, as had happened in previous years, "to the police station," Clerise had told the children, "and when he gets there," she added, "they fingerprint him to see if he has ever been a thief. Then, they keep an eye on him. They think if he can climb so well, he'll have no problem getting into people's houses at night."

At the end of the holiday season, soon after Three Kings Day, Rose-Marie helped take down the Christmas tree, and save the decorations for the following year.

"Tell Clerise I hope to see her when I return for vacation," she said to her mother before leaving for boarding school.

A short while later, Mardi Gras once again started a new cycle in the life of the town.

CHAPTER 5

Changing Times

When we spoke again about her mother, I told Nicole, "I remember how everybody was excited during the electoral period, when I was in my teens. When I went home on vacation, your mom used to say, 'Rosie, tell me all you saw in Port-au-Prince.' She also updated me about everything that happened in Les Cayes."

"Well, I certainly heard about it!" Nicole answered. "And I understand that the excitement was not just in Les Cayes, but all over the country."

"A lot of what we are seeing now relates directly to that period. Your parents also became engaged around that time. By the way, how is your dad?" I ventured.

"Hanging in there," Nicole answered.

"Your mom and I used to talk a lot about him."

I remembered Desil, a serious young man who worked as a clerk for several years in my uncle Andre's store. According to family lore, Clerise's demeanor had impressed Desil while he observed her from afar. Since he knew that any romantic involvement between them would have to be taken seriously, and because he lacked the means to get married, he refrained from expressing his interest beyond polite greetings and casual words when they happened to meet. On an errand one day, my aunt Adeline Visel caught him looking at Clerise in an unguarded moment.

"Simone," she told my mother, "what do you think of Desil who works for Andre?"

"I don't know him much. But I see him as a serious and polite young man. Why are you asking?"

"I saw him looking at Clerise. I think there is some interest there."

"Then, we should get them married. It's about time for Clerise, anyway."

From there, the women started a swift matchmaking campaign in which they involved their husbands. Together, they coaxed, encouraged, and helped both parties in the subsequent courtship, toward what they saw as a perfect match. Clerise was then twenty-one, and Desil in his late twenties. At the time, I was seventeen; and in my memory, their involvement is linked to what happened then, in the larger political context.

1956

The country was in turmoil. The older Juin children had just returned from Port-au-Prince for their summer vacation. After the evening meal, they rushed to the kitchen where Clerise, now in charge of the personnel, presided. Like her aunt Elia in Port-au-Prince, she carried keys to the various household hutches and storage areas, although her supervision was considerably more benign than that of the older woman.

"Tell me all about what I missed," Rose-Marie asked.

Clerise and Danny started to speak almost at once.

"You should have seen those big guys from the Lycée running from the police!"

"I went to pick up Danny from school. People were terrified. They just wanted to grab their children and run home."

"The secondary school students took to the streets. They said they were going to all the other schools to have them close. The kids in my school said they would make all of us march with them. I heard people shouting outside. The kids said the police were going to beat us if we went out. I was scared. I was among the last ones left in the school. I was so happy when Clerise and one of the guys who works for dad at the store came to get me," Danny explained excitedly.

"When I arrived, there were only a few kids in there. Your mom thought it would be safer inside the school than out in the streets. She said to wait for things to calm down before going to get him."

"Desil who works for Uncle Andre also came to pick-up Ti-Louis and we all left together."

"Ooh... Desil...!" Rose-Marie sang as she looked at Clerise. "We'll have to come back to that."

"There's nothing to come back to. I was doing my job and Desil was doing his. Your mom, your dad, and your uncle told us what to do," Clerise answered as she started to apportion the staff's dinner in individual plates.

"Okay. But tell me, what did you see when you went to get Danny?" Rose-Marie conceded.

"By that time, the police had already broken down the demonstration. From what I understand, a lot of the soldiers came out with their *rigwaz* and their *kokomakak*, their billy-clubs. The students started running all over the place. They went inside houses and everywhere else they could hide."

"I was told that some of the leaders stayed for a while at the Dominican consul's house. Did the police do anything to them when they came out?" Pilou asked.

"I don't know."

"Me neither."

Danny paused. "I think I saw some of those students going to school in their uniforms some time after that," he offered.

"Magloire will have to go," Pilou stated, referring to the then General-President who, at the end of his constitutional mandate, was showing unmistakable signs of his determination to remain in power, even by force if necessary.

By midyear, strikes and unrests had started all over the country, including in Les Cayes where students had destroyed furniture, fixtures, and material in the newly-built and modern Lycée Philippe Guerrier, the local public high school. Somewhat considered a symbol of the ostentatious expenditures, graft, and corruption of the government, the lycée bore the first brunt of the protest before the students took to the streets toward other schools to demand their closing in support of the strike. Soon, panicky parents ran all over town to pick up their children. Businesses closed their front doors as *rigwaz*-carrying gendarmes chased striking secondary school students through the streets.

"How long did the whole thing last?' Pilou inquired.

"Not very long," Danny answered.

"It only lasted a few hours," Clerise said as she passed the food. "But there sure was a lot of commotion."

Later that evening, while the children and their parents sat in rocking chairs on the balcony, Simone Juin added a few details. "The police did not actively pursue the students," she said. "The students either went in hiding or sought refuge at the Dominican consulate on First Main Street. A few weeks later, they resurfaced to go back to school. Meanwhile, all kinds of political rumors buzzed around town and opposition to the government reached a new height."

"Spies were said to be everywhere, many apparently sent from Port-au-Prince, so that citizens speaking ill of the government could be jailed," Edmond Juin added, as a warning to the children.

In the rumor mill the General-President and his cronies were accused of fraud, mismanagement, graft, corruption, illegal enrichment, desecration of churches for evil purposes, tyranny, arbitrary arrests, violation of free speech, torture, political assassination, and above all, attempt to remain in power for another term. Soon, various underground songs circulated, recounting instances of government's malfeasance, and poetic license often left room for exaggeration. One song — *Fò l jije*, He Should Be Tried — particularly popular in Les Cayes, attributed the fairly recent death of two prominent local citizens to the president and his brother, although the deceased had apparently died of natural causes and were not known to be government opponents. Since they had not been detained, arrested, or tortured, the general assumption was that they must have been poisoned.

By the time Rose-Marie returned for Christmas vacation, the General-President was already gone. A spontaneous and exuberant demonstration in the streets of Les Cayes had celebrated his departure for exile outside the country. From the Juins' balcony, Clerise and others in the household had watched the parade of stunt-performing bicycle riders, motor scooters, horn-blaring cars and trucks, followed by throngs of people singing, shouting, and dancing. In the midst of the commotion, a dark, medium-built young man emerged from the crowd and moved toward the Juins' house.

"Here is Desil," Danny said, rushing to greet him.

"Mr. Edmond asked me to check with you on my way, to see if everything is okay. As he told you on the phone, he is closing the store and will be home in a little while," Desil told Simone Juin.

"What did you see on your way here?" she inquired.

"All the stores are closing, the demonstration is getting bigger. People are on porches, balconies, and all over the street. There is celebration everywhere."

Caught in the moment, Clerise asked: "Did you hear that when he left for exile, Magloire said that the country was like a cigar lighted at both ends?"

"I heard that," Desil laughed. "Maybe that's what he wishes!"

"Do you know the latest song? Danny inquired, following the young man down the stairs, as he left.

"Which one?"

The boy started to sing at the top of his lungs:

> *"Maglwa se yon gannstè*
> Magloire is a gangster
> *Li piye nou rapyetè*
> He stole everything from us
> *Li pran lajan Kiben*
> He took money from the Cubans
> *Li pase nou nan tenten*
> And played us for fools
> *Mayifikat, Mayifikat!*
> Magnificat, Magnificat!
> *Ala yon bon delivran ...an ...se!*
> What a good riddance!"

Fixing her hair in front of her dresser, Simone Juin recounted the events of that day to her daughter. Then she added with an exasperated sigh: "I thought that things were going to start moving between Clerise and Desil. But until now, nothing has happened."

Rose-Marie laughed. "We are only talking about a couple of weeks," she replied as she stretched on her mother's bed. "Has Desil shown any further interest in Clerise beyond the 'look' that Aunt Adeline caught?"

"We don't want to appear to push Clerise on him. But your uncle Andre casually touched upon the matter of marriage with him in one of their conversations."

"What did he say?" Rose-Marie turned on her side, facing her mother.

"From what I understand, Desil does not feel that he can afford to get married yet. I think that he is helping to support some relatives. He also needs time to save enough to buy the furniture and everything else that is needed to start a household. You know how it goes."

"Well, that can be arranged. Can't it?" Rose-Marie stretched again, sat on the bed, and prepared to get up.

"We thought that we could coordinate more efficiently between our houses and the stores for the help that we need during the holiday season. Since Marie is getting old, Clerise can work on that with Desil," Simone Juin said with a wink. "He is going to come here to begin the process. You and I need to think of ways to get things to move a little."

When Desil arrived later in the afternoon, Rose-Marie and her mother were waiting. "Have Mr. Desil come to the living room," Simone instructed Antoine, the now adolescent *timoun kay*. "Also, tell Ms. Clerise to join us."

"She is nearby, I'll get her now," Rose-Marie offered as she wondered about Desil's possible reaction to the unusually formal reception.

Respectful as usual, Desil betrayed no surprise when the Juin women greeted him with unaccustomed handshakes, while Clerise uneasily followed suit.

"Please have a seat, Desil," Simone Juin offered graciously, indicating a nearby chair. "How is everything for you?" she continued as she and Rose-Marie sat on the sofa and left for Clerise the chair facing Desil's.

"I am fine, thank you, Mrs. Juin. Quite a bit of work at the store now," he answered.

"Over here, too. And with the political situation so uncertain now, we really need to plan carefully on the work that needs to be done, especially during this holiday season. Don't you think so, Clerise?" she asked.

Clerise appeared slightly perplexed. "Yes, Madam," she answered.

Simone Juin nodded pleasantly. "From the top of my head, I know that we'll need help to take the pine branches inside for the Christmas tree, to handle bulky items, and to do some other work. Perhaps some of the workers at the stores can help. Clerise, you need to arrange that with Desil," she instructed.

"May I get you something to drink?" Rose-Marie offered promptly. "A light vermouth? Cinzano? Dubonnet?" she inquired around, while Clerise shot her a puzzled look.

The day after Desil's visit, Rose-Marie came for an early afternoon chat in Clerise's room during the siesta time following lunch. She sat near Clerise on the bed. "What do you think of Desil?" she asked.

"I have known him for a while. What do you want me to think?" Clerise sounded slightly annoyed.

"Why are you so touchy? I was just asking," Rose-Marie protested.

"Listen Rosie. I know what you are trying to do. But I'm not interested. I don't want any involvement with anyone right now. Why don't we talk about something else, like the elections for example?"

Amid what was to become a succession of provisional governments, the electoral process had started in full blast in Les Cayes in 1957. The town overwhelmingly supported Louis Dejoie, a mulatto candidate, who promised to create jobs on a platform of agricultural development. An agronomist and industrial entrepreneur, Dejoie was the great-grandson of General Nicolas Geffrard, a local hero of the Independence war on whose tombstone a monument had been built in *La Place d'Armes*, the town square; he was also the grandson of General Fabre Nicolas Geffrard, a former president of the country. In 1860, the then President Geffrard signed with the Vatican an accord known as *Le Concordat*, which made Catholicism the official religion of Haiti. As a result, the clergy recruited from France received a stipend from the government, became an official partner in public and private education, discouraged the practice and development of Protestant religions, and took an active part in persecuting Vodou practitioners. In the climate of nationalist fervor that emerged during the American occupation of 1915 and continued thereafter, various Haitian intellectual and political sectors, including the *Noiristes*, condemned and reviled that legacy.

Although not born and raised in Les Cayes, Dejoie reclaimed his local heritage after a stint as a young agronomist in the town and surrounding areas. Soon he turned entrepreneur and established a factory in Ducis, the village not far from Les Cayes where the Juins and their friends spent part of the summer. There, Dejoie produced essential oils for export from his fields of *vetiver* and huge tracts of *ilan-ilan* trees spread throughout the region. He also encouraged local farmers to cultivate those aromatic plants, which they sold at prices, apparently deemed acceptable, to his factory. The long-term environmental consequences notwithstanding, the flow of capital, job creation, and increased prosperity in the area made the *elite*-bred Dejoie immensely popular. His democratic and unpretentious style further enhanced that image, as he lived and worked among the farmers, albeit in more modern and comfortable conditions. With strong employee loyalty, Dejoie's local enterprises continued to prosper after he became a senator in Port-au-Prince. Later, he challenged the General-President during the last year of his government.

"What do you think of Dejoie?" Clerise asked Desil after one of their planning meetings in the Juins' backyard.

"I don't know much about him. But many people really like him and want to vote for him," he answered.

"I know that he will be a good president," she replied with conviction. "He has already created so many jobs in this area. I am all for him, because he has already shown what he can do!"

"You may be right," he replied. "Time will tell."

"I wonder whom Desil supports," Clerise commented to Rose-Marie. "It could be Duvalier," she added, as she made a disgusted face.

Dejoie's electoral campaign started almost immediately, with Les Cayes as a major national stronghold, and the bourgeoisie in the lead. It was a passionate affair opposing the Dejoist "Forces of Good" to the "Forces of Evil." The latter group included everyone else, but particularly the partisans of Duvalier, Dejoie's major opponent. A self-described humble country doctor, Duvalier had the allegiance of the old *Noiriste* coalition, with mass support in the northern and central part of the country, as well as in the southwest near the town of Jeremie, and in some other areas. Otherwise, the entire South was Dejoie's country. Following a historical trend, the majority of the influential and largely mulatto *elite* endorsed the mulatto candidate nationwide, while the traditional black bourgeoisie and the majority of middle class intellectuals mainly supported Duvalier and two other leading candidates.

In that context, the impact of national politics on the neighborhood's social climate became clear to Rose-Marie when she returned home for Easter recess. Then, her mother, other women with their children in tow, and sometimes a few men, often gathered after dinner in various backyards or kitchens to exchange the latest political information, including insights from the household workers' network.

For Dejoists, Duvalier was the devil incarnate. They distrusted his character, passionately and militantly opposed his endorsement of Vodou as well as of other aspects of the national African heritage, and feared his *Noiriste* slogan of social promotion for the masses. Consequently, although some Haitian Catholic priests and most of the Protestant churches generally supported Duvalier, the large and foreign-born majority of the Catholic clergy enthusiastically joined the crusade against his candidacy. In addition, "the humble country doctor" was accused of trying to influence the outcome of the elections through secret alliances within the military, and political maneuvering.

"I still don't know for sure who Desil's candidate is," Clerise told Rose-Marie a few days after she arrived. "He doesn't speak against Dejoie, but he's not hot for him either. I heard that some of his relatives are Protestants, so you never know."

"I see him coming in the evening now!" Rose-Marie giggled. "With all the strikes going on, I understand that you still have to work together. Tell me," she added "how do you like him now that you see him more often? Anything new between you two?"

"He's a nice guy. We talk about different things, and that's all."

That evening in the backyard, Rose-Marie observed Desil's low-key interaction with all present, and his patience with the children. She also noticed that, on his way out, Clerise walked him to the front door and waved good-bye as he left.

Dejoists' anger later turned to fury when two young military officers lost their lives near Port-au-Prince in an explosion, which led to the indictment of some of Duvalier's partisans. The implicated Duvalierists went into hiding amid accusations that they were attempting to create confusion in the country and assassinate other political candidates. In a much-publicized incident during an otherwise well-received and attended stop at the beginning of a campaign tour in the South, members of Dejoie's security force were accused, in turn, of the shooting death of a man who had defiantly yelled his opposition to their candidate.

Thus, Duvalier never tried to set foot in Les Cayes throughout the electoral period, or even later. During the campaign, safety considerations prevented such a visit because of the climate of political passion. In that context, an early, unsuccessful attempt by another candidate had resulted in his hasty retreat under a volley of stones and conch shells at the outskirts of town in Kat Chemen.

In contrast, Dejoie received a glorious welcome in Les Cayes. An endless sea of jubilant partisans sang his praise, waived his pictures, displayed signs and banners, and carried him on their shoulders. He promised to provide a radio station to the town, amid thunderous cheers and bursts of songs. The clergy treated him as a sitting president rather than a candidate, and celebrated in his honor a *Te Deum* Mass in the Cathedral. At the end of the ceremony, he placed a flower arrangement on his ancestor's monument on the *Place d'Armes* across the street from the church.

In the general euphoria, Clerise joined Rose-Marie and her friends in the Juins' downstairs study room to comment on the events. "I don't know Dejoie," Clerise said. "I only saw him perhaps once or twice from a distance when he came to town. But what I heard about him is good enough for me."

"Dejoie is so handsome. He's elegant and suave with his wavy hair, and the nice way he brushes it back when the wind blows through it, and he says 'A vote for Dejoie is a vote for work!'" Michèle Visel claimed, with an appropriate demonstration.

"He looks just like a movie star," chimed another of Rose-Marie's friends.

"Look at this picture," joined Clerise. "This is nothing like that nasty, ugly one-eyed Duvalier *jepete* who looks like a real devil behind his thick glasses. He's the worst of the worst, a true werewolf, a real *lougawou.*"

"All over town, the priests, the nuns, and lots of other people talk about his evil magic," remarked Louise who was cleaning the study where the girls had gathered.

"They say he does horrible things so that he can become president," Michèle added.

"I heard people say they don't understand how Duvalier can even think of becoming president when he

172 – Marie-Thérèse Labossière Thomas

couldn't even have a private medical practice. Dejoie created jobs and he plans to develop the country," Rose-Marie mentioned.

"The worse part is that Duvalier and his people are criminals who are making bombs to kill Dejoie and who knows who else," Clerise concluded with a passion that many in town shared.

On the national scene, the larger political picture evolved in shifting alliances among the major presidential candidates for control of the electoral process. As provisional governments succeeded each other under allegations of being pawns of various interests, Duvalier patiently cultivated the all-powerful army, while Dejoie chose to enforce his political demands by relying on his business supporters to paralyze the country through general strikes. While the Dejoist radio *La Voix du Sud*, The Voice of the South, controlled the airwaves in Les Cayes, other broadcasting stations, mainly from Port-au-Prince, Cuba, and the Dominican Republic, also kept the local citizenry informed of larger developments at home and abroad.

As political passions intensified, Dejoie's representatives in Les Cayes enforced, in increasingly coercive ways, the general strikes that he ordered. At first, a loudspeaker mounted on a vehicle circulated throughout the city to pass the word: "Parents, keep your children home. Do not send them to school. The strike continues until the nomination of the constitutional provisional government." Later, the campaign used various communication devices to hurl public insults and threats at opponents, as emboldened supporters of Dejoie carried partisan acrimony into private lives and relationships. Political independence became suspicious, dissidence an affront. The situation exploded when Dejoie's *Rouleau Compresseur*, his human steamroller, took to the streets to enforce his latest strike order. Modeled on the masses of people from the shantytowns of Port-au-Prince who could be summoned almost instantly by Fignolé, a leading populist candidate, Dejoie's *Rouleau* in Les Cayes included people from all social classes determined to block all activities in the city.

It was one of those clear days typical of Les Cayes. Following a series of public treats against anyone who would not participate in the strike, those who had stayed home anxiously awaited the day's developments. News came that the *Rouleau*, which had continued to grow as more people joined, had gone to the nuns' school to demand its closing. While the Canadian Mother Superior negotiated with the rioters, other nuns ensured an escape route through the backyard for the few non-Dejoist students who had shown for class. Word was that a known partisan of another candidate, who had come to get his daughters from school, had to hide at first behind the Mother Superior, and later under a bed in the nuns' dormitory, to be saved from the mob.

By mid-morning, Antoine, the Juins' *timoun kay*, arrived at the house disheveled and breathless.

"Where have you been? What happened to you?" Clerise exclaimed.

The boy bent down to catch his breath. "Nothing, Miss Clerise," he managed to answer. "The *Rouleau* went to the marketplace. They got everyone out. People ran and left their things everywhere. I was near the vendors of fried food. You should have seen all the goodies I found there!"

Now at center stage, Antoine continued to recount the story to various members of the household, providing new details to the information already gathered from neighbors, friends, and acquaintances. It appeared that the reportedly Dejoist military officer in charge of the police did nothing to establish order. Thus, once having secured the marketplace area, the main streets, and the schools, the *Rouleau* decided to carry its activities to the sugar factory, a semi-governmental operation at the outskirts of town, which had remained open. On the way, the mob stopped at houses of leading Duvalierists and promised to return in force after closing the sugar plant.

As Antoine told his story, Clerise's grew restless. She covered her eyes, shook her head in disbelief, and rested her chin on her fingers. Then, she got up and began to pace. "Did they go to Lan Savann? Have you seen Mr. Desil?" she asked.

"I didn't see them go there, and I didn't see him either," Antoine answered.

Simone Juin dismissed the young man and put an arm around Clerise's shoulders. "Desil is not going to have any problem," she said. "People know him and he attends Dejoie's rallies sometimes. We are not sure where his relatives in Lan Savann stand politically, which means that they don't attract attention. There is no need to worry."

Moments later, Clerise stood on the Juins' balcony and watched the *Rouleau* pass in front of the house on its way out of town. She thought of Desil and felt a knot in her stomach. Amid a sea of branches and pictures of Dejoie, the mob moved in a cloud of dust and an uproar of threats against opponents. Many covered their faces with handkerchiefs and, in an unprecedented sight, several women of the bourgeoisie participated fiercely in the vociferation.

The *Rouleau* did not invade the sugar factory as threatened. Instead, a manager well-liked and respected in town met the leaders at the gate and persuaded them to leave peacefully. Thus, the armed soldiers positioned nearby under the command of the colonel in charge of the military department, did not have to intervene. Rumor also had that, unlike the Dejoist officer in town, the colonel meant business. On the way back to Les Cayes, the mob used huge stones and boulders from the nearby banks of *La Ravin* to ransack and destroy the home of a then obscure Duvalierist. Severely beaten, the man was hospitalized, while his wife escaped unarmed. Toward the end of the afternoon, the military restored order and the crowd dispersed without further violence. The day ended on that note.

Not long after, the colonel left for Port-au-Prince to become the new Army chief of staff. That development occurred at the end of a crisis that had culminated in a one-day civil war between factions of the military in Port-au-Prince. The new general quickly overthrew the established provisional government and assumed power at the head of a three-member junta. Thus, the machinery to bring Duvalier to power through fraudulently controlled elections was set in motion. Passions in Les Cayes as well as in the rest of the country continued to escalate.

"So, mom told me that you were very concerned for Desil," Rose-Marie mentioned casually when she arrived home for summer vacation.

Near the kitchen, Clerise continued to iron a stack of clothes. "Yes. I see him quite often now," she answered without looking up, "and I didn't want anything to happen to him."

"Come on Clerise, admit it! You care for the guy. There's nothing wrong with that."

Clerise stopped ironing and glanced around. They were alone in the room. She seemed at lost for words. "Rosie, I have something to tell you," she finally began. "Desil spoke to me the other day. He likes me and wants to marry me."

"Really!" Rose-Marie clapped and jumped. "And what did you tell him?"

"Nothing yet. Please, listen quietly to what I have to say. He told me that he is not ready to get married right now. He is saving some money for that. But he wants to talk to your mom once I give him a response."

"Then, what are you waiting for? Don't you like him?"

"I need to think about it a little more. Yes, I like him. But, as you know, it's not that simple."

"Mom told me that you were very concerned about him when the *Rouleau* was out."

"And I was so happy to see him after that. He must have noticed. I think that may be why he spoke to me the way he did."

"Do you want me to tell my mom?"

"Just give her an idea. But I don't want to talk about it yet."

The subject was not discussed directly. The next morning after breakfast Simone Juin made a passing remark, "Clerise," she said, "why don't you sit in the living room with Desil when he comes in the afternoon? You will be more comfortable there."

"No thank you, Madam. Downstairs is fine."

"Leave her alone, mom!" Rose-Marie intervened before her mother could protest. "What were you telling me a moment ago about the last strike?"

"I was saying that I did go to the hospital to visit the man that the *Rouleau* had beaten. That was a sorry sight!"

"Mom! Why did you go to see him? Did you know him?" Rose-Marie nearly yelled.

Her mother's tone remained calm. "No, I didn't know him. But that day, I happened to meet one of my former classmates who was on her way to the hospital. She invited me to go with her, and so I did."

"People must really think that we are Duvalierists!" Rose-Marie exclaimed.

Out of Simone Juin's sight, Clerise vigorously nodded her agreement.

"What happened to that man was just not right," Simone Juin replied tersely. "Besides, everyone knows where I stand. I don't know Mr. Duvalier. I have known Louis Dejoie for years. How could I be a Duvalierist?"

"Then why did daddy have Danny and Antoine remove the pictures of Dejoie that they had put in front of the house when Dejoie was coming to town!"

"Your father wants to stay neutral. As a citizen, he is profoundly distrustful of politicians and their games. He thinks that all politicians are crooked, or will turn to be that way."

"But why?"

"When he was younger, he helped in the political campaign of a friend that the Vincent government had endorsed. Anyway, your dad felt so disgusted by the cheating that he decided never to cast a ballot again."

"Mom, I understand that dad doesn't let you, Clerise, or Danny go to any political rallies."

"Unfortunately, that's true. It's not that I don't want to, but I am not going to have problems in my family because of politics. Not that I am thrilled about that! Some of my friends are giving me the cold shoulder because I don't join them in their political activities. But your father would not even hear about it! All I know now is that I am going to vote for Dejoie when the time comes. Nobody is going to stop me from doing that!"

"In that case, can we return to Port-au-Prince for the summer vacations? Things are different at Aunt Lina's. I don't think that I can stay here this way."

"I'll talk to your dad. But you also have to understand that he has a business to manage. Like other established businessmen in town, he knows what problems Haitian citizens can have when they get involved in partisan politics. Enraged mobs may come and loot their stores, and that can lead to financial ruin. To your dad, whatever is going on now is not worth it."

"What about the Syrians who have really thrown themselves in Dejoie's corner?"

"When they came here, they were peddlers carrying their merchandise on their back. With typical arrogance, people looked down on them. Now, they have prospered and most of them have adopted nationalities other than Haitian. Foreigners who do business here often benefit from political problems by supplying the various factions. Often, they receive reimbursement for any claimed damage, through their embassies and consulates. As we know, even warships were involved in the past."

"Is that why most of the Haitian businessmen here cooperate with the Dejoists' demands, but don't make enemies with the other side?"

"That's true. I should also say that while most have personal esteem for Dejoie, many have concern about the prejudices and arrogance of his entourage, which is somewhat the case for your father. I agree with him on that to some extent. Still others are rooting for Dejoie privately while they are very cautious in public."

Thus, with Edmond Juin's approval, the children prepared to leave for Port-au-Prince.

"I am happy for you that you can go, Rosie," Clerise said while helping her prepare for the trip.

"I wish you could come too. It must be terrible not to do anything here! But that's not really true for you. I know that you wouldn't want to go right now. You're lucky to have your mind busy elsewhere," Rose-Marie replied.

Clerise's face lit in a smile. "Well…" she started. Then, she continued in a more serious vein. "Some of your Mom's friends are very upset with her. They ask me what the matter is. But some of them are doing things I don't think your mother would ever do. I saw respectable ladies curse out people in the middle of the street and argue like fish sellers with little street vendors — all because of politics."

"That's what dad says. He feels that the way some people are acting is nothing into which we should be dragged. Mom feels so too. Given a choice, maybe she would have thought like him, but as it stands now, she just has to go along with what he wants."

"That's what makes things more difficult for her. But she doesn't show it at all. When you hear her outside, you would think that whatever she does is her own decision. Among her Dejoist friends, I should say that Mrs. Jobert has been very supportive. But anyway, your mom promised that she's going to take me to vote with her on election day. She says that no matter what, she's not going to miss the election in which Haitian women have the right to vote for the first time. I just can't wait for that!"

Best friends since childhood, Simone Juin and Solange Jobert shared a special bond. Their husbands and off-spring of corresponding age also got along well, and they were godparents of each other's children. Solange Jobert's progeny had increased with alarming regularity to the extreme pride of her husband who felt his virility thus constantly proclaimed. As most other women in similar circumstances, Solange was considerably less pleased with the situation, to which she referred as her "enslavement." While presenting a brave front to the public, she was candid with her friend Simone. Rose-Marie remembered one of their conversations that she had overhead a few years before.

"I'm tired of all those comments about my being constantly pregnant," Solange Jobert had said. "As if I liked it! But René cannot wait. As soon as the forty days are over after the birth of one child, he wants to be at it again. Sometimes I try to put him off, but then I feel guilty. I know that he has needs, and I don't want him to go elsewhere. As a Christian, I have to do my wifely duty, otherwise I'll be in sin and also responsible for his straying. Sometimes, I dread going to bed. We have tried the Ogino method without being able to stick to it faithfully. I don't know what to do! But after this one, I don't think I can take another pregnancy."

"Hang in there, girl! You know we are here for you. As a woman, you can't really push him to go outside, although with men, one never knows. But at least, it's worth keeping a clear conscience. Have you talked to your mother about it? What does she say?

"The same as you. Sometimes I am tempted to leave. But then, how would I take care of all those children! Besides, I am tired of being treated like a child myself. René gives me most of his money, and he keeps part of it for his own expenses. If I need more, he always assumes that I am wasting money, and requests a detailed accounting. I find it insulting!"

"Men are like that. Edmond does the same to me. When business is good, he doesn't mind that much, but when things are not going well, it's another story. But then, one has to spend to keep up appearances. Who wants everybody to know about one's business. My mother always told me about Mrs. Vendome, a proud woman who would make rocks boil in water so that the neighbors, seeing smoke coming from her house, would not know that the Vendomes did not have any food for the children that day."

"No money, no one knows you anymore. As soon as you can't pay your dues, they stop inviting you to the clubs. And then what happens to your children? Whom are they going to grow up with as friends? Who knows what manners they will pick up? On top of that, before you know it, they lose their French and are only comfortable speaking Creole. And then, that's it! That's how families *font le plongeon*, plunge into middle class."

"Also, these kids should be dressed properly, and that's expensive. Men don't understand these things."

"Tell me about it!"

"That's why a couple of times when things were not going well, rather than asking Edmond for more money than he could give me, I prepared those pastries and sent them for sale outside. I pretended that it was just for fun so people wouldn't know about my business. You remember?"

As she recalled that conversation, Rose-Marie wondered if it really made sense for anyone to get married under those circumstances. "That's life," Simone Juin had commented that day. "But we also need to look at the good side. Hopefully, things will get better for our daughters."

Now, women have the right to vote at least! Rose-Marie thought while she and Clerise finished packing the various jams, candied nuts and other local goodies that she would take the next day to her relatives in Port-au-Prince. Their work done in that process, her mother and Solange Jobert went to sit nearby in the study.

"Simone," Solange Jobert said, "I know that things must be difficult for you now. It's good that you are letting the kids go to Port-au-Prince. Given the current climate, the situation here would be too hard for them. How are you doing yourself?"

"Well, the best I can. What I find hard is when old friends give me the cold shoulder because of politics.

Some of what they do can be quite hurtful, like when they change the subject as I join a conversation, and suddenly 'have to leave' one by one."

Solange touched her arm. "I know how it is for you. Men do not act that way toward each other on those matters. I am sure Edmond doesn't have such a tough time with the other guys."

"Men are more careful with each other than we are, because they are more violent. They know that things can take a bad turn rather quickly."

"Then try not to let it bother you too much. Deep down, people know you are with us. But with all the excitement going on, they resent that you don't jump into all the activities like most everyone else. The proof is that no one has confronted you publicly, cursed you, or insulted your family through the loudspeaker," Solange laughed.

"It must not be easy to decide whether or not to get married after hearing all of that," Rose-Marie mentioned to Clerise a little later.

"That's not the question," Clerise answered. "Life is not perfect."

Rose-Marie stopped packing. She turned toward Clerise and stared incredulously. "Does that mean you are going to accept Desil's proposal?" she asked.

"I'm thinking about that. But before I do, I need to have a serious conversation with him. If everything goes well, I'll tell your mother."

"She's already making plans for your wedding! She even wants me to tell Elia to expect some important news soon."

Thus, Clerise's engagement occurred during Rose-Marie's stay in Port-au-Prince. The national elections also proceeded in an increasingly repressive political climate, and Duvalier was declared the winner. In Les Cayes, the new government closed the radio station and seized Dejoie's properties. Soldiers tore down his pictures throughout the city and ordered those inside private homes destroyed. Arbitrary arrests, beatings, house searches, and intimidation of former opponents became routine.

In that charged environment, popular wisdom had that, although Duvalier might have stolen the election, his government was not going to last. Exiled abroad, Dejoie kept calling upon his partisans to rise and get rid of the monster. As nothing of the sort was possible under Duvalier's tight rein, repeated harassment and explicit threats from the military, those whose names Dejoie called on over the airwaves started to resent the painful consequences of his patriotic appeals. Thus, when Rose-Marie returned for vacation, she found that an uneasy coexistence had developed in Les Cayes between the military-Duvalierist establishment and the now leaderless local population.

Passive resistance spread in many ways within an outwardly calm situation. The extremely efficient rumor mill, the *teledyòl*, kept alive the constant hope of impending governmental doom, while the clergy and the faithful fervently expressed their defiance in seemingly innocuous religious songs. *"God of clemency, God of victory; save, save Haiti, in the name of the Sacred Heart,"* became a staple of various special religious ceremonies. However, playing one against the other, Duvalier consolidated his power and progressively removed any potential rival or opponent from the higher echelons of the military, beginning with his former benefactor, the general who had brought him to power. He then turned on suspicious members of his own party, fellow *Noiristes* supporters of other candidates, as well as potentially dangerous members of the Dejoist opposition, in what was to become a long series of arrests, torture, rapes, horrific murders, kidnappings, and resulting disappearances initially perpetrated by hooded men under cover of darkness. Thus were born the much dreaded Tonton Macoutes. For terrified Haitians, the Tonton Macoutes became the Duvalierist version of the bogeyman of childhood tales, whose name was now only spoken in whispers.

PART III

Nicole

CHAPTER 6

Full Circle

I know the story of my parents' marriage. Their engagement was brief. Gifts from various members of the Visel–Juin–Mussain clan, including Matant Elia, helped in preparing my mother's trousseau and procuring the furniture and other necessities for the future household. They were married early one morning in the L'Hospice *chapel of the hospital compound where Clerise often went to Mass, in a small, simple, and quiet ceremony.*

I also remember a conversation with my mother as we began again to bond after my rebellious adolescent stage.

"When I was little you used to get us ready in the afternoon, before Dad returned from work. We waited for him on the porch and ran to him as soon as we saw him turning the street corner," I said.

"And I still can see him smile, bend to kiss you and your sister, take you in his arms and carry you home while he held your sister's hand," Clerise added.

"You told us stories," I said. "And Dad taught us riddles before we went to bed."

I could almost see my mother smiling at the memory of past happiness. And as I fell asleep, I returned to the Les Cayes of my childhood.

1961

Their first home in Pon Gonbo was a small, one-story house with a tin roof gleaming under the sun. In the front, two double doors with wooden shutters opened on a porch leading to the street. During the day, while the doors were open one set of shutters always remained closed to insure privacy while the other stayed ajar to accommodate Clerise's small retail business, her *boutik*, which she conducted from a console in the doorway. There, she sold brown sugar, Chalonais butter, bread by the piece, cassava, lard, tomato paste, and other miscellaneous items, to a clientele who mostly lived from meal to meal. In that context, her past experience as a *timoun kay* had proved invaluable.

Because she sold such minute quantities of each item, she set her price by agreement with the client, and also gave a little more than average on each order to keep bargaining at a minimum. With a well-deserved reputation for quick and efficient service, she kept her *boutik* open from early in the morning to as late as possible at night for the convenience of her customers. Soon, the business developed and the other shutter of the double door had to remain open for a second console of displayed items.

Mr. and Mrs. Juin had provided the initial loan for the venture. The main witnesses at Clerise's wedding, they were affectionately called *Nennenn,* Godmother, and *Parenn,* Godfather, in her household.

Now Madame Desil Fleurantier, or Mrs. Desil to her clients, Clerise sat on her porch that afternoon to keep an eye on Nicole who played with her doll, awaiting her friends' arrival. After his day at work, Desil joined them to relax and chat a little with the neighbors.

"How did business go?" he asked Clerise.

"Things are moving, and people keep coming. Soon, we may need more space. Who knows, if we find something that we can afford near Kafou Orèl, that would be good. People there can afford to buy more, and still it will be close enough for me to keep the clients I have here. But first I have to give Nennenn Simone her money back. Then I will ask her to recommend me for credit because I'm going to need more things."

"I don't want to go anywhere! I want to stay with my friends," Nicole said before her father could comment.

Nicole was three years old. In the morning, she stayed in the house and sometimes played with a couple of other little girls who met her mother's standards. In the afternoon, she sat on the porch on low chairs with her friends to play with her favorite doll or improvise games under Clerise's watchful eye. Unlike most other children, Nicole seldom visited other homes in the neighborhood. Her mother selected her friends according to definite criteria, including manners and upbringing.

Ania, a girl of about seventeen who had come from the countryside, assisted in Nicole's care. Ania also cooked, ran errands, and helped serve clients and keep the house clean.

With occasional assistance from Clerise and Janine, Nicole's older sister, Ania also took care of the family laundry. Janine was nearly six years older than Nicole. She spent a lot of time with the Juins who were somewhat raising her. Mrs. Juin's had sponsored her to attend the Canadian nuns' private school for girls near the Cathedral. There the students came from the upper classes and from moderate income families able to afford the tuition. Mrs. Juin, Nennenn Simone, insured that Janine memorized her assigned texts and completed her homework every day after class. She paid the monthly tuition at the school, stayed in touch with the nuns, and had Janine at her house for lunch every day. Sometimes, Janine also stayed there during vacations and on weekends.

In their two-bedroom house, Nicole sometimes heard her parents argue about the arrangements concerning Janine.

"Those people treat us like children. They act like we can't to take care of Janine," Desil said. He sounded irritated.

"What do you want me to do, Desil?" Clerise's tone began to rise. "Do you want me to hurt Nennenn's feelings? Do you want me to get her angry? I have to have that little business for you, me, and the children's future. Things are going well now. What will we do if you lose your job or if something happens to you?" She briefly paused. Then she resumed even more animatedly. "You know I'm most busy when school is out for lunch. You know I can't give Janine all the help she needs to study in the evening. I didn't go to school that much. So, what do you want me to do?"

Desil spoke with contained anger. "At least, have her come home for lunch. She's old enough to help you a little with the clients, or to help Ania with her sister."

"*Ay, ay, ay*, Desil!" Clerise exclaimed. "You want to create trouble for me! It was hard enough to work things out with Mrs. Juin to have Janine for dinner with us. She does all of that because she loves the child. You know what help they are giving us now. They are doing for Janine what neither of us can do. Why rob her of the chance?"

"Look! Don't tell me about doing for that child what neither one of us can do!" Desil exploded. "How can you say something like that to me? Have you lost your senses? Those people act like we can't do anything for Janine! Every time they're in the picture you seem to lose your mind! I'm tired of taking that from you, from them, from everybody!"

"Desil, this is hard on you, on me, on all of us." Clerise's voice was now full of tears and her bed creaked. "Do you think I like it any more than you do? Do you think I have liked it all my life? Nennenn isn't a bad person, she doesn't mean to hurt us, she only wants to help. She has done a lot for me. But if we make her angry, if she thinks we're ungrateful, she can become very upset, and you know we can't afford that now. *Ala traka pou malere!* Poor people's life is not easy!"

Desil's voice softened. "Clerise, stop crying," he said, and again the bed creaked. "I know you're working hard. I'm not blaming you for what's happening. But we need to talk to Janine. We need to remind her of who she is. One thing you can do is go less often to Mrs. Juin in the evening with the kids. Cut it down to once a week, or once every two weeks. Can you do that?"

"I'll try….."

Nicole strained to hear more while she fought her need to sleep. Soon, she lost interest in the subsequent giggles, suppressed laughter, muffled sounds, and other unintelligible noises coming from her parents' room. "I need water, please!" she yelled. All the noise stopped abruptly. "Water… please!" she yelled even louder.

Ania appeared quickly at her side with a cup. "Sh…" Ania said, one finger on her lips. "You're going to wake up everyone here," she added as Nicole took sips of water.

"I can't sleep," Nicole said, rubbing her eyes. She continued to complain while Ania had her use the chamber pot in front of her bed to avoid all possible accidents during the night.

"If you continue to make noise," Ania warned, "Tonton Macoute, the bogeyman, will put you in a satchel and take you away. That's what happens to naughty children," she concluded. Nicole kept silent and closed her eyes.

A thin partition and door enclosed the parents' bedroom between the parlor in the front and the dining area in the back of the house. Nicole and Janine slept in what was originally an open space across their parents' room. To insure their privacy, a colorful drape extended in what would have been their doorway and created a small corridor in the middle of the house. In each of the bedrooms, a double bed took most of the space. Clerise and Desil had a dresser with a mirror and an *armoire*, a hutch, where they kept their clothes and locked the household's prized possessions. The girls hung their dresses in a space behind a homemade curtain along the outer wall, and stored other garments in cardboard boxes underneath. They kept their toiletries on a shelf in front of a medium-sized mirror set on the dining room partition.

In the small and sparsely furnished front parlor, Clerise took pride in her red imported plastic flowers and hand embroidered doilies, wedding gifts that she still treasured. A current and colorful calendar from one of the businesses in town, as well as some religious imagery, and other pictures cut from calendars and magazines decorated the walls. In one of the parlor's corners, Clerise kept her sewing machine, a hand-operated Singer that the Juins had given her as a wedding present. There, she made all of Nicole's clothes, but fewer and fewer of Janine's, since those now mostly came from Simone Juin. Once a year, Clerise sewed one or two dresses for Ania who saved those new clothes for special occasions while she used the ones from previous years on ordinary Sundays, and hand-me-

downs from Clerise or Simone Juin when she worked at
home or ran errands in the neighborhood.

Ania slept on a straw mat in the parlor in the front of
the house where Clerise's business, her *boutik*, was set up
during the day. On evenings and Sunday afternoons,
they pulled inside the two display cabinets of the *boutik*.
Then, business was officially closed and only one set of
shutter doors remained open for socializing. The last to
go to bed, Ania disturbed no one by sleeping in the
parlor. Her presence there was also useful in case a thief
tried to enter the house at night despite Desil's
precautions in locking the two front doors with large
metallic latches. Before she went to sleep, Ania also
extinguished the last light from the kerosene lamp since
there was no electricity in the house.

The morning after her parents' argument, Nicole
woke up early. As she often did, she pretended to help
Ania in her daily routine, which began at five in the
morning when everyone else was still asleep. First, Ania
folded and carried her straw mat for storage in the little
back room where she cooked and ironed on rainy days.
From there, she took a *recho*, a portable cast-iron range,
which she carried outdoors to the backyard to start the
morning fire to prepare coffee. Nicole watched her fan
the burning charcoal with a piece of cardboard. Sparks
flew, and Nicole ran for cover.

The coffee ready, Ania put it in a pot, which she set
on a tray with two *demitasses* in saucers and a sugar bowl,
and took to Clerise and Desil in their bedroom. Nicole

eyed her parents cautiously. They were already awake, and everything appeared in order. She ran to Clerise's side, kissed her, climbed on the bed, and settled in the middle. She turned to Desil and gingerly pecked his cheek. *"Bonjou Papa,"* she said quickly, and she hid her face in her hands to begin their morning game.

"Hmm..., where is she?" Desil growled. He moved his unshaven face toward her and briefly grazed her hand with his cheek.

"It stings!" she giggled at the touch of the prickly hair.

"Then, I am going to take it off," he continued to growl as he got out of bed and started to move about the room.

Nicole rolled onto his empty space and kept her back to him. He tiptoed to the bed and tickled her lightly. She kicked her legs and dissolved in peals of laughter. Clerise briefly joined in the merriment, then also got up. Nicole rolled all over the empty bed and made circles with her arms. Then, she jumped off and ran to the dining room to "help" Ania set the table for a quick breakfast of bread, butter, and coffee for Janine, and *Poban* plantains with salted herrings, for the adults. In the meantime, as everyone else showered and prepared for the day, Ania emptied the chamber pots for the whole family, in the outhouse at the end of the small backyard.

After a lengthy nap, Nicole joined her mother at the *boutik*, and sat quietly, still dozing a little. A moment later, Ania returned from the public fountain at the corner of the street with water for cooking and drinking that she stored inside the house in big and small clay jars, *kannari* and *krich*. Then, she washed Nicole with cups of rainwater kept in large basins and pails for laundry, bathing, and housecleaning, in an enclosure in a corner of the backyard. To Janine's discomfort, Ania shared that shower facility with the family.

A few days later, Nicole overheard her sister ask her mother why Ania had to use the family's shower enclosure and outhouse. Janine was concerned because Nennenn Simone's friends, who had similar facilities in their home, usually made separate ones for their hired help. Surprisingly, Clerise became extremely angry. "And where do you want her to go?"

"Maybe we can make something for her."

"Listen! Who do you think you are? Ania is a person just like you and me, and Mrs. Juin, and her stupid friends. What's the matter with you? Desil may be right. You stay too much over there. I really have to start looking into that!"

"But..., "

"Don't you tell me anything else, and I'd better never hear that kind of talk from you! Now, go and study, or help Ania at the *boutik*."

Puzzled, Janine left, ready to cry.

"Is Janine very bad? Are you going to spank her?" Nicole asked her mother.

"No... she is a good girl. She just has to learn some things. I'll go and talk to her."

Then, Clerise took a deep breath and went to the girls' room where Janine sat on the bed, wiping her eyes. "Go and play in the backyard for a moment," she told Nicole.

Somewhat shaken by her mother's uncharacteristic behavior, Nicole wisely tried to keep herself occupied for the longest possible time, making mud pies, thinking, and wondering. In her nearly four-year-old mind, she did not understand exactly what it all meant. She knew that the relationship with the Juins was a source of problems for the family, and that it needed to be viewed with a measure of suspicion. Then, bored and curious, she went back to the room and found Clerise and Janine speaking quietly and about to end their conversation.

"Look at that child!" Clerise exclaimed. "Nicole, where have you been?"

"Whew!... Let me go and clean you up," Janine volunteered.

Afterwards, the two sisters went to buy some candies, and Janine gave her *senk kòb,* a whole five cents coin, so that she could get a *piwouli,* a real treat of a lollipop.

While observing adults, Nicole had learned to keep some of her thoughts to herself. Thus, she wondered why a big and strong person like Ania did not herself carry home the pails of water from the public fountain in Pon Gonbo. Instead, she paid a few cents to a couple of the little beggars hanging around the fountain to transport the water atop their heads. Nicole knew that she would not have been allowed, or even been able to lift the pails. She wondered why children, not much bigger than she was, were asked to strain under their weight. Could it have been for the money? That seemed to make sense, since five cents could buy such an enjoyable *piwouli*.

"Is Ania very rich? How much money does she get?" she suddenly asked Janine.

Her sister gave her a quizzical look. "What's the matter with you, nosy little girl? That's none of your business."

But Nicole already knew. She had heard Clerise mention to Desil that if the *boutik* went well, they should think of raising Ania's salary so that she could earn *douz goud*, two dollars and forty cents a month, instead of the *di goud*, the two dollars that she was presently getting. No longer a *timoun kay*, but not yet a full-fledged maid, Ania was on her way to receiving the customary three or four dollars per month paid to beginners in more affluent households.

Di goud! She must be rich! thought Nicole. She could not even begin to imagine all the lollipops such a fabulous sum would buy.

The flood happened shortly afterwards. Earlier that evening, at the news that the river *La Ravin* was rising, Edmond Juin had stopped at the Fleurantiers' home to offer his hospitality in case of need. Clerise and Desil had profusely thanked him, and sent their love to his wife. The stopover was an unusual occurrence, as

Parenn Edmond almost never visited their house, and Nicole could not remember having seen him there before. Nennenn Simone came once in a while, sometimes in the afternoon when Janine was still in school, to chat with Clerise. That day, Parenn Edmond did not stay long, not even having time to sit, he said. After he extended his invitation, he went to take care of other business.

"I wish we don't have to go over there," Clerise remarked after he left, "I came out of their house. I'm not ready to go back!"

"We don't have to go there," Desil said. "If worse comes to worst we can always go next door to Mrs. Lifaite's house. They have already told us to come. The water will not reach their second level."

"Don't even think about it!" Clerise answered promptly. "We can't do this to Mr. Edmond. He'll be very offended."

Desil's voice took a sharp edge. "If we go next door, we will all be able to keep an eye on the house and clean up more quickly. That way, we'll return home sooner."

"Nennenn will be very hurt," intervened Janine timidly. "She is the one who sent Parenn here, to make sure we will come to their house."

"Then you all can go, and I'll stay."

Clerise's voice rose with alarm. "Desil, how could you do something like that? How could I leave you all by yourself? You know how worried all of us would be. You realize how Mr. and Mrs. Juin are going to be hurt and offended. Nennenn sent you her own husband! The man came personally all the way here. They must have been very concerned to go to such an extent. You can't hurt them like that without reason!"

"Let's stop talking and get moving now. We'd better try to salvage what we can if the water really comes." At that, Desil went to the back of the house, gathering items here and there in preparation for the flood.

They all worked quickly, placing whatever they could on top of furniture which they tried to elevate as much as possible on any wooden piles or cement blocks they could find. The neighbors also kept busy, and more than the usual traffic took place from house to house in order to borrow or share protective covers and other items.

Clerise and Desil packed family papers, a change of clothes and other essentials in a bag to be quickly grabbed on the way out of the house, if the need arose. Ania and Janine also gathered a few items. All Nicole took was her doll, her most prized possession. Her godmother, the midwife who had helped deliver her at birth, had given her the doll, Lisette, the first of that size that Nicole had ever owned. However, unlike the baby-size imported dolls, who could say "mommy" when turned over, wore real clothes as well as shoes and bonnets, had hair that could be combed, and eyes that could open and close, Lisette merely had painted eyes and hair, only a blanket for clothing, and could not make any noise. Nevertheless, she was much bigger than the minuscule, finger-sized or crudely made rag dolls that Nicole had owned in the past. Furthermore, Clerise had provided a couple of hand-made dresses, which had increased Lisette's trousseau, as well as Nicole's fun in changing her outfits.

That night however, no one seriously thought that *La Ravin* would rise to any appreciable height. Consequently, the Fleurantiers had made rather perfunctory arrangements. The sheer magnitude of the flood caught everyone by surprise. *La Ravin* came all the way from Lan Gabyon, and suddenly covered the entire neighborhood. The swift rise of the water forced the family to gather quickly a few essentials, secure the house from possible looters, and leave in the middle of the night for the Juins' residence. There was no time to save some of Clerise's inventory.

Under the rain, holding tightly to each other, with Nicole riding on her father's shoulders under one umbrella while Clerise, Janine, and Ania huddled under the other, they carefully made their way to safety, stopping briefly once in a while to exchange quick comments with neighbors who, like them, were seeking refuge in other parts of town. Nicole remembered the scene vividly: the rain splashing in the darkness, the wind howling amid the roar of the invading river, their careful and almost silent advance in the surrounding tumult. Since they did not own raincoats, they were thoroughly wet and cold as they tried to keep the umbrellas from turning in the gusts of wind. At last, they arrived at the Juins' house.

Nennenn and Parenn greeted them with effusion. They offered coffee and gathered their servants for all the necessary arrangements. Janine settled immediately. All she had to do was to occupy one of the empty rooms on the second floor where she usually slept when she spent the night with the Juins. Clerise, Desil, Nicole, and Ania remained downstairs in the study area of the now-gone Juin children, which had hurriedly been converted into an all-purpose room. There, the parents had a double sofa-bed, Nicole a cot, and Ania a straw mat to be unfolded at night in a corner. A table and four chairs already in the room provided adequate furnishings for family meals, which could be taken in private, as the Juins diplomatically mentioned. Although they had already arranged to increase the normal household rations to accommodate everyone, Nennenn and Parenn also made their kitchen facilities available to the Fleurantiers, as needed upon coordination with the cook.

Built at the turn of the century, the Juins' large, two-story house had been partially renovated to include modern plumbing facilities on the top floor. They were for the exclusive use of the Juins and their customary guests, including Janine who, for all practical purposes, was considered to be informally adopted. Two sets of outhouses remained in the courtyard, one that the Juins still used on occasions and the other for the help. The shower house stood nearby. Nennenn and Parenn graciously placed their downstairs facilities at the Fleurantiers' disposal.

Once settled, Ania and Nicole fell asleep right away, while Clerise and Desil remained restless. Desil left at daybreak to assess the damage to their home and Clerise remained to take care of their new living arrangements. Her first task was to awaken Ania to assist Mrs. Juin's staff in preparing the morning coffee. That proved difficult, since Ania loved to sleep and felt particularly tired after all the happenings of the night. However, Clerise remained firm, since she did not want to seem to take advantage of the Juin's hospitality without shouldering her share of the workload. Therefore, she dispatched Ania to the nearby kitchen where Mrs. Juin's maid immediately had her start the morning fire in the built-in cement stove counter in preparation for the coffee.

After a while, the activities from the kitchen disturbed Nicole's sleep. She began to cry and complained of hunger.

"Sh…" Clerise said. "Don't make any noise right now. People are sleeping upstairs."

Since "people" meant the Juins, Nicole took the opportunity to escalate her protest, almost to the point of howling, when a frustrated Clerise gave her two resounding slaps on the behind and threatened to use a belt if the whole scene did not stop immediately. From past experience, Nicole knew that it was better to compromise. Thus, she continued to cry as long as she could and kept her face buried in the pillow to muffle the sound, knowing that her mother would soon feel sorry. Concerned about their situation and careful not to make too much noise, Clerise quickly patted her hair. "Come on, be a big girl, stop crying!" she whispered. Finally, Nicole relented and let herself fall back to sleep, all the while blaming Parenn and Nennenn for the turn of events.

Moments later, Desil arrived with bad news.

"The water is still high, but it's going down somewhat."

"How far has *La Ravin* arrived?" Clerise asked.

"Not beyond the corner of Pon Gonbo. But there's damage to the house."

"How bad is it?"

"Well, there's quite a bit of water and mud inside the house. It's kind of bad. We can't go back until the house is fixed."

"Can we do it ourselves?"

"I don't think so. The roof also leaked pretty badly. I believe I should go and talk to the owner, Mr. Visel, to let him know what happened."

"I'll ask Nennenn Simone to talk to him too, since he is her brother. Then, maybe he'll have things fixed more quickly, so we can go home."

In fact, Louis Visel owned several rental properties in town. Since the Pon Gonbo house was close to the bottom of his income sources, any speedy repairs would require adequate persuasion.

Thus, Desil supplied Clerise with some additional clothes, a few pieces of bread, as well as some butter and sugar taken from their house, and left for the Visels' residence. Meanwhile, as she waited to meet Simone Juin, Clerise undertook to establish and enforce the new rules of their current living conditions. After she prepared Nicole's breakfast of buttered bread and diluted coffee with a lot of sugar, she spoke to Ania.

"First, as soon as you wake up in the morning, take the straw mat from this room and put it with your other things behind the kitchen. You understand?"

"Yes, *Madanm*."

"After that, see if Mrs. Edmond's people need anything. Do what they tell you to do, and be very nice and polite with them. You understand that too?"

"Yes, *Madanm*."

"The other thing you have to do, and that is your own responsibility, is to continue to take care of Nicole and keep an eye on her. But, if the people of the house need anything from you, let me know, or let Janine know, or take Nicole along with you. You understand that too?"

"Yes, *Madanm*."

"I don't want Nicole to do anything that would inconvenience anyone here. In the little space that we have, you need to watch her and make sure everything goes well. You can also open the shutters and let her play on the porch in front of this room, once in a while. But don't let her go in the street, because more cars are passing here than near our house. You understand that very well? Don't you?"

"Yes, *Madanm*."

Furthermore, Clerise instructed Ania to set the table for meals and wash the family's dishes. Last but not

208 – Marie-Thérèse Labossière Thomas

least, she would make sure to wait until all preparations
related to the morning coffee had ended before taking
chamber pots to be emptied in the servants' outhouse,
which she also was to use.

"What about me?" Nicole said.

"I expect you not to make noise, especially early in the
morning or late at night when people may be resting,"
Clerise answered sternly. "You don't go anywhere outside this room, until you get permission first. You
understand?"

"Can I go out with Janine?"

"Yes, you can."

"Can I go with Ania?"

"Yes. But you don't go anywhere by yourself. Always,
remember to ask first if you want to use the outhouse
or do anything else. That's how nice children behave."

At first intrigued, Nicole became quickly bored.
Parenn and Nennenn, who had eyes only for Janine,
gave her scant attention. Because her mother insisted
that she be at her best behavior in their presence, she
always felt resentful and self-conscious when they were
around. She did not appreciate all the problems that the
Juins indirectly caused in her family, and to her, that
included their staying out of their neighborhood.
Consequently, she missed her friends, the excitement of
the flood, and the spectacle of onlookers wading in the
water.

She knew better than to continue to provoke her
mother, and adopted an exemplary behavior, which

continued throughout their forced stay at the Juins, to the puzzlement of her family. By the second night, however, she started to wet her bed. Consequently, the nice and clean little cot that Nennenn and Parenn had gotten out of storage especially for her, as everybody had emphasized, became repeatedly soaked.

To complicate matters, after their full or partial washing, the soiled mattress and bed sheets had to be left to dry in the courtyard, and progressively became a less than aesthetic sight. At first, everyone had assumed that the problem would end with ordinary precautions at night. When that failed, and following a conference with Parenn, a somewhat annoyed Nennenn gave Clerise a plastic sheet to protect the mattress. The solution, which might have been adequate earlier, came too late as large and stubborn stains had already developed. In addition, the Juins' domestic staff began to voice muted complaints about the unpleasant traffic and malodorous smell that started to become an early-morning feature, from the kitchen area near Mrs. Desil's quarters to the courtyard. There, day after day, struggling to keep her balance and sense of direction, Ania carried the offending sheets and mattress in front of her, in full view and like a shield, sometimes staggering when she tried to move fast as she valiantly ignored hostile stares and snide remarks.

The once cordial relations between Clerise and Simone Juin began to show signs of strain. When not busy in her house in Pon Gonbo, Clerise kept more and more to her quarters instead of spending long periods of time with Nennenn to help supervise the household and exchange the latest gossip. Ania, now ostracized by the Juins' servants, spent most of her time taking care of Nicole. Away from her friends, the little girl played with her doll and went over and over the old French magazines discarded by the Juins that her sister had given her for distraction. At work most of the time, and otherwise busy with the inspection of his home, Desil felt the general tension somewhat marginally. However, he started to notice the increasingly distant attitude of the Juins toward him, and began to resent it.

By then, Clerise and Ania would go in the afternoon to visit friends in their old neighborhood and sell what they could of Clerise's remaining inventory. Nicole and sometimes Janine came along. As her estrangement from Nennenn deepened, Clerise spent more time with her next-door neighbor Mrs. Dieujuste Lifaite. While Ania ran errands and Nicole played with Mrs. Dieujuste's daughter Marie-Carmelle, the conversation focused upon the Juins. "Nennenn takes such good care of us!" Clerise said. "She and Parenn don't even know what else to do for us. As for Janine, she's right at home with them. You can't imagine how they spoil her!"

"They seem to be good people," Mrs. Dieujuste answered. "Mrs. Juin always has a smile and a nice word for everyone."

"They're like my mother and father. They raised me since I was little."

"Not everyone is like that."

"Yes, and Desil also works for Mr. Juin's brother. They pay him what they can and we manage. Nennenn also helped me quite a bit with my little business."

"Doesn't your house also belong to Mrs. Juin's brother? "

"Yes, and he doesn't charge us much for the rent. I wish he would fix it a little more quickly. Nennenn says he's so busy with the repairs at his other houses."

"Well, he'll come around to fix yours…"

"Oh yes, I know that. But no matter how nice Nennenn and Parenn are, I really need to come back home. It has been two weeks now since we left. I need to take care of my *boutik*. I have things to do!"

The burgeoning friendship between Clerise and Mrs. Dieujuste continued to grow. Next door neighbors, the two women had only been distantly cordial to each other in the past. Mrs. Dieujuste was a *Madan Sara*, an itinerant business woman, who traveled to various rural areas on market days selling goods that she had purchased from the city. She was on the road three times a week, although her trips rarely extended overnight. A girl of about Ania's age assisted in the household chores and the care of her three children. The youngest, Marie-Carmelle, was one of the neighborhood children with whom Clerise allowed Nicole to play.

Mrs. Dieujuste's husband, Boss Dieujuste Lifaite, a mason and carpenter by trade, usually called by his title and first name, had recently renovated their home into a two-story masonry house. Nearing middle age and somewhat older than Clerise and Desil, the Lifaites were becoming increasingly prosperous, thanks to the wife's business and to her husband's government position. A long-time partisan of Duvalier, Boss Dieujuste belonged to the political establishment as a minor public servant and member of the local militia. For that reason, Clerise as well as others in the neighborhood had maintained a polite reserve with the Lifaites, keeping cordial relations on the surface, always careful not to offend or appear overly distant. The situation had started to change. Desil and Boss Dieujuste were also beginning to converse more often.

"I am sick of it!" Desil said as they stood in his backyard looking at damages to the house. "That man keeps putting me off about fixing this place. I need to be done with that whole thing! It's taking too long!"

"Why doesn't he send someone to do it? Don't you pay him rent?"

"Yes, but this little house isn't that much to him. He takes care of his other places first."

"*La Ravin* didn't arrive in his neighborhood. So, what does he care!"

"The bad part is, I can't afford to go anywhere else with that much space. I just have to wait. But I'll see if Mr. Juin can help speed up matters."

"Mr. Juin is a good man. But you can't let people push you around like that. Bourgeois are bourgeois. They don't really care about poor people. Under Lescot they used to say *'Jòn pa kite van pase.'* You know what that means? It tells the light-skin people not to let the wind flow through, meaning us, the black people that they can't see in the dark. So, when Estimé took power, we started to sing *'Mwen pap travay pou boujwa pou granmesi*, I will not work for free for the bourgeois.' Later, when 'General' Magloire became president, he didn't care for poor people. Black as he was, he was too busy drinking and carrying on with bourgeois of all colors. That's why I am a Duvalierist. Duvalier is Estimé's heir. He'll make things change."

"Well... I just do my work and come home. I'm not really interested in politics," Desil answered as he began to pick up some debris from the ground.

"You should really think of what I said. You can't let people push you around like that. If your house was mine, it would have been fixed by now. I bet they don't pay you much. You have a growing family. I can help you do better for yourself."

During the past electoral campaign, Boss Dieujuste had belonged to the tiny local minority of Duvalier's supporters. Now part of the group in power, he still struggled to overcome the polite reluctance that he perceived from many, while enjoying the exaggerated friendliness and business opportunities that others anxiously offered.

After the elections in Les Cayes, Duvalier's core group of civilian supporters had not actively participated in the persecution of Dejoists by the military establishment. Even the man beaten by the *Rouleau* did not retaliate against his well-known tormentors, at least not openly. Apparently close-knit, the Duvalierists moved to various government positions, especially at the *Régie du Tabac*, the Office of Tobacco Control, a tax collection agency whose increasingly broader base became a private treasury for the new government.

As Duvalier consolidated his power, previously unknown, unsuspected, or newly converted working-class Duvalierists emerged in Les Cayes, and became more visible while stories grew about the Tonton Macoutes' reign of terror in Port-au-Prince. When Duvalier officially created the militia in 1958, after the first unsuccessful invasion and attack against his government by a small commando of exiled former military officers, the local "little Duvalierists" joined the lower ranks of their party's core establishment and progressively organized as the first contingent of VSN or *Volontaires de la Sécurité Nationale*, the Volunteers for National Security. Trained by the military, they rose in prominence while the old Duvalierist leadership increasingly faded into the background. In that context, Marcel Octavien, a former construction worker who had moved to Les Cayes a few years before, became the militia commander, and Boss Dieujuste Lifaite an early member of that group.

"I would be careful with Boss Dieujuste," Clerise said to Desil as they sat on the sofa after dinner, in their room at the Juins'. On her father's lap, Nicole was about to fall asleep.

"I know that," Desil agreed. "But he understands what we are going through and I try to stay away from politics with him."

Her voice down to a near whisper, Clerise continued. "With those people, you never know. They fight among themselves and they arrest others anytime they think an exiles' invasion is preparing. Remember that young guy who always dressed well and disappeared a couple of years ago. He was one of theirs. Until now, no one knows what happened."

"I heard he was rising too fast," Desil replied in the same tone." After they take people away, some come out of jail, some just disappear. Many people, even Duvalierists, are going to Africa for that reason. I hear they get contracts and lots of money from the United Nations and the French-speaking countries that have just become independent."

"Now the government is trying to keep some from going. I hear that people like teachers and doctors need to have permission to leave. They also send a list of names of everybody who apply to leave the country to the National Palace for approval, before they let them go."

"So far, people who didn't actively join one group or another during the electoral campaign have not been bothered. Let's knock on wood!" Desil joked, lightly taping on the table nearby.

"Yeah!..." Clerise joined. "But do you see that many who were very hot in Dejoie's campaign are now going

out their way to be chummy with the Duvalierist
authorities?"

"... and the military, and also with anyone with a gun,
a Macoute uniform, or even a low-level connection,"
Desil chuckled.

"Boss Dieujuste's business must really be booming!"
Clerise laughed, as they stood to take Nicole to her cot.

The next afternoon, Clerise took Janine and Nicole
with her to Pon Gonbo.

"When is our house going to be fixed?" Janine asked.

With Nicole's hand in hers, Clerise continued to walk.
"Soon, I hope," she replied wearily. "Yesterday, I was
talking with Mrs. Dieujuste about that. It's just taking
too long!"

"Mom, you know what? Parenn and Nennenn also
want to see our house fixed," Janine continued.

"I know that. I can only hope it will be done soon."

"Parenn is upset because he has to look at Nicole's
sheets drying in the yard every day. So, he keeps complaining to Nennenn. She tells him there's nothing she
can do about it. So, they start arguing. That's why
Parenn doesn't come home for lunch now. Nennenn
told him that when he stays at the store, it gives her
more work because she has to pack his lunch and have
someone bring it to him. Today, Parenn started complaining again. Nennenn looked at me, then she gave
him a sharp look, like that," Janine demonstrated with a
frown, "and then she started talking about something
else."

Clerise stopped in her tracks. "I don't know what else I can do!" she exclaimed, almost letting go of Nicole's hand. "So, he came and got us from our house! Now his brother-in-law is not fixing it! And he's complaining! What do they want me to do?"

In a situation fast becoming intolerable, an apparently sweet and innocent Nicole literally continued every day to add fuel to the fire. By the third week of their stay at the Juins, Desil began to consider an offer from one of his out-of-town relatives, who had proposed to help him find a job soon to be available in Port-au-Prince. The possibility of moving became even more tempting because, since their conversation in the backyard of his house, his neighbor Boss Dieujuste had eagerly pursued their relationship along uncomfortable political lines. A few days later, he had even introduced Desil to the local militia chief with whom he was playing dominoes near Lan Gabyon.

On an errand that day, Desil had noticed a half-dozen men, including Boss Dieujuste, involved in the game on the porch of a militiaman's home.

"Desil, come here my friend!" Boss Dieujuste called effusively. "You know everyone here, but I'd like to say something about you. Commandant, this is a good man. I want you to know that!"

Absorbed in his game, the Commandant merely grunted, and Desil left after a few awkward moments. The next day, Boss Dieujuste brought him a card, signed by the militia chief, requesting from authorities assistance and protection to Mr. Desil Fleurantier, as may be needed. Desil thanked his neighbor and wondered how to approach Clerise on the matter. After careful consideration, he decided to postpone any disclosure, at least until they had returned to their own house. In that context, the perspective of moving to Port-au-Prince became somewhat of a relief.

Her patience nearly exhausted, Clerise proudly made the announcement of Desil's possible departure to Mrs. Juin. From what Clerise later understood, Nennenn Simone left the house shortly thereafter to confer privately with Parenn in his store.

"You realize that Desil may not even find that job in Port-au-Prince?" Nennenn said.

"And if he does, it may take him months to send for his family. The little girl's problem is certainly to be considered."

"I agree. But Edmond, look at it another way also. Clerise does not know these people much. We raised her with different manners, a different upbringing. What about Janine? Port-au-Prince is not Les Cayes. It's a big place. By the time they reach my mother or Elia, if they are in need, who knows what can happen?"

"Clerise is married to Desil now and you have to realize that Janine is her child. They will manage. But I know that it will be difficult for Andre to find someone as dependable as Desil for the store. Let me talk to Andre. Maybe we can help arrange things differently."

Consequently, Desil saw his salary increase slightly to thirty-two dollars per month, while Edmond and Andre Juin successfully dissuaded him from going toward the uncertainties of Port-au-Prince. Furthermore, that same night, Nennenn and Parenn went together to the Visels' home for a visit. To their surprise and discomfort, they found that Boss Dieujuste Lifaite, who had contacted Louis Visel that same afternoon to offer his services, had already been hired to work on the house. The next day, Desil and Clerise received notification that repairs to their house would begin immediately. In addition, Mr. Visel promised to have the house wired for electricity without raising the rent of *quarante gourdes* — eight dollars — per month, in compensation for their losses.

Satisfied, Mr. and Mrs. Desil Fleurantier returned home with their family, amid feelings of peace, harmony, and cooperation. However, their relationship with the Juins never fully recovered from a tinge of uneasiness. In a final display of generosity, Nennenn and Parenn gave Nicole, to take home, the folding bed that she had used, just in case she had a visitor. The cot remained in the small room behind the dining area for possible use in the future. Nicole's "problem" stopped the first night at home to the amazement of her puzzled family, who tried for a long time to find a satisfactory explanation to the phenomenon.

By then, Clerise's pregnancy was fully showing.

CHAPTER 7

Interaction

1962

Not long after the flood, Nicole started to attend kindergarden, *le jardin d'enfants*, and proudly wore her blue and white uniform. Ania prepared her clothes and took her to and from school twice a day for the morning and afternoon sessions, depending on Janine's busy schedule. Nicole was able to benefit from an affordable reduced family rate at the nun's establishment since the Juins already paid her sister's tuition.

The logistics of Nicole's schooling, and the fact that Clerise had to make her read, write, and count every night, considerably increased the workload for the Fleurantiers. While old clients returned to the *boutik*, Clerise's growing reputation as a dressmaker generated more orders in the neighborhood. Thus, Clerise and Desil decided that they needed additional help and sought a new *timoun kay* through relatives in the countryside, since they could not afford to pay anyone but Ania.

Jesula, a twelve-year-old girl, arrived around noon on a Saturday with her father and a bundle of clothes. They both sat in the backyard with Clerise.

"What's your name?" Clerise asked.

"Jesula ...*wi, Madanm*... yes, Ma'm."

"Are you a good girl?"

"Yes."

"Yes, *Madanm*. Jesula, you know that's how you address your elders. Mind your manners!" the father corrected.

"Yes, *Madanm*," Jesula whispered. She sat stiffly at the edge of her chair and kept her eyes on her bare feet.

"Will you do a good job here?" Clerise continued.

"Yes, *Madanm*." Again, the answer was almost inaudible.

"Are you happy to come here?"

"Yes, *Madanm*."

Clerise turned to the father. "How's her health?"

"She's fine. Never sick."

"Good. I hope things will work out."

"Mrs. Desil, Jesula is a strong girl. She knows how to take care of children and of a house. She is good-natured and doesn't eat much."

"That seems to be what I need. But I want to make quite sure that she understands something important. It's about the business of having friends. That can really put her in trouble. It can keep her from doing her work, and make her pick up all kinds of bad habits. I'm not telling her not to speak to other children. But she can only do that when her work is done and when she's near the house. That way, she can be reached when she's needed."

"You hear that, Jesula? Will you do as Mrs. Desil says?"

"Yes, Papa."

"Say 'Yes, Mrs. Desil.'"

"Yes, Mrs. Desil."

Then, Jesula raised her head and saw Nicole who had come to stand by her mother's chair. For the first time, the country girl looked more at ease. Nicole smiled at her, with reserve.

"I heard some good things about you," Clerise continued to tell Jesula. "I hope you'll do a good job to make your father happy."

"Yes, *Madanm*, she will. She's not a bad girl at all," the father intervened. "You'll see!" Then, he turned to his daughter. "Jesula," he said, "don't embarrass us. Be a good girl with Mrs. Desil. Ok?"

"Yes, Papa."

"Very well then," Clerise said. "All she'll have to do is take care of Nicole, run some errands, and help around the house. We're not rich, but we'll give her food, clothing, a straw mat, and a place to sleep. If she does her work well and finishes on time, we may send her to school in the afternoon, if we can afford it. Has she ever been to school?"

"No, *Madanm*. We couldn't send her."

"Well, you never know. She may have a chance to learn how to read and write here. We'll see how it goes. Now let's find out what she brought with her."

Jesula's belongings included a dress and a pair of panties in addition to the clothes that she wore. Since

she had no shoes, Clerise promised to buy her a pair of
locally made sandals, as soon as possible. To seal the
agreement, Jesula's father offered a bunch of plantains
that he had brought. Then, Clerise and Nicole left him
alone with his daughter for a short while.

After that private moment, Jesula's father assured
Clerise that she had full power over his daughter. "I told
her again to behave. She shouldn't be any trouble. But
let me know if you ever have a problem."

Afterwards, Clerise took them both to the little back
room, then to the parlor, to explain the sleeping
arrangements, which were to be similar to Ania's. As she
said good-bye to her father, Jesula cried a little.
However, she followed his instructions, and immediately
began to get acquainted with the household.

Nicole, who had liked Jesula right away, found the
whole hiring process rather strange, and always
remembered it with a faint sense of guilt. However, to
her and to the rest of the household, the family that
Jesula had left behind remained rather abstract and
became increasingly remote.

Free to delegate part of her work to Jesula, Ania spent
more time with Clerise in the *boutik* until she became
quite competent and entirely reliable. Rather busy
herself, Clerise continued to prepare for the baby's
arrival, take care of Nicole's schooling, help Ania and
Jesula in the housework, and do some sewing while she
supervised the *boutik*.

Jesula washed clothes, ran errands, emptied the chamber pots, started the charcoal fire each day, escorted Nicole to and from school, and also had to fetch water from the public fountain. However, unlike Ania, Jesula carried the full pails of water herself, either on top of her head or with arms extended down her side, since she was only a low status *timoun kay*.

During Jesula's adjustment period, Janine, who needed more time to study for school, stayed longer at the Juins' residence and sometimes even slept there for days when preparing for her exams. However, she took a keen interest in the new *timoun kay* whose religious instruction became her major project as a *Croisée de l'Eucharistie*, a Crusader for the Eucharist, at the nuns' school. The *Croisées* met about once a week after school, under a nun's supervision. They listened to heroic stories of incredible suffering that young people of other times and places had endured for the Faith at the hands of nefarious and heathen torturers, including the Romans, the Saracen, or a more immediate menace, the Communists of Russia and China. In addition, the Crusaders wore an insignia, sang valiant tunes, attended special Masses once a month at the bishop's compound near the Cathedral, and performed good deeds.

Thus, Janine began to prepare Jesula for her First Communion, as mandated in the *Catéchisme*, the official manual of Catholic doctrine that all elementary school children in town had to memorize. Consequently, she took Jesula to catechism sessions conducted for *timoun kay* at her school on Sunday afternoons.

One day, Nicole came along and sat patiently, while her sister drilled a group of *timoun kay* in memorizing questions and answers from the catechism book. As the lesson progressed, Nicole noticed that some of the pupils, including Jesula, appeared older than Janine. After nearly a half-hour, Nicole welcomed the opportunity to rush outside for recess with the pupils, through the classroom door which opened on the schoolyard.

"Nicole, come here," Janine called as she began a conversation with the adult in charge and the two other young volunteers on duty.

While she waited in the classroom for her sister to finish talking, Nicole heard a melody of children's voices drifting from the yard. *"Ti si ni dekoumande; Laverans, dekoumande ...,"* they sang. The unfamiliar tune intrigued her and she tried to decipher the meaning of the words in Creole which, in any case, was forbidden on the schoolyard on weekdays. Only much later did Nicole learn that the original song *"See, see me dear Commander; Reverence, dear Commander ...,"* might have dated from the British invasion of the island during the French colonial period.

Then, Janine turned to her sister. "Let's go outside now," she said.

Not allowed or invited to play with the *timoun kay*, Nicole observed them from afar. She noticed that they no longer appeared shy or subservient as they interacted with each other.

"Let's play *'Malerèz kou m Malerèz,* Poor, as I am,'" one of them said.

After a brief discussion, the children selected two older girls for specific roles. While the entire group lined up behind one of the girls, the other stood facing them, and started to sing:

"*Rich kòm mwen rich,*

Rich, as I am

Ala m pèdi tout ti pitit an mwen"

I have lost all my little children"

Then the line leader responded with the same tune:

"*Malerèz kou m malerèz*

"Poor, as I am

Ala m genyen tout ti pitit an mwen "

I have all my little children."

The "rich" character then moved forward. "I'll take one…, I'll take two…," she said, trying to capture the poor "children" who did their best to hide behind their "mother" while they shrieked in terror. Meanwhile, the "mother" extended her arms protectively and moved in mother-hen fashion to counter the assault.

While she did not fully realize that her own mother had once been one of those *timoun kay* attending catechism, Janine continued to work seriously toward Jesula's First Communion. She vaguely knew that her mother, an orphan from a nearby village, had been "taken in" by the Juins, who had raised her as "their own child." In spite of her doubts about some aspects of the story, as well as various hints gathered here and there, Janine never really pursued the matter, preferring not to know. A quiet and observant child devoted to her family and her loving Nennenn, she had few social friends. However, her teachers constantly praised her behavior, academic performance, and involvement in local parish activities.

On that matter, Father Justin, the new rector of the Cathedral, an irascible and swarthy Breton with bushy eyebrows and a perpetual scowl, became the talk of the town. Recently transferred from a rural parish, the priest had thunderously assumed his new post, constantly chastising his parishioners.

The first hint about the situation came from Ania when she returned from Mass on a Sunday. *"Madanm,"* she said to Clerise, "the new Father Rector said women can't come to church if their dress doesn't cover up to their neck and their sleeves aren't half-way through their elbows, right here," she demonstrated.

After that announcement, the situation continued to escalate. The next day, Clerise found that Father Justin's standards of decency and level of zeal in their enforcement had become the source of puzzled, infuriated, or downright amused comments all over town.

"That Father Justin refused communion to several people, including little girls, because they were wearing lace or embroidery that he calls indecent," commented Solange Jobert, about to take her leave from Simone Juin's porch. "He must have some kind of hawk eyes to find anything immodest in some of those dresses."

"He just ignored some people at the communion table and he made some kind of curt remark to others," Simone Juin added.

"He said that when he refuses communion to people, it should teach them not to present themselves again with indecent clothes. He also said that this is a sin that should be reported at the next confession," Janine offered.

"What's his problem?" a neighbor inquired.

"I can understand that he reminds women not to come to church in slacks, tight dresses, or décolletage," Adeline Visel said. "In the past, people who wore those kinds of clothes were either asked to leave the church from the pulpit or privately notified and escorted to the door. But now, it seems to be going pretty far."

By late afternoon, Mrs. Dieujuste Lifaite added some comments of her own from her porch in Pon Gonbo. "I don't think we ever had one like him. What's the matter with that priest?" she concluded.

A few days later, when Clerise stopped at the Juins for an evening chat around the dinner table, she found Parenn fulminating. "That Father Justin! What does he think! This is really going too far! In this town, men have always stayed in front of the church to talk among themselves during the four o'clock in the morning Mass. Of course, we always come inside to stand and pay our respects during consecration. Now, that priest demands that we stay inside for the entire Mass, to kneel and stand at his command! He should know whom he can order around like that! Who does he think he is?"

Father Justin's unfolding drama continued to generate comments, gossip, curiosity, interest, outrage, and a fair amount of jokes among all segments of the population, including the youth. His most forceful sermons occurred during the *Mès Katrè*, the traditional four o'clock in the morning Mass held every Sunday, to accommodate domestic workers and others who, because of their chores, would have otherwise been unable to fulfill their religious duties. Consequently, diplomatic requirements were less stringent at that service. That obvious appeal and the fact that the Mass was held before dawn, made it somewhat of a rite of passage for adolescents of the upper classes during school recess. At the conclusion of the service, they often walked to the old fort *L'Islet* at the end of town, or took a stroll on the pier to see the sun rise.

Thus, because of Father Justin, Janine started a subtle campaign to attend the early church service sooner than anticipated. Still too young for the related teenage group activities, she wanted to link her request with Jesula's religious instruction to convince her parents of the validity of the project.

"Some of my friends have already been there with their relatives. I need to go with Jesula to help her with her *Katechis*."

"Your mother is pregnant. You don't want to wake her up that early in the morning," Desil said.

"But dad, she wakes up anyway when you get ready to go. And I won't make a lot of noise," Janine promised.

"I'll take you if it's okay with your mom," Desil conceded.

Nicole did not want to be left out. She had to be part of the adventure. Through a whole campaign of crying and begging, she pestered her parents to be included, while Janine resisted the idea.

"Mom, aren't you making my Sunday uniform?" Nicole whined. "I'm going to be old enough to go to the six-thirty Mass with my school at the Cathedral now! So, why can't I go to the four o'clock Mass?"

"Because you're still too young," Janine answered. "Don't you see that when you start going to that little short six-thirty Mass, I'll move to High Mass, the *Grand-Messe*, at eight. It's much longer and more beautiful. That's why only older students go there. Not babies like you!"

"I'm not a baby," Nicole protested. "Marie-Carmelle's brother is older than you. He doesn't go to your stupid *Grand-Messe*. People from the *Lycée* don't have to go to church."

"Nicole, watch your language," Clerise said. "You are not helping yourself at all!"

"She called me a baby!" Nicole whined. "She's acting up because Nennenn and a bunch of other fancy women go to that Mass with their hats, their gloves, and their high heels."

"That's why you can't go there," Janine replied. "You wouldn't know how to behave and keep quiet. I'm going to sing with the men and women of the choir and the kids in my school. It sounds beautiful with the organ! And you aren't about to do any of that!"

Desil started to laugh. "Well, that's definitely the place for elegant ladies to be seen on Sundays. When am I going to see you there, Clerise?" he teased. "Father Justin is much more mellow there than at the four o'clock Mass."

Clerise postured. "I am the elegant lady of the six o'clock Mass, right near here at *L'Hospice* chapel on the hospital compound. When my beautiful girls go with me, we are devastating!"

"Please, mom! Please," the girls begged.

"Okay, now, let's see. Since I am pregnant now and need lots of sleep, it's going to be better for me to wake up only once and take care of all that has to be done for church. So, Nicole will have to come too. Then, later, I'll get some rest with her. How does that sound?"

That Sunday before daybreak, Ania remained to watch the house while the rest of the household went to the Cathedral. It was dark, and somewhat cool. Nicole held her parents' hands as she walked through the quiet streets. She paid no attention to their almost whispered conversation or to the catechism review between Janine and Jesula as they walked in front. To her, the houses lining the street appeared quite different with their doors closed in the dark, while street lamps in the middle of intersections created islands of light. Here and there, a door opened almost in silence, and people emerged to head quietly toward the Cathedral. After a brief exchange of salutations, the few passers-by moved on, while the Fleurantiers walked slowly in step with the very pregnant Clerise. Past Kafou Orèl, they came face to face with Boss Dieujuste Lifaite and Marcel Octavien, the commander of the militia.

"Well, Desil, how are you?" Octavien said. "I see you are out with the Missus and the little family!"

"Oh, I'm fine! We are just taking the children to four o'clock Mass. Commandant Marcel, this is my wife. Clerise, you know Commandant Marcel!"

"Good morning, Commandant," Clerise said quietly. Nicole felt her mother stiffen and hold her hand so tightly that she looked up. However, she could not read anything on the polite mask that Clerise's face had become.

"I told you, he's a good man, Commandant!" interjected Dieujuste cheerfully. "Good morning Mrs. Desil! How are you, children?" he continued.

Janine now stood close to Clerise who had placed a protective arm around her shoulder. A little on the side, Jesula waited patiently.

"Good morning, Boss Dieujuste. We are fine, thank you," Clerise answered.

"Waiting for the heir! I wish you a boy," Dieujuste joked.

"And me too," said Marcel Octavien. "We have to get going. Desil, I'll see you around," he continued, waving good-bye.

The Fleurantiers stayed close to each other and silently walked the short distance to the Cathedral.

The church was already nearly full when they arrived. However, they were able to find a bench where they could sit together in one of the lateral chapels before the Mass started.

"Can we go and sit over there?" Nicole whispered to her mother pointing to the more comfortable benches and pew still empty in the nave.

Clerise bent toward her and put a finger on her lips. "No, we are okay here," she whispered.

Later, Nicole learned that parishioners rented church seats and pews according to assigned fee schedules. Those able to pay inserted a card with their family name in the pew so reserved, with the right to displace anyone sitting there at any time. Because of the consequent humiliation, many chose instead to sit on the backless benches of the two lateral chapels in the aisles of the church, which contained no pews. The Fleurantiers settled uneasily there, still deeply troubled by their previous encounter. Sensing the tension, Nicole remained relatively quiet, almost ready to fall asleep. Even Desil stayed inside, and did not step out for a brief chat with some acquaintance, as he often did when he attended Mass.

What happened next was also quite unusual. That Sunday, Father Justin began with the expected fulminations against Protestants, indecent women, and the falsely proud men with whom his standoff continued. Then, he decided to target one of the many dogs which, quite naturally, had followed someone inside the church and briefly made his presence known. Since no one usually paid attention to an occasional bark, the fact went unnoticed until the priest, who had abruptly stopped talking, suddenly resumed his speech.

"Silence!!!" he thundered. Startled, a couple of other sleepy dogs responded with a concert of their own. "Silence!!!... Silence!!!" Father Justin hollered.

The subsequent contest between the rector screaming his exasperation and shouting directions through a microphone set at its loudest in his determination to gain the upper hand, and the terrified dogs yelping, running, barking, and trying to escape, led to utter pandemonium. While volunteers tried to seize the dogs for eviction, the dogs kept on dodging them, biting innocent legs found on their way, thereby forcing even the most dignified parishioners to climb on benches. In the midst of the tumult, a middle-aged male volunteer about to catch a dog fell on his prey, and joined his howls to those of his victim amid the horrified exclamations of nearby spectators.

The episode with the dogs awakened, somewhat scared, and later amused Nicole and her family. For a while, the story generated considerable mirth in town, while Father Justin appeared to mellow with time.

Later that afternoon, after Janine and Jesula had gone to the catechism session and Ania to evening Mass, Clerise, Desil, and Nicole were alone in the house. While the little girl rested, Clerise closed the outside window facing the Lifaites' residence and insured that the front doors were shut before returning to her room. Almost in a whisper, she asked Desil, "What was it all about this morning?"

"What was it about? What you saw is what I saw too. I assume that you are talking about those guys that we met."

"They aren't 'those guys.' They are Tonton Macoutes."

"Boss Dieujuste is our neighbor. I talk to him all the time. You also talk to his wife. So, what's the problem? What's so wrong?"

"His wife is not a Tonton Macoute. And I didn't know you were friends with the Macoute commander. Where have you met him? What's going on?"

"I just met him one day. I was passing by, and Dieujuste called me and introduced me to him."

"Desil," Clerise said with alarm, "be careful with that Boss Dieujuste stuff. You don't know where all of that can lead you. Those people are evil! You'd better stay away from them."

Desil stood up. "What do you think you're telling me? As if I don't know what to do? You talk to me like I am a child. I know what I should do. I don't tell you how to deal with Mrs. Dieujuste. So, don't tell me what to do either!"

"Oh my God!" Clerise answered. "Look at those people's crimes, and see how you are talking to me! I never talk about Duvalier with Mrs. Dieujuste, because all she does is take care of her children and her business."

"Clerise, you know you're pregnant. This is no time for you to get angry. Just understand what I am going to say. I am an adult and I know what to do! Don't worry about any of that. Just forget it!"

"I would really hope so, because I wouldn't want to have anything to do with those people," Clerise said. "By the way, Desil, I have one last thing to ask you. Did you send Boss Dieujuste to Mr. Visel to have this house fixed?"

"I didn't ask Boss Dieujuste for anything and I don't know what happened between him and Mr. Visel. Now, can we stop talking about this?"

"I think I'll get some rest," Clerise said. "I'd better do that before Nicole wakes up."

"I'll wait until Ania comes back before going out. I'll be in the front."

Feeling the child inside her move, Clerise laid down on the bed, thinking. She patted her belly and turned to her side for a better position. She was tired. She needed to rest. On the bed near her, Nicole whimpered in her sleep. "Sh…," Clerise said, as she lightly touched her daughter's eyebrow, and rocked her a little.

More than ever, Clerise needed her mother. She felt the injustice of Oliante's early death and remembered the stories of her childhood. Grasping at vague memories of her mother, she sought to bask in the warmth of that early love and wondered what her life would have been, had Oliante lived. With mixed emotions, she recalled her father, Josaphat. Again, she felt an old resentment toward him and toward the strangers that she had been made to serve and who had treated her so unlike their own children.

She had wanted a chance to go to school longer, to learn and study more. "You're not a boarder!" she had often heard as a way to remind her and other *timoun kay* that they had chores to do throughout the day. For them, going to school full-time was totally out of question, and doing so on a regular basis was more than often a matter of luck. In that instance, Clerise felt privileged to have been able to learn a trade, after outgrowing her one-room school. Her longevity at the Juins' household had also allowed her to be ready for a First Communion, which she still remembered fondly and with quite a bit of pride. That memorable day remained one of the most important of her childhood.

And now, she thought of Janine's First Communion, which had been sponsored by Nennenn in more modest proportions than that of her daughter Rose-Marie, but with infinitely more opulence than her own. In her mind, she also saw her daughter standing in the Juin's balcony in her own right as a visitor, almost a child of the house, a *pitit kay*, not subservient to anyone. *We've come a long way!* she felt. Suddenly bothered by a nagging feeling, she said almost loudly, "Nennenn has done a lot for us."

Nicole opened her eyes and looked at her.

The following evening, Clerise walked the short distance to the Juins' residence with Nicole in tow. The conversation mainly revolved about Father Justin's peculiarities since the last episode still remained a source a considerable amusement in town. On her way out, Clerise asked, "Nennenn, what did Boss Dieujuste tell Mr. Visel about our house?"

"When?"

"When he got the job to fix it, after the flood."

"Oh!" said Simone Juin with the little tight smile that Clerise only knew too well, "I don't know."

"Did he threaten him in any way?"

"Oh no, dear! What an idea!" The little tight smile was still there.

"Because I asked Desil about it. He didn't know that Boss Dieujuste had gone to Mr. Visel."

"But Clerise, the house would have had to be fixed anyway! It was better to have a neighbor do the job."

"I just wanted for us to be clear on that," Clerise said, taking her leave. For her, the overly cheerful answer, as well as the little tight and diplomatic smile, had said volumes. Desil's relations with Boss Dieujuste and the Tonton Macoutes had become a cause for concern.

Because she had lived so long with Simone Juin, Clerise could read beyond her words and sense hidden meanings through subtle cues. Not long before, an interesting situation had occurred when Edmond Juin had been summoned to Port-au-Prince together with other local business owners so they could be notified of the amount expected by the government for their "voluntary" contribution to the new project of National Renovation. Administered by a high-ranking Duvalierist official, the Movement for National Renovation was an extortion scheme that forced business owners, civil servants, and ordinary citizens to contribute funds to vaguely projected government initiatives, through cash donations, imposed payroll deductions, road tolls, and other miscellaneous taxes. While government officials led an increasingly lavish lifestyle and were rumored to have accumulated large accounts in Swiss banks, basic services had deteriorated throughout the country.

Somewhat worried about her husband's summons to Port-au-Prince, Simone Juin had shared her concerns with Ermance, her former maid, and Clerise, who had both come to lend their support.

"Madam, a man is asking for you downstairs," one of the current maids announced.

"Who is he?" Simone Juin asked, somewhat alerted.

"I don't know. But I think he's a lottery vendor."

Puzzled, Simone Juin looked at Clerise and Ermance. "Let's go downstairs," she told them. She turned and said to the girl, "Go to the study and open the front shutters. Then tell the man that I'll be right down and take him to the study through the front porch. I'll see him there."

While Clerise and Ermance waited within earshot in the kitchen, Simone Juin graciously greeted the visitor. "Good afternoon, sir. You wanted to see me?"

"Good afternoon Mrs. Juin," the casually dressed man answered. Apparently in his mid-thirties, he carried a bulging pouch of the type used by official lottery vendors. "I had to see you," he continued, "because I had a good dream for you last night. Your father told me to bring you a lottery number. I have the tickets for you right here."

"Thank you so much," Simone Juin answered warmly. "Unfortunately, I took a holy vow not to play the lottery. So, I regret very much not to be able to buy from you."

Clerise and Ermance quickly glanced at each other and covered their mouth to keep from laughing.

"Perhaps, your husband will be interested. May I talk to him?" The man continued.

"My husband is out of town, but I thank you for stopping by," Simone Juin replied.

"When is he coming back?" the man persisted.

"He may be back any time, but I don't know for sure…"

"Is he one of the people they told to come to Port-au-Prince for that Renovation business? That's a shame. People work to make their money and those people over there try to take it from them!"

"Sir, don't you know that in every country of the world governments collect taxes from their citizens," Simone Juin answered in a calm and reasonable voice. "Without taxes there would be no roads, no schools, no public services. How would governments pay to pick up trash? … People should think seriously about those things," she added.

By then, Clerise and Ermance nearly fell off their chairs, stifling laughter. They heard the man hastily take his leave.

"Thank you, Madam," he answered. "What you said is true. I'll come back some other time."

Coincidentally or not, Edmond Juin returned home sooner than expected and the amount required for his "voluntary contribution" was less than anticipated. Although summoned a few more times to the military barracks in Lan Gabyon for additional payments by the then Duvalierist commander, he was not humiliated, mistreated, or jailed, as were others in town.

Still amused at the thought of Simone Juin's performance that day, Clerise felt calmer walking home. Later, as she waited for Desil to return from a visit to his aunt in Lan Savann, she reflected on their fight, and wondered whether or not she had overreacted to the encounter with the Tonton Macoutes. *Desil is a good man!* she thought. However, she remained puzzled at his angry reaction, especially since she was about to give birth, and decided that something was not clear. During their years of marriage, Desil had often been stubborn, opinionated, sometimes bossy, but generally thoughtful and considerate. He really wanted that child and hoped that it would be a boy. Lately however, he had become ill-tempered and impatient as if dealing with some kind of problem. The situation was tense and Clerise felt her concerns mount. Then she tried to remember happier times, especially their honeymoon at the Visels' vacation home not far from Les Cayes.

They had arrived there after their wedding and a quick reception at the Juins' residence. Louis Visel and Simone Juin had driven the newlyweds to their glorious honeymoon. For Clerise, those six days became an oasis of happiness, an unforgettable time of cherished memories to which she retreated for strength and renewal.

"You're so beautiful," Desil had said.

"Beautiful! Me?" Clerise laughed. "There's no beauty there. Don't you see all those beautiful people in town? You must be kidding!"

"You're my beautiful black woman. You feel good. You're like chocolate."

"If you say so! But how often have you had chocolate?" Clerise teased. Then, she really started to feel beautiful, reveling in her womanhood and blossoming with each moment of that time, which was theirs alone. Soon, she lost all notions of passing days as if time itself had ceased to exist. No longer an appendage to the Juins, she relished in her newly found freedom and felt whole at last. The empty house was all theirs to enjoy. They spent hours in bed, made love, talked, discovered each other. They went out for long walks, bathed in the river, and played like children. For the first time in their lives, they luxuriated in total relaxation, while the caretakers of the home, who lived nearby, prepared and brought them their meals. That week, Clerise truly fell in love with Desil.

In the glow of her memories, she wondered about the cause of his present behavior. Later that evening, when he came home and tentatively kissed her forehead, she responded and greeted him as usual.

"How's your aunt doing?" she asked to his surprise, for the first time in years.

While the swift and efficient preparations for their wedding had generated a flow of activities among the Juins, Visels, Mussains, as well as Matante Elia, Desil's Aunt Amanthe became somewhat of a problem along the way. On the surface, it had to do with religion. A relatively new convert and fervent Protestant, Amanthe, who had raised Desil, had unsuccessfully tried to attract him to her congregation. To that end, she had planned on a good Protestant girl who could bring her nephew to the fold. She reluctantly accepted Clerise, who was not only a Catholic but a chambermaid — mannered and somewhat high class, but nonetheless a *gadmantèg*, and a dark one at that. She saw Clerise's redeeming value in her polished manners, her reputation for intelligence and seriousness, as well as the connections that she would bring to the marriage. However, when Desil took his fiancée home for a visit, Amanthe was rather distant and she later found reasons not to attend the wedding. Clerise, who disliked Protestants, started to resent her with a passion.

The controversy was an old one in Les Cayes where Protestants formed a small minority and functioned in tight-knit enclaves within their social groups. On average, they coexisted peacefully with Catholics within the bounds of that tacit agreement, and the larger population usually ignored their proselytism as long as it took place among the disadvantaged and in the countryside. In spite of their different denominations, they were all grouped under the single label of Protestants and expected to respect the modus vivendi as far as everyone else was concerned. Any deviation from the status quo was guaranteed to provoke a veritable barrage, tantamount to a declaration of religious war, from the Catholic hierarchy.

Such a series of events had occurred several years earlier, when a new and enterprising Protestant minister had attempted to conduct a public procession of his parishioners near one of the major streets. The virulent diatribes of incensed Catholic priests determined to bring an end to the sacrilege had intensified the resulting scandal. While the more affluent remained above the fray and maintained cordial relations with their Protestant counterparts, Clerise and other maids and *timoun kay* had embraced the cause with fierce outrage. Retreating to the status quo, the Protestants limited their worship to the privacy of their church, and thus restored peace in town.

To Clerise, Desil's religious connections offered some positive influence, which she reluctantly acknowledged. Protestants, especially those newly converted to American-imported sects, totally opposed Vodou, which was openly or secretly practiced by large numbers of Catholics, who, as the dominant group, observed their religion much more casually. Legal marriage and a display of pious austerity were the professed norm for most recently converted Protestants. In contrast, many of those who officially described themselves as Catholics followed the traditional pattern of common-law marriages, or, if legally married, often had extramarital affairs or semi-official mistresses, depending on their inclination and means. Catholic priests seldom interfered in the latter cases, which were tolerated by law and custom. However, some of the clerics strongly objected to birth control by their married parishioners, and Clerise's pregnancy had occurred in that context.

After the complicated birth of the stillborn baby who had followed Nicole, Clerise had sought advice from Simone Juin on a safe and religiously acceptable method of birth control. The recommended Ogino method gave her good results. However, in the confessional booth, the old French priest who had known Clerise since her First Communion and was tying up loose ends before his departure for retirement in his country, had quizzed her on the matter. Angrily, he refused her absolution and told her to return for the sacraments only after she had ceased such a sinful practice. Clerise became pregnant shortly thereafter.

With Desil at work, and Janine and Nicole in school on the day Michel was born, Mrs. Dieujuste Lifaite and Ania took Clerise to the hospital at the first signs of labor. They left Jesula in charge of the house and the *boutik.* A few moments later, Janine and Nicole came home and waited impatiently for any bit of news. Desil arrived in the evening to announce the birth of a big and healthy boy. The following day, they all went to see Clerise in her semiprivate room at the hospital. The baby was dozing in her arms when Mrs. Dieujuste Lifaite came a little later.

"Clerise, you sure were ready to have that baby," she joked. "Good thing I told you to drink a glass of okra water every evening for the last month. That made him slide right out. See! All you had to do was boil the okra in water and drink a glass of it and you almost didn't even wait for the doctor and the nurse to arrive for the delivery. Hey, little man, you couldn't wait to come out!" she added, touching the baby's chin.

"When I got the word at work, I rushed here. But I only waited outside the room for a little while before the doctor came out to tell me I had a son," Desil said with a broad smile. He sat on the bed close to Clerise and gingerly touched the baby.

"Do you want to hold him?" she asked.

"I don't like to do that when they are so small."

The women laughed, and the girls crowded around the bed. "Desil," Clerise continued, "we need to have Janine and Ania go out and let people know of the baby's birth."

As they made plans to proceed with the announcement to friends, neighbors, relatives, and acquaintances, they received *bouyon pijon,* the customary pigeon soup, to restore Clerise's strength after her labor from Nennenn and Parenn, who had already been notified. Nennenn also sent word that she would come to visit shortly.

"Have you already chosen the child's godmother?" Mrs. Dieujuste asked, hoping to be selected for the coveted role.

"I had to promise Janine that she was going to be the godmother," Clerise answered diplomatically. "She would have died otherwise! She pestered me so much for that, I almost went crazy."

"Then, the next one is mine," Mrs. Dieujuste replied. To mask her disappointment, she continued, "Mrs. Juin really takes good care of you! Let me give you some of the *bouyon*."

Happy and proud, Desil seemed unable to take his eyes off his wife and son.

"Our baby is beautiful," Nicole said enthusiastically. "Can I hold him now?"

Mrs. Dieujuste laughed and rose to help. "Don't repeat the first thing you said," she chuckled. "You'll give the baby *maldyòk*, and he'll have bad luck. Clerise, I'll bring you a little bracelet to put on him against *maldyòk*."

"Nennenn's boy, Danny, was bigger when he was born," Clerise ventured to change the subject. "I remember how pretty Nennenn was after she gave birth to him, with her pretty hair loose on the pillows and all that lace and embroidery around her."

Desil stood up suddenly, and looked at Clerise almost with contempt. "I have to go," he said, "I have things to do. You need anything?"

248 – Marie-Thérèse Labossière Thomas

"No thank you, I am okay." She looked at him with surprise.

"Then, I'll see you later. Good-bye Mrs. Dieujuste." He turned around abruptly, and left after a brief talk with the girls who were admiring their little brother, unaware of the unfolding drama.

Mrs. Dieujuste showed a flicker of surprise. She quickly glanced at Clerise and seemed to try to find something to do. "You like the *bouyon?*" she asked.

"Desil doesn't like me to talk about Nennenn," Clerise blurted, almost with tears in her eyes. "I don't understand, but he has been quite tense lately."

"Don't pay attention. It'll pass," Mrs. Dieujuste said reassuringly. "Men are like that. If you let that bother you, your milk will go to your head. Here, take the baby. Janine may be his little *Marenn*, but I am his big *Marenn*. That's a big man with two godmothers. He'll be president of the country some day! "

"What happens to people when milk goes to their head?" Janine asked Ania when she got home.

"It can make them crazy."

"What makes milk go to someone's head?"

"That can happen if a mother gets very upset and angry soon after her baby is born."

"I hope it doesn't happen to mom," Janine said.

Nicole clutched her doll a little more tightly.

CHAPTER 8

The Politics of Everyday Life

1963

"You are going to be the godmother of that baby!" the neighbors had often told Mrs. Dieujuste when she showered the very pregnant Clerise with attention. With great modesty, the would-be godmother had always demurred. However, she secretly wished to be selected for the role which would have boosted her stature and acceptance in the neighborhood. When Clerise chose Janine instead, Mrs. Dieujuste concealed her disappointment while she continued the friendship and gradually took her distance.

In spite of her genuine liking for Mrs. Dieujuste, Clerise had never considered her as a potential godmother for her child. Although she would have been a logical choice under normal circumstances, Boss Dieujuste's position in the current political context made the situation difficult.

"The only thing we can do," Clerise had told Desil when they discussed the situation, "is to let Janine be the godmother. We can't possibly choose anyone else without getting Mrs. Dieujuste all upset. I'd hate to do that. She's really nice to me. Also, Janine will be so thrilled."

"You're right. Plus, we have to be very careful with Boss Dieujuste and his wife. They may think that if she can't be the godmother, her husband or one of her sons should be the godfather, and we don't want that either."

"So, what are we going to do?"

Desil paused, then taped his forehead. "Okay," he said, "let's keep it in the family. Why don't we have my cousin Eugene be the godfather. That way, there'll be no problem. Everybody will understand."

Desil's cousin, Eugene Fleurantier, was the son of his aunt Amanthe, his mother's younger sister, and Clerise's Protestant foe. Raised in Lòtbò La Ravin, on the other side of La Ravine river at the outskirts of town, the young Amanthe had later moved to Lan Savann when she entered a short-lived common-law union, which resulted in one son, her treasured Eugene Fleurantier.

Lucia, Desil's mother, had started work very young as a *revandèz*, who retailed produce for local *Madan Sara* wholesalers. Her sister, Amanthe, a quiet girl, enjoyed spending her days by the river, half-naked under the hot sun, while she exchanged gossip with other washer-women. In contrast, Lucia loved the excitement of traveling and meeting different people at all hours of the day and night. Thus, with her large open box, her *bak*, placed on her coiled cloth *tiyon* atop her head, Lucia sold a variety of products in the streets, the marketplace, and by following organized groups during Mardi Gras, Rara, and other occasions in Les Cayes and surrounding areas. Desil was conceived during one of those nights when, intoxicated by the pounding drumbeat and ambient sexuality of the Rara band, she had followed Desulien, one of her occasional suitors, into the shadow of a recessed porch, setting aside *bak* and *tiyon* on the ground and turning off her makeshift lamp. After that, she became one of his women.

Born nine months later, Desil remained with Lucia's family, while his mother continued to travel until she settled in Port-au-Prince. By then, her affair with Desulien had ended, and they both regularly contributed some money or produce to the care of Desil, who had been informally adopted by his grandparents and his aunt Amanthe, then still single. Until his cousin Eugene was a toddler, Desil stayed in Lòtbò La Ravin with his maternal grandparents. However, since Amanthe needed someone to help her keep an eye on the baby when she washed clothes on the riverside or was busy ironing for wealthier families living near her house, Desil joined her in Lan Savann as a *gadò*, an informal guardian of his cousin, bringing with him the modest resources that his parents provided. That mutually satisfactory arrangement had moved the little boy closer to established local schools, which he started to attend as soon as his cousin no longer required constant supervision. A few years later, his aunt was able to hire a *timoun kay* to run errands and perform other chores.

Much younger then, Amanthe had worked long and hard. Because she was conscientious, efficient, in need of money, and with plans for the future, she developed a steady and faithful clientele. Over the years, Desil attended school as time and resources permitted, while his cousin Eugene was regularly enrolled at the school for boys run by the Brothers of the Sacred Heart, near the church of the same name across the street from the marketplace. Since his formal education had started relatively late, and because of the precariousness of the family's resources, Desil was always among the oldest in his classes in the various establishments through which he passed. Painstakingly learning the basics of French, reading, writing, and arithmetic, he knew that he would not get very far in his studies. However, everyone expected him to learn enough to earn a decent living, assist his aunt Amanthe in the care of Eugene, and eventually provide some support to his mother and siblings in Port-au-Prince, if needed.

He had nearly completed the primary cycle of studies when Lucia died. Heartbroken, he and his aunt made the trip to Port-au-Prince where they joined his stepfather and two siblings for the funeral conducted in the Protestant temple where Lucia's family worshipped. Profoundly moved by the heartfelt Creole songs and the congregation's support, Amanthe contacted a local minister upon her return to Les Cayes. Thus, she began her conversion, which culminated in her Protestant baptism some years later.

After his mother's death, Desil no longer received financial support from Port-au-Prince. Thus, he left school to contribute to the household. By that time, Amanthe was also in transition, from the hard work of ironing clothes – she had long ago subcontracted the washing — to the establishment of a new business. On that matter, she developed a partnership with Desil's godmother, an aging *Madan Sara* wholesaler, who brought Amanthe produce from the countryside for distribution to the *revandèz*, the women who sold in the local market. For a while however, Amanthe continued some of her previous and fairly lucrative business, supervising the woman who came to her home to press the clothes.

Initially, Desil ran errands for his aunt and insured the liaison first with his godmother, and later with the additional *Madan Sara,* who also became associates as the activities developed. As the business grew, to satisfy the demand from the resellers, Desil started to buy items from local stores on behalf of his aunt. Thus, he developed a steady relationship with Louis Visel from whom he purchased flour and other imported products. To supplement the household's income, Desil also sold official lottery tickets to relatives, friends, associates, acquaintances, and others that he happened to meet. In the proper tradition of a responsible young man, he turned his earnings to his aunt, keeping only some pocket money for miscellaneous expenses. Those were few, since he did not drink or smoke, except for an occasional puff as a concession to some essential re-quirement of machismo. Conscious of his family obligations, he had no time or resources for a steady girlfriend, and opted instead for a variety of more or less brief and inexpensive encounters with available women.

Desil's demeanor had impressed Louis Visel, who recommended him to Andre Juin for an open position in his store. By then, Amanthe's business had developed sufficiently to provide dependable resources to the family. Her son, Eugene, who had almost completed his secondary education at the Lycée, was about to move to Port-au-Prince where he would continue his studies at the University. There, he planned to live with Lucia's family. Amanthe would then have to send additional support besides Desil's regular contributions for his younger siblings. Thus, Amanthe welcomed the opportunity that Louis Visel offered her nephew. Desil, who had started to yearn for financial independence and resent his aunt's prodding for conversion to Protestant-ism, was elated.

Upon completion of his university studies, Eugene returned to Les Cayes where he started to teach at the Lycée. The resulting freedom from financial obligations allowed Desil to get married and start a family of his own.

About to leave for Congo on a foreign contract, Eugene enthusiastically accepted Desil's invitation to be baby Michel's godfather. However, because travel prepa-rations often took him in and out of town, the baptism date needed to be arranged to meet his schedule.

"I have something to tell you about Eugene," Desil whispered to Clerise, motioning discreetly toward the Lifaite's house. On that Friday evening, at the end of the holiday season, they had lingered to converse at the dinner table while the girls went to join Ania and Jesula on the front porch.

Puzzled, Clerise arched her eyebrows. "Can't you tell me here?" she whispered.

"You really need some fresh air and exercise," Desil replied in a normal tone, again pointing cautiously in the Lifaites' direction. "Why don't I take you for a walk with the girls?"

"I'll get the baby ready for bed, and since it's Friday, we can go out around the girls' bedtime. Ania and Jesula will watch the baby and the house."

On their way past the Lifaites sitting on their porch, the Fleurantiers exchanged greetings. "I'm taking Clerise for a little walk," Desil said as he waved.

At the plaza near the pier, Clerise and Desil sat on one of the benches facing the sea while the delighted girls played with the waves. With an arm on the bench behind Clerise, Desil turned sideways, so that both could see anyone approaching. In the night breeze, the sea shone under the moonlight.

"Walls have ears sometimes," Clerise said amid the murmur of the waves.

"We're okay here."

"What about Eugene?"

"He's getting married this weekend."

"Whom is he marrying? Why so suddenly?" Clerise exclaimed keeping her voice low.

"His girlfriend whom you know. She's distantly related to one of the priests who is quite active in exile circles.

Eugene is keeping things quiet because he fears that she'll not be able to leave the country if the government knows that she plans to go with him. That's why they are going to keep their marriage secret. All her papers will be filed under her new name. That way, she'll be able to pass the checkpoint at the airport in Port-au-Prince."

Clerise put a finger on her lips. *"Je wè, bouch pe,* The eyes see, the mouth remains silent," she answered with an old saying.

"We need to decide on a time for Michel's baptism."

"Let's have it after Carnival, during Lent. We'll plan around Eugene's schedule."

As they paused to watch the children play, Nicole ran to them. "Mom, dad, look at what I found," she said flashing a seashell before she ran back to her sister near the water edge.

"Girls, try not to get wet," Clerise admonished. "You don't want to catch a cold."

Alone on the beach, the girls continued to play quietly, as their parents watched. Then Clerise sighed, "Things used to be so simple. Now, everywhere you turn, there's trouble. Look at that new building that the *Juvenia* club built right behind us, near this plaza. They only held a few events there. Now, it's not even used anymore."

"When the club's president kept that Duvalierist official from entering the Mardi Gras ball, that was it! You know how I feel about these rich people and their airs. It serves them right in a way, but what happened was no reason to arrest the guy."

"Now that the Military Club is closed too, you see how the *elite* girls and the young officers keep their distances. They don't marry each other as often anymore. With all the changes Duvalier made in the military, the soldiers who are for him become officers before you know it. Even those young guys who go to the Military Academy are mostly Duvalierists. At least, that's what I hear."

Desil looked around. "We already know how some people are in this town," he said, "but bad things also happen from the other side. Those officers who are connected with the Tonton Macoutes arrest and beat people for no reason." His voice down to a whisper, he continued, "Remember how that Duvalierist colonel made a point of driving slowly around town. No one dared to pass him anymore, since the day he stopped some people who had, and said he was going to arrest them... ."

Clerise chuckled. "...and he told them he would lock them up if they ever again cause dust from the road to get on his car and make it dirty."

"That really shook many people up. What's going on is so bad, it even gets funny at times," Desil chuckled.

They remained silent for a moment. Then Clerise whispered, with a hand nearly covering her mouth. "When they take you to jail, even for the silliest reason, you never know what can happen. You may disappear, or they may beat you so badly that you end up in the hospital. It's better to leave town before they get to you."

"Sometimes you may not even know why and when they'll take you. That's why I am so happy Eugene can leave."

"Let me know what day will be good for him for the baptism," Clerise said. "It's getting late. We need to go back home," she added. Desil helped her stand and went to get the girls.

While the old social structures struggled to survive, a new *elite* had emerged in Les Cayes. With the Tonton Macoutes' rise in prominence, *les gens de famille* — the people of "good family" — which included the traditional and largely mulatto *elite*, the black bourgeoisie, and some of the upper-class *Noiriste* intellectuals now in power, forged new ties of friendship and social bonding. Thus, the town's traditional way of life remained largely intact through a complex and informal network of alliances, which often extended as far as the highest levels of government in Port-au-Prince. This network insured a measure of protection to the old *elite* as well as a politically acceptable avenue of social advancement to the upper middle class.

In a climate of intimidation, harassment, and genuine terror where legal recourse had vanished, those whose relatives had "disappeared" kept a low profile and often befriended well-placed military personnel to learn the fate of loved ones. With the brutal suppression of newspapers and radio stations nationwide, as well as the imprisonment, forced exile, and disappearance of journalists, writers, teachers, student leaders, and union organizers, communication fell under total government control. In Les Cayes, private telephone exchanges abruptly ended when the central telecommunication office mysteriously caught fire on a summer day and was never repaired. Local calls became impossible, and out-of-town communications could only be made from one central location where conversations were monitored. No longer delivered, the mail had to be collected from the post office, preferably at the moment it arrived in town from the lone military plane flying once or twice a week from Port-au-Prince. Otherwise, leftover envelopes were opened, scrutinized, and often discarded, should their content be deemed suspect.

While services continued to deteriorate, municipal trash collection also came to a halt, providing vagrants and paupers an opportunity to collect garbage from residences and, for a small fee, dump it on remote vacant lots. Amid the internal tension, external pressure, and increasing scarcity of national resources, repression and fear intensified. However, the assassination of the then Dominican consul still came as a shock in Les Cayes.

The news exploded on a Sunday afternoon, before the carnival season started to unfold. Unlike the previous long-tenured Dominican consul, the slain man had only been in town for a few years. Rather than moving to the large masonry house on Main Street where his predecessor had stayed with his family, the new consul lived alone in a large wooden house on a side street near

Pon Gonbo and generated a number of comments in the neighborhood.

"That man is weird!" said one of Clerise's clients who had come to try on her new dress.

"Who?"

"You know! That Dominican consul who stays all by himself in the big house where the Freyons used to live," the woman explained as Clerise adjusted a sleeve. "On my way here, I saw him on a bike carrying home some ice wrapped in paper. I hear he has no maid or *timoun kay* working for him to run those errands. That's a strange guy!"

After she left, Ania who had overheard the conversation while serving clients in the *boutik*, added some information. "Mrs. Desil," she said during a lull, "I also heard some things about the man who lives in that big house when I was buying some *fritay* at *Manzè Mama's*."

Clerise was amused and curious. "People talk so much in this town! Anyway, what did you hear?" she inquired while she continued to sew.

"They say he walks naked around the house. They also say that the people who live next to him in that other balcony house have to keep their side windows closed all the time because of that."

"Oh!"

Encouraged, Ania continued. "I also hear that the only people who come to see him in that house are women… women who are doing… you know… the bad kind of women," she added with embarrassment.

Sometime later, the Dominican consul moved to the residence in Lan Gabyon where he was assassinated. The murder had been particularly gruesome, with the head almost severed from the body, which was found in the front yard of the bungalow. Aside from the local authorities, no one seemed to have known the name of the consul who had mostly kept to himself. While his death remained a mystery, the attitudes of Haitian as well as Dominican authorities further baffled the citizenry. No obvious search for suspects occurred, as would have been expected under the circumstances. Then the Dominicans discreetly retrieved the body of their envoy without issuing an official statement or protest. The only known arrest in the matter was that of an American student apparently engaged in archeological research in *L'Île-à-Vaches*, one of the islands off the coast of Les Cayes. While kept at the military barracks in Lan Gabyon, he often sat in plain view on the front porch at the end of the courtyard, conversing with the soldiers. Soon the word spread in town, and the white American prisoner, the *blan*, became a local curiosity.

"Instead of going to the pier this Sunday afternoon, let's walk to Lan Gabyon to look at the *blan*," one of Janine's friends proposed. The girls had just been allowed to go out with others of their age for short strolls on the pier and occasional matinees at the movie theater.

"I'll ask my mom if we can go to Lan Gabyon instead of the pier. I think it'll be o.k.," Janine said.

"I'm going too," Nicole announced. "I want to see the *blan*, also."

"What's the matter with you? Why can't you play with kids your age? And then you're going to tell mom, and she'll make me take you."

"If you go see the *blan*, why can't I see him too? I'll tell Mom to make you take me."

"Let's get her friend Marie-Carmelle to go along and we'll make the two of them walk in front of us," offered one of the girls as a compromise. "Maybe I'll have to take my brother, too. Those kids are pests!" she added.

Thus, the traffic in front of the barracks in Lan Gabyon increased considerably as a large number of mostly young or otherwise idle pedestrians leisurely strolled by to catch a glimpse of the *blan*. As no one dared to look too much inside the barracks' yard, or inquire further about the killing, the issue died down. However, rumor was that a young soldier had lost his mind at the Colonel's house in connection with the Dominican consul's murder.

"That's what I heard," Janine explained animatedly to her mother and Ania, while casting cautious glances toward the street. She continued to speak as she dropped her schoolbag near Clerise's sewing machine. "You saw him before," she said. "That's the one people mistook for an officer sometimes because he used to wear the fine khaki uniforms. That's the one who became crazy."

While her sister spoke, Nicole made funny faces at her baby brother contentedly propped on her mother's lap. Meanwhile, she also kept an eye on the street to make herself useful in case of need. "Here comes Marie-Carmelle's mother!" she suddenly shouted in warning.

"Janine and Nicole, you need to go inside and change your clothes." Clerise said promptly. "Wave to Mrs. Dieujuste before you go."

"I hope she didn't hear you," Janine whispered to her sister on their way out of the room.

"Bonjou Mrs. Dieujuste!" Clerise exclaimed cordially as the woman stepped on the porch. "Janine," she called, "have your sister wash her hands before she changes her clothes. We don't want them to get dirty. Those children!" she added with a resigned sigh, turning to her neighbor.

"How're you all?" Mrs. Dieujuste said. "Here, give me my big boy. *Bonjou* Michel?" she cooed, holding the baby at arms length and bouncing him lightly. "Aren't you a big boy? Yes, you are!" Michel giggled with delight. "Even if they didn't let me be your godmother, I'm still your grand-godmother, your *gran-marenn*," she continued to coo as she took a seat. "They didn't think I was good enough for you, right? But no matter, you're still my big boy."

"You know we had promised Janine," Clerise replied, managing to convey a mixture of regret and annoyance, as Mrs. Dieujuste continued to fuss over Michel.

As the baptism ceremony approached, Nicole shared Janine's excitement and called herself the baby's little godmother, his *ti-marenn*. Nearly six years old, the little girl often had mixed feelings toward her new brother. While she enjoyed playing with him and getting him to laugh by making funny faces and noises, she often resented the attention that everyone lavished on him, since she was practically excluded from assisting in his care. Thus, she would make a display of anger to protest his crying which, she claimed, annoyed her and disturbed her activities. She tried to carry him as often as she could however, taking him from Ania, Jesula, or Janine, as they would allow.

Janine understood the honor and responsibility of being chosen as a godmother, and took her new role very seriously. "You may not understand what I am going to say, but I am going to try to explain it anyway," she told Nicole as they went to bed. "The godmother and the godfather should be able to get along well with each other, in case they have to replace the parents. Then, they are like the father and mother of the child. That's why parents have to like and trust the people they choose to be godparents. They also have to make sure those people will be able to help the child in the future, if need be."

"I can do that too," Nicole said, half-asleep.

"Yes, but I am the oldest," Janine replied before she turned on her side.

While the parents projected simple arrangements for the baptism, Eugene insisted on doing everything in style. Thus, when Carnival ended and Lent began, he sent a nicely wrapped gift, along with roses and a card, to announce his visit to his "distinguished *commère*, his co-parent, the baby's godmother." Janine was so pleased that she called everyone present in the household to admire her flowers, and placed them on display with the card and the gift in the parlor. For a while, she kept running back and forth when she forgot to act as a mature young woman worthy of formal consideration.

"Where are my flowers?" Nicole asked. "I'm the baby's *ti-marenn*, his little godmother."

"The flowers are for both of us," Janine answered magnanimously. "Mom, we really have to take care of my dress, my hair, and the baby's clothes for the baptism," she added.

"You'll look fine. And we're going to use Nicole's baptism clothes for the baby."

"But, the godmother is supposed to give those," Janine said.

"Yes, but it doesn't have to be done like that all the time. Many people keep the same baptism dress for all their children, as long as that's all it's used for. Nicole's things are brand new, just like when her godmother gave them to her. She only wore them that one time. We'll use them for Michel. He'll look great!"

Nicole's baptism outfit was one of the ready-made, inexpensive varieties with a long white gown and camisole with matching bonnet, socks, plastic pants and shoes, which could be found in the lesser shops. More affluent families ordered custom-made embroidered or laced outfits with hand-made or imported leather booties. However, for Clerise and her daughters, the carefully packaged outfit that they took from the bedroom hutch and unwrapped on the bed, looked simply marvelous. Desil arrived.

"What are those flowers in the front room?" he asked.

"They are Janine's. Her *compère* Eugene sent them to her," Clerise said.

Excited, Janine took Desil to the parlor with Clerise and Nicole in tow. "Look at my card and gift!" she said

"The flowers are for me too," Nicole interjected, talking at the same time.

Desil smiled broadly. "That man Eugene! Always so grand!" he joked with a touch a pride.

"Well. We'll also greet him in style when he comes," Clerise said. "You and I and Janine will put on our nice clothes and sit with him in the parlor for a formal visit. We'll make polite conversation and Ania will serve refreshments."

"What about me?" Nicole asked.

"You'll also put on your nice clothes and come to greet your uncle. Then you'll go play outside with your friends. Jesula will watch you."

"I'm not going to put on my suit for Eugene," Desil said. "What's the matter with you Clerise?"

"All I know is that your cousin is trying to do things very nicely before he leaves. That's his way to thank you for all you did for him. We should also show him our appreciation."

"Children, remember not to tell anyone that Eugene is going anywhere," Desil warned. "Well..., we'll see about that polite business!"

As godmother and baby lived in the same house, Eugene took advantage of his visit to Janine to bring the baby's gift, which consisted of some cash in an envelope that he gave to Clerise with profuse apologies.

"What I really would have loved to give him is a silver cup," he said. "But you know how things are right now. I cannot do yet what I would have liked; but that will come."

"Why?" Clerise said. "The other kids don't have silver cups. Don't worry about it at all. We're family."

"Eugene, I see that you're already a bourgeois," Desil laughed. "You read too many of those books. But that will help you someday. You'll get there!"

"You have opened the way for me," Eugene said. "I'll never forget how you sacrificed to help my mother raise me. I will always be there for you and yours."

Consequently, the day of the Christening, Eugene arrived in one of the town's two or three private cars used as taxicabs, whose drivers could be summoned from their homes or the curbside in Kafou Orèl by the *timoun kay* dispatched for the occasion. Ready, Janine waited for him in a new dress, hair freshly pressed and curled, while Ania, clad in her Sunday's best, carried the baby in his baptismal glory. While the godparents sat in the back of the car, after exchanging appropriate greetings with the driver, Ania handed Michel to Janine before she crammed in the front seat with Nicole and Marie-Carmelle Lifaite, also in their Sunday's best. It was Nicole's first car ride, an unforgettable experience that left her rather dizzy as they arrived at the Cathedral's rectory. Then Ania took the baby from Janine and carried him the whole time except during the actual church ceremony when she handed him back to his godmother.

Meanwhile, in the Fleurantiers' home, Clerise, Desil, Mrs. Dieujuste, and Jesula prepared for the reception to begin as soon as the baby returned from church. For that event, Eugene had offered a bottle of decent champagne, some sweet liquor, several bottles of *kola*, the locally made soda, as well as cakes and sweets. Boss Dieujuste brought a bottle of local rum, the Juins sent meat patties, and Mama, the corner *machann fritay*, offered some of her fried food as a gesture of goodwill to her long-time customers.

The Christening party arrived among the cheers of the assembled relatives, friends, and neighbors. After everyone settled, the festivities began with the godfather's much- practiced and awaited traditional toast to the godchild, the parents, and the ever "charming," and "distinguished" godmother.

Because of the Lifaites' presence, Eugene's bride did not attend the celebrations. Shortly thereafter, the young couple left the country.

In the month following the baptism, *Dife nan kay la*, The House Is on Fire, the theme song of Duvalierists in times of turmoil, continuously played on the radio. Bombs had detonated in Port-au-Prince and a plot discovered against the regime led to a massive purge in the military. Throughout the nation, the government dismissed, jailed, and killed officers of all ranks, along with former military personnel. Many sought asylum in various embassies in Port-au-Prince.

"We really need to get a radio," Clerise told Desil as he went out for an update on the latest news.

"Once I find a used one we can afford, I'll definitely get it. That will also help with your *boutik*. You'll be swamped with clients. The woman down the street is doing very well since she put that radio in hers."

"In that case, we may have to move," Clerise laughed. "What we have here will be too small. Anyway, last night when I went to Nennenn for an update from their radio, everything was still the same. I'll help the children get ready for school."

Later that day, while breastfeeding Michel in her bedroom, Clerise heard a car screech in front of the Lifaites' residence. The sounds of *Dife nan kay la* wafted almost constantly from their open windows. *The house must really be on fire!* Clerise thought.

Jesula nearly ran into the bedroom. "*Madanm,*" she said, "Ania asks you to come to the *boutik* when you can. Someone told her there's big trouble in Port-au-Prince and the schools have to close. Boss Dieujuste just came back home in a government pick-up truck."

"I'll be right there," Clerise exclaimed, rushing to the front with the baby.

"Ania, put your shoes on. Get the children from school, and take them to Nennenn," she instructed. "I'll take over the *boutik.*" As she spoke, she saw Boss Dieujuste emerge from his house in full militia uniform carrying a rifle. He looked straight past her and climbed in the cab of the truck, which took off at full speed.

"They tried to kidnap Duvalier's younger children on their way to school," one of Clerise's customers said. "The children escaped unharmed, but their bodyguards were killed."

As the latest news developments made their way to town, Clerise learned that an enraged Duvalier had accused a young lieutenant originally from Les Cayes of the attempt against his children. The officer was a member of a sharpshooting team that had recently won a contest abroad. Recently dismissed from the military, he was among the many who had received political asylum in foreign embassies. Although his family had moved to Port-au-Prince when he was a teenager, they had kept solid ties in town. In what became one of the most terror-filled days in the nation's history, a squad of Tonton Macoutes invaded the home of the officer's parents, machine-gunned them, and set the house on fire. The fate of his toddler son who had also been in the home remained unknown. In an orgy of killing, the Tonton Macoutes shot on sight any possible enemy. Blood flew in the streets of Port-au-Prince.

In Les Cayes, where the officer's family had been well liked and respected, the population was shocked, numbed, and horrified. Friends paid discreet visits to the relatives. The town mourned silently. The Tonton Macoutes kept quiet.

The government officially closed schools throughout the nation as the crisis escalated in Port-au-Prince. Tonton Macoutes attempted to invade the Dominican Embassy where the accused officer had sought asylum, although by then it was known that he had not participated in the failed kidnapping. In response, the Dominican government threatened to invade Haiti. In fiery speeches over the radio, Duvalierist officials vowed to burn the country to the ground should Dominican troops cross the border. *The House Is on Fire* played all day long. That night, the sound of Tonton Macoutes drum beats, harsh voices, and loud footsteps in the deserted streets punctuated the mounting tension, as citizens behind their locked doors prepared to face the unknown. Through the cracks of her wooden house, Clerise saw Marcel Octavien, the Macoute commander, lead a prisoner carrying a metallic drum atop his head. They went toward the gas stations in Kafou Orèl. Terrified and powerless, Clerise kept silent. The night passed. The Dominicans withdrew from the border. The Duvalier regime faced international condemnation.

Later, rumor had that Marcel Octavien had been determined to set fire to the city on that fateful night. Apparently opposed to the plan, the old-time Duvalier partisans succeeded in having it stopped, with support from the politically well-connected military department commander. The latter, it was said, had vowed to execute Octavien publicly on *La Place d'Armes* the next day if even a single miserable hut had burned in Lan Savann.

The subsequent political lull did not last long. Continuous attacks and threats from the exile community, dissent among core Duvalierist supporters concerning the government policies of violence and corruption, and more or less overt contention by some Catholic bishops and priests, as well as from other sectors of society forced the regime to remain on a state of alert. Frequently on the offensive in what often appeared to be a policy of random violence, the government struck in all directions. Catholic and Protestant bishops were expelled and foreign priests deported. Students, educators, trade unionists, suspected communist sympathizers, exiles' relatives, and ordinary citizens were jailed, tortured, killed, forced to leave the country, or simply disappeared. Once again, the Tonton Macoutes were on the warpath.

In that context, a new wave of repression started in Les Cayes. Led by Lieutenant Darville, a young Duvalierist officer who had arrived in town nearly a year before, teams of soldiers and Tonton Macoutes entered homes and brutally arrested citizens. Luc Derat, the paraplegic former journalist and movie theater owner, was thrown from his wheelchair and forced to crawl in the street near his home. Jailed and beaten, he died a few months after his release. The long list of those brutally snatched from their homes kept growing.

Around dusk one evening, Desil and Boss Dieujuste politely greeted each other from their respective backyards. Since the arrests had begun, their relationship had grown somewhat distant. Although Desil felt concerned by that turn of events, he could not bring himself to renew the easy and burgeoning friendship with the other man in the current political context. Dieujuste also appeared to avoid him, and they had reverted to their formerly reserved interaction.

"I'd like to show you something that I saw in your yard," Dieujuste said rather suddenly. "You may have to fix it."

Desil managed not to show his surprise. "Come in, Boss Dieujuste."

"Over here, I'll show you," Dieujuste said, moving to a corner of the yard where he bent, as if looking at something on the ground. The younger man followed suit.

"Your people, the Juins, are on the list to get arrested," Dieujuste said in a low voice.

"Is that true?"

"Yes, tell them." And then he continued loudly, "See, I told you. That must be a big rat to make a hole like that on the ground. Let's cover it. I think that rat comes to my house too. Let's set a big trap for it."

Later that evening, as the children slept, Desil informed Clerise in the barest of whispers. "Tell Nennenn and Parenn. They are on the list to be arrested."

"I'll go there tomorrow."

With tears in her eyes, Simone Juin hugged Clerise and thanked her for the information. However, as Clerise later found out, Nennenn already knew. Her crime was that she had organized a group of mothers who had met with the bishop a few years earlier to request a Catholic secondary school. For that act of treacherous elitism, the women, along with their husbands, were placed on the list to be arrested. "I'll keep a toothbrush stuck in my bra at all times, since I don't know when they will come to get me," Nennenn said to Clerise. There was no escape. The Duvalierist machinery had penetrated the countryside through the rural police and most of the Vodou establishment. There were no embassies or consulates in which to seek asylum in Les Cayes. Teams of soldiers and Tonton Macoutes stopped and searched travelers at roadblocks. The military had confiscated privately owned guns.

An avid hunter, Edmond Juin had been forced to surrender his rifle to the local police. However, not long before the previous political crisis, a military acquaintance had offered to help him get the gun back, so that he could go hunting again. Sensing a possible trap, Edmond Juin had refused on principle, and viewed the man with a measure of suspicion. The officer was transferred from Les Cayes during the purge of the military, and rumor had that he had been executed, along with others suspected of plotting against the government. When he heard of his own impending arrest, Edmond Juin remained resolute. "I am an honest and independent man," he said. "I don't get mixed up in politics. I don't hurt anybody. I don't bother anyone. If they come to my home, they won't take me alive." However, the threat did not materialize. Lieutenant Darville was summarily transferred out of town after his brutal arrest of a citizen with powerful but discreet family connections in Port-au-Prince, and the entire operation came to an end. The relationship between the Fleurantiers and the Lifaites remained cordial.

CHAPTER 9

The Eye of the Storm

1964

A restless period followed on the political scene. Still without a radio, the Fleurantiers continued to rely on the *teledyòl*, the ever efficient rumor mill, and as they pursued their outside activities, they could also hear the increasingly violent speeches and songs broadcast continuously all over town. A show of defiance toward international assistance to the exiles set to overthrow the government, the theme was also to consolidate Duvalier's power by making him president for life, strike terror among the population, and discourage any support for the *kamoken*, the enemies of the regime.

"We will make a Himalaya of corpses," the Duvalierist president of the national Red Cross, himself a medical doctor, had declared in a harangue endlessly repeated.

"Did you hear that? Did he really say that?" Nennenn asked, the first time that she heard the speech on her living-room radio. She held her face in her hands and appeared stunned.

"The 'corpses' thing?" Janine answered with fear in her voice. "Yes I heard!" she said, and they both resumed their intent listening. Nicole sat quietly and refrained from asking questions.

The sinister broadcasts continued during the following weeks. In a fiery and menacing speech, a congresswoman who was a *Fiyèt Lalo*, the female equivalent of a Tonton Macoutes, contemptuously compared Dominican airplanes that had dropped anti-government leaflets on the capital to nothing more than "little butterflies." Amid the escalation of threats and competing pledges of allegiance, Duvalier declared his fierce determination, as well as physical stamina, while his followers cheered wildly. "They say that I am not a man. Ask Mrs. Duvalier!"

Government employees, students, business people, citizens from the provinces, and throngs of people from rural areas forcibly transported to Port-au-Prince were compelled to participate in "spontaneous" demonstrations of support. Trucks and buses, commandeered by the local authorities in Les Cayes, roamed the countryside to carry loads of human cargo; other citizens ordered to participate in the massive show of support either secured rides in private cars, or remained secluded inside their homes, as did Edmond Juin. Since each household was to be represented in the capital by at least one member, Clerise stayed with the children, while Desil traveled with Andre Juin, who also lived not too far from known Duvalierists. Without consultation, and since their presence could not be monitored in Port-au-Prince, both men remained inside their relatives' homes.

Not long after, all schools and businesses in Les Cayes were made to close for a day, while students at all levels, their teachers, and all public employees had to take to the streets for a demonstration in support of Duvalier's intent to become president for life. Smiling and cheering government officials encouraged the noisy crowd to march to the tempo of brisk new Duvalierist tunes. The younger set enthusiastically shouted slogans, while many of the other marchers either paid lip service, or remained grimly silent when not being directly observed. "I like Duvalier," Nicole said to her mother after the march, "he gives children nice vacations."

A new scandal erupted in town, when a recently arrived lieutenant fell in love with a local girl. According to rumor, the man was already married to one of the most prominent *Fiyèt Lalo* of Port-au-Prince, and the marriage had been personally ordered by Duvalier, "in the interest of the great Duvalierist family," at the woman's request.

The young, gregarious, charming, politically secure, and rather handsome Lieutenant Polin, who had arrived in Les Cayes without his wife, struck a friendship with some *elite* youngsters and apparently started a romance with the local girl. As the situation evolved, many in town whispered their concern, especially because of the precarious political position of the girl's family. The matter took an interesting turn when the lieutenant's wife, the reportedly fierce and prominent militiawoman, the *Fiyèt Lalo* Bertha Carmonot Polin, decided to pay a visit to her husband in Les Cayes. Once in town, she also undertook to whip the local contingent of Tonton Macoutes into shape.

On their porch, Clerise and Desil sat as usual, commenting on current events and enjoying an easy banter in the June afternoon. The baby on her lap, Clerise noticed Boss Dieujuste arriving from the corner. He looked unusually grim, quite different from his usual jovial and pleasant self.

"Desil," he said without preamble, "I need to talk to you."

Alarmed, Clerise looked at Desil, and sensed a subtle tension.

"When do you want to talk, Boss Dieujuste?" Desil asked, the strain almost palpable in his voice.

"Can you come to my house with me?" Boss Dieujuste answered somberly. He did not look at Clerise or the baby.

"Clerise, I'll be back in a moment," Desil said as he rose from his chair and left for the house next door.

He emerged moments later, petrified, visibly struggling to walk the short distance home with a degree of composure. Clerise had not moved from her chair.

"What is it?" she said, as he passed her and entered the house without a word.

Janine and Nicole were out. "Jesula," she called, "tell Ania to watch the *boutik*; and you, come and take care of the baby for a moment."

In their room, she found Desil sitting on the bed with his head in his hands.

She felt her stomach knot and put a hand on his shoulder. "De, what is it?"

Still, Desil did not move, or look at her.

She closed the bedroom door, sat on the bed near him, put an arm around his shoulders, and gently caressed his hair. To her surprise and dismay, Desil was crying. Silently. With tears running through his fingers onto the back of his strong hands.

Clerise fought her panic and rocked him lightly. "De, tell me what it is."

He wiped his eyes, regained his composure, and stood up facing her. "Clerise, I don't know how to tell you."

"Just sit down and tell me," she said bracing herself.

"Boss Dieujuste has just told me that I will have to wear the Macoute uniform and come to march in the parade that Mrs. Polin is organizing."

"How can he tell you something like that? You are not a Tonton Macoute. He knows it!"

Desil got up, walked to the dresser, and leaned there with his back turned. In the dark little room, it seemed to Clerise that the world she knew was rushing away, never to be the same again.

"Things are not that simple," Desil said without looking at her.

"What is not that simple? Are they forcing you?" she asked uncomprehendingly. "Are they going to force people in town to do that now? So, where is that going to end?"

"They are not exactly forcing me. They are just telling me to do it."

"Why?" She was incredulous, refusing to accept what she knew was going to come. She remembered flashes of their encounter with Octavien, Desil's knowledge of the Juins impending arrest, his friendship with Boss Dieujuste, his impatience of the past few months. At times, the change in his behavior had made her think that he might have had another woman, a possibility that she had promptly discarded, as he continued to turn over to her his entire salary on payday, drawing only his usual pocket money.

"Why?" she repeated.

"Clerise, there is something I didn't tell you."

"Tell me now. I am listening." The blood was draining from her. *I can take whatever comes*, she thought, *for my children*. Resolute, she looked at him, her hands folded on her lap. "Desil," she asked. "What do you have to tell me?"

"It was not that I was trying to hide it from you," he said wearily while turning toward her. "You were pregnant at the time and I didn't know how to tell you. After that, the baby was born; and then, as time went by, I never could find the right moment."

"Now is the time…"

"Right after the flood, Boss Dieujuste introduced me to Marcel Octavien, and soon after that he brought me a protection card. He was just trying to be nice. I could not say no. You know that would have put us all in danger. I didn't want to upset you, so I put the card where I knew you wouldn't find it."

"Where is it?"

"I left it at my aunt's…"

"It figures… Now, what is the situation?"

"According to Boss Dieujuste, Mrs. Polin has decided to organize a great demonstration of all the *VSN*, the Volunteers for National Security of the town and surrounding areas. She wants to make it very big, and somehow my name came up in connection with the card. Dieujuste said that he tried to have them leave me alone, but that he could not push too much. Mrs. Polin wants a big group, with uniforms, to scare the people in this town. Dieujuste said that I was not the only one in my situation."

"And what else have you been cooking up with your aunt? I think that she will also be the one taking care of your uniform," said Clerise scornfully. Her tone was glacial.

"First of all, I was not cooking up anything with my aunt. As I already told you, I just didn't want to get you upset during your pregnancy, knowing how you feel about Duvalier, his people, and the *VSN*," Desil answered, his anger mounting.

"The *VSN* now! They are no longer the Tonton Macoutes, I see!" Clerise laughed bitterly. "And that is why, all that time, you were acting so nastily with me. Sharing your precious secret with your Duvalierist aunt, and passing your anger all on me!"

"My aunt is not a Duvalierist. She may not happen to be a *tisousou*, subservient to the bourgeois like you, but that doesn't mean anything else. She is a proud woman. More than I can say of many others."

"Then why don't you go to her? That's where you have always belonged, in any case. What other secrets do you have that I don't know? Are you going to denounce me now to your buddies? Are you going to have them come and get me, and kill me too? That bunch of criminals!"

As she spoke, Desil's fury had changed to incredulity and to an expression that she had never seen. "Clerise," he said with chilling calm. "I'd better leave this house before something dreadful happens."

"Okay Desil," she answered. "I'll see you marching at the parade."

As he left her between pain and anger, she breathed deeply and refused to think of his love, betrayal, tenderness, rage, condescension, and unknowing cruelty. She walked out of the room, nearly blinded by the last rays of the sunset.

"When is daddy coming home?" Nicole asked a couple of days after Desil's departure.

"I don't know exactly," Clerise answered.

"Marie-Carmelle told me that now my daddy is a militiaman just like her dad. Is that true?"

Janine was indignant. "That's not true! They're only making him wear that uniform to go to their parade!"

"Nicole, don't you repeat that to Marie-Carmelle. Janine, you'd better watch what you say!" Clerise interjected quickly.

"Mom, it's not just to dad they are doing it," Janine continued still fuming. "Nennenn's neighbor told her about other things that this Mrs. Polin is doing. She's going to have a big thing on *La Place d'Armes* after the parade and she'll make a lot of people speak for Duvalier as President for life. I also heard that the people that Lieutenant Darville arrested, and others who were strongly for Dejoie, have been told to make those speeches. I hate that woman!"

"Does Nennenn know about your father?" Clerise asked wearily.

"She doesn't know yet. And I haven't said anything, either."

"I'll have to tell her before she hears it from someone else."

Nicole sensed that something was dreadfully wrong.

"Is Papa Desil's uniform going to be like Marie-Carmelle's dad?" she inquired.

"I think it will be," Clerise said, as she suddenly fought back tears and tried to keep herself busy.

"Why is he going to wear the uniform?"

"Because they make him!" Janine answered. She was still quite angry and unable to accept the situation.

"Is his parade going to be like mine?" Nicole wanted to know.

Janine was thoroughly disgusted. "Your parade? That was those people's parade! They made us go and march, just like they are doing it to Papa Desil now! You don't understand anything!"

"Janine," said Clerise, "she's only six years old!" Then she turned to Nicole. "I don't know how that parade is going to be. But I really don't think it will be like the one in which you marched." Exhausted, Clerise sat on a chair, feeling that she no longer had the strength to handle any more questions.

"Is daddy staying with Aunt Amanthe now?" Nicole asked.

"For now, yes. We'll see about later."

Desil's Aunt Amanthe now lived not too far from Lan Savann, in the area that extended near the marketplace. The night he left the house, Desil dispatched one of his aunt's *timoun kay* to tell Clerise that he would be sleeping there for the night. The next day, the child returned with a message. "Mr. Desil says to please send him some fresh clothes."

"Tell Mr. Desil that if he wants his clothes, he'll have to come and get them," Clerise answered.

Desil came home, as the girls were about to leave for school. "Clerise, I need to talk to you," he said.

"Okay. We can sit in the dining room."

They pulled chairs and sat tensely, facing each other. Her hands clasped on her lap, Clerise waited as Desil leaned on the table with eyes downcast. He shook his head in disbelief, took a deep breath, and then looked at her.

"First of all, let me say that I am sorry for what happened the other night, and for what you have been through for the past few months," he began. "I didn't know how to tell you about that protection card. Believe me if you will, I didn't want things to turn out the way they did. I understand your anger, but I swear that I never have, and will never do anything to hurt you. I will lay down my life for you and the children. And that is why I will march in that parade, because I have no choice, other than putting all of us in danger. But, I will not bring the Macoute uniform in this house. They told me that I will have to take some training to march in that parade. I don't know what's going to come next, and that's why I am staying at my aunt's. But I will come to see you and the children, because I am going to miss you very much. Besides my aunt, I won't let anyone know that we have been fighting over that matter."

"So, what are you going to say?"

"For right now, we can put it all on Eugene's departure. Aunt Amanthe is getting old. She has not been feeling well. She lives practically alone now. That will do."

"If you stay there, you will have to contribute some money to your aunt."

"Yes, but it won't be much. Eugene gave her a little something before he left, and he'll continue to send her money from abroad. But, I still have to give her something."

"It will be tighter for us here, but we'll manage," Clerise said, leaning her head on the back of the chair.

"I know."

"Have you told Mr. Juin at the store?"

Desil shook his head wearily. "Not yet. But I am going to. Have you told Mrs. Edmond?"

"Not yet, either. But I will go to see her."

"How are the children taking it?"

With a glance at her husband, Clerise leaned on the table, her hands were clasped. "Nicole doesn't understand yet," she said. "But Janine is very upset; not at you, but at Mrs. Polin."

"I wish things were different."

"I wish so too," she answered without looking at him.

For a moment, they remained silent. Then, Desil slowly rose. "I will miss you Clerise. I will miss the children too, especially the little man. I wanted to be with them. I wanted to be, for them, the father that I never had. Now, things seem to be changing."

"You can still see the children, Desil," she answered quietly. "You can't be more hurt about what happened than I am. I know that most of it was beyond your control. But, I am your wife. There is no excuse for your not telling me about that card and putting me through that misery for all those months. If you were so concerned about me, you would have cared a little more and not hurt my feelings so much, even when I was in the hospital, having the baby," she added as she stood. "What you told me the night before was no accident. It had been building up. You have changed, Desil. You are not the man I married. But, I also understand what you are going through, and feel for you. That makes the whole thing even harder. Now, if you'll excuse me, I have to go to the *boutik*."

As she passed by, he touched her shoulder, lightly.

With the new living arrangements, Janine and Nicole began to visit Amanthe's home more frequently, increasingly enjoying her many little gifts and snacks. The children also liked to help her in her business, and observe her clientele, which differed from that of their mother. While Clerise's focus was on the piecemeal needs of neighborhood households, Amanthe sold her resellers larger amounts of products that she obtained from local stores and traveling *Madan Sara*, such as rice, beans, corn flour, locally-made bars soap, coffee, millet, imported wheat flour, sugar, and other items.

For Amanthe, the girls were becoming the daughters that she never had. However, at Desil's request, she refrained from trying to convert them to her faith, save for a few brief and occasionally veiled comments. Instead, she entertained them with stories about her growing up, Desil's early years, and her beloved Eugene.

"Your father was just a baby," she said, "the day of that big commotion at Kafou Machatè."

"That's where the big cross is in Lòtbò La Ravin, just as you leave town, on the other side of the river, isn't it?" Janine inquired.

Nicole was curious. "What happened there?"

"I was a young girl then, and that's where we lived. For a while, there was a lot of commotion in Les Cayes. People were angry. They wanted the Americans, the *blan meriken*, to leave the country. We heard that the workers had taken to the streets. To scare them, the Americans dropped bombs over the sea. That got everybody enraged. The next day, I remember it was December 6, of 1929, lots of people with machetes, sticks, knives, cutlasses, pikes, whatever they could find, came together from the countryside. They passed my home. They were about to cross *La Ravin* to enter Les Cayes. The Americans told them to stop. They said 'No.' I was the only one left home to watch Desil. I heard the people shouting. It was like a big roar. Then later, before night fell, I heard the shooting 'takatakata'. The Americans had a machine-gun. They didn't want any more trouble in town. My father was wounded. Others were wounded, too. Many people died."

"Is that why they put that cross there?"

"Yes, that's why. It was put there not long after. Lots of people came for that. They came from Les Cayes, from all over. There were ceremonies, speeches, songs… you name it. It didn't take too long for the *blan meriken* to leave after that."

"What else happened?"

"Then I moved to Lan Savann."

"Did dad come with you?"

"Not until after Eugene was born. Your dad was always a good kid," she began.

Since Desil barely knew his mother, Amanthe had become the central figure of his childhood. He loved her dearly, and was grateful for the opportunities that she had allowed him to have. To him, she had been a good, stern, pragmatic, and loving educator who sacrificed for her two boys, and instilled in them a sense of purpose, family responsibility and solidarity. She insisted upon cleanliness of attire and proper behavior, and did not hesitate to enforce a healthy measure of respect for her rules with appropriate doses of *rigwaz* spanking.

"What about dad's father?" Nicole asked.

"Your Grandpa Desulien? He used to come here and visit us often when your dad was growing up. Now that he is getting old, he seldom comes to town," Amanthe said.

From what she gathered then and over the years, Nicole understood that, following his affair with Desil's mother, Desulien had married and settled on the piece of land that his family had owned near Les Cayes since the second Haitian Empire of Soulouque, more than a century before. To increase his income, he leased large pieces of land where he hired farmers to work for him as *demwatye*, an arrangement by which they gave him half of the crops and kept the rest for themselves. Desulien had grown into a portly and jovial man. Still fun loving, he never made a secret of his inability to resist any fetching woman who caught his eye, many of whom became his farmers and were allowed to keep a larger portion of their harvest. Permitted by law to proceed as he saw fit outside his legal domicile, he professed great respect for his wife and the conjugal roof. Although his only officially acknowledged children were those born within the bonds of matrimony, he took pride in and care of his many offspring, both in and out of wedlock. Of the latter category, Desil was one of the few reluctantly allowed to visit him at home, since his existence had been known to Desulien's wife before their marriage. Those born later, from Desulien's adulterous affairs, were barred from his official residence.

Cementing their bond, Desulien also instructed Desil of their special family traditions at the service of the *lwa*, the Vodou spirits through which they could trace their ancestry all the way to Africa. Thus, he took him to the appropriate Vodou services conducted at various times during the year and asked him to remember.

Caught between his aunt Amanthe whose practice of Vodou and Catholicism had been lukewarm prior to her conversion to Protestantism, and the love, pride, and legacy of his father, Desil chose to retain the status quo, while obliging Desulien during appropriately scheduled visits. Those became more sporadic as the years went by, and contact between father and son grew infrequent since Desulien, now in semi-retirement, seldom visited Les Cayes.

Prior to their marriage, Desil had prudently refrained from mentioning anything to Clerise about the religious aspect of his paternal heritage. He continued to remain discreet about the details of his rare visits to his father, when he realized the extent of her fears and revulsion toward Vodou. She had not probed him on that matter or queried him on issues of sexual fidelity, preferring not to know about whatever did not happen under her roof, according to local mores. While she set for herself the most rigid standards of behavior, she only demanded public respect and a measure of peace at home, as did other "respectable" women. However, the

Tonton Macoute protection card was another matter altogether. It had to do with issues of values, lives, and safety of the whole family. Clerise felt that she should have been told.

The women that Clerise knew had extended support networks of family and friends. However, she could only count on Simone Juin for emotional sustenance. When she had left her family, her training as a high status *timoun kay* had discouraged independent relationships with her peers. Thus, she developed a reserve which prevented close personal associations outside her immediate circle. For a while, Mrs. Dieujuste had appeared to be an exception. However, the political situation prevented the development of their friendship. Remembering the good times that they shared, Clerise thought with sadness that, at the moment, Mrs. Dieujuste was the last person to whom she could turn. With regret for what could have been, she recalled the easy banter between Simone Juin and her friends when they returned home from various church devotions. She also thought of the confidences overheard, of the love, concern and support between Simone Juin and her friend Solange Jobert. Desolate and longing for understanding, she left for the Juins residence.

"Nennenn, did you suspect something?" she inquired. "I did not quite like the way you answered me when I asked you about Boss Dieujuste."

"I did not know anything about that card. But I found it strange that Boss Dieujuste had gone to my brother on behalf of Desil. I can understand that he was trying to drum up some business for himself when he asked to fix the house. But the way he put it seemed a little weird, somewhat personal. That gave us a funny feeling."

"Desil didn't ask for that card, and he could not say no when Boss Dieujuste gave it to him. I did not know anything about it, because he didn't want to upset me when I was pregnant. The whole thing is very hard for him. He is staying at his aunt's now, because of the children."

"I wish he had told one of us, Andre, Edmond, Louis, or me. That would have made things easier on everybody. Many people are going to be shocked to see Desil in that uniform."

"It is tough on Janine. She is very upset," said Clerise. "I have to keep telling her not to let anybody outside know how she feels. But she loves Desil and sees what that whole thing is doing to him and to all of us."

No longer able to fight back her tears, she started to cry. Simone Juin put a comforting arm around her shoulders, and passed her a handkerchief.

"Nennenn, why does this have to happen to us!"

"I know it is hard, Clerise. But you are not the only ones. That woman, Mrs. Polin, is doing so much mischief over here. I don't know why she had to come!"

"We will all be on the porch, as the parade passes by," Clerise said to her daughters. "We will stay there quietly, and show nothing. That's the least we can do for your father, and for our own protection."

Holding her son, she watched impassively as the motley of blue denim-clad Tonton Macoutes walked the street under the command of the mighty Bertha Carmonot Polin. From her starting point at the barracks in Lan Gabyon to her destination in *La Place d'Armes,* the *Fiyèt Lalo* put on a show as she barked orders at her small band of hastily trained militiamen. With determined and fierce expressions, many of the parading "Volunteers" wore red scarves and brandished machetes while shouting menacing slogans. Among the privileged who wore guns in hip-hugging holsters, their attempt at studied rugged elegance often lead to the most comical effects. Also clad in blue pants and shirt, with matching hat, red scarf, and dark glasses, the commander looked suitably ominous. Alternating between short runs and walks, she managed to lead her entire troop, including a few old stragglers, to *La Place d'Armes,* in some semblance of order.

As he passed near Pon Gonbo, Boss Dieujuste threw a quick glance at his house. "Here's daddy," Marie-Carmelle said proudly to her mother. Desil looked straight ahead. Then, after the briefest salutation to the neighbors, Clerise and the children entered their house. Like them, the population remained impassive, and not even the Lifaites attempted to cheer the passing "Volunteers."

Catching their breath on *La Place d'Armes,* which had been equipped with loudspeakers for the event, the militiamen and the "invited" population listened to music and speeches extolling Duvalier. The various speakers, including government officials often clad in Macoute uniforms, and known opponents of the regime, who had been forced to come and pledge their allegiance, performed with varying levels of enthusiasm.

Bertha Carmonot Polin left town a few days later, and her husband resumed his discreet romance with the local girl. The uniformed Volunteers for National Security, the VSN, remained mobilized, however. Thus, Desil stayed at his aunt's home and, since he did not come to visit his family for a few days following the parade, Clerise sent the girls to see him, along with Ania carrying Michel. That day, Amanthe saw the baby for the first time.

Nicole did not know exactly why, but for some reason, on a Sunday morning not long afterwards, she had gone to Mass at *L'Hospice* at six thirty in the morning with her mother, Janine, Jesula, and her baby brother Michel. As the few people in attendance left in different directions after the shortened early-morning service, Clerise showed some concern.

"Let's get home quickly," she encouraged the children.

"Is that because of the elections?" Janine asked.

"Yes, we'd better make it home before all kinds of activities begin."

Now alone in the narrow and unpaved back street leading to their house, they saw, coming toward them, a rifle-carrying Tonton Macoute in blue denim uniform.

"Let's move, kids," Clerise said, as she gathered her brood and tried to appear calm.

The man approached without a smile or greeting. "*Madanm*, come to vote," he ordered sternly.

"I am only going to take the kids home. I'll be coming back to vote," Clerise said.

The Tonton Macoute was adamant. "Come and vote now. And with those kids too. All of you are going to vote. The Doc has to remain President for life. Everybody should vote today."

He escorted them to a nearby voting station, led them to the door, and pointed to someone inside. "Go to that lady," he said. "She'll tell you what to do."

In the nearly empty room, Clerise and the children were each given a referendum ballot already prepared, and told to place it in a box nearby. "Here's one more, Madam. Put it in for the baby," said one of the election workers.

Politely, Clerise and Janine exchanged the required salutations with those present in the room, including the Duvalierist officials standing by. Under Clerise's watchful eyes, Jesula was curious but suitably reserved, Nicole excited but cautious. To her, the whole affair appeared to be some type of grown-up game in which she was invited to participate. One by one, they deposited the required bulletins in the ballot box. The baby remained quiet, dozing and sucking his thumb. In the room, the mood was jovial.

"You know what you just did? You voted for Papa Duvalier to remain our president for life," one of the men said to Nicole with a big smile.

As Clerise and the children left the station, rifle-toting Tonton Macoutes instructed more passers-by to go there and vote. On the way home, Clerise herded the children through the larger streets and stopped at the Juins' residence where Janine had planned to spend the day. Nennenn was still in her night clothes, and Parenn nowhere to be seen.

"Nennenn, you should know what just happened!" Clerise said, recounting the story, as Janine added details.

"You are both so shaken! You should have some *tibom* tea. But first, let me get you some cold water," offered Simone Juin, who called her maid for the necessary arrangements.

"I'll only take the water now. I have to get home before someone else stops me again. I'll have Ania make the *tibom* tea."

"You are right! We'll take care of Janine here," Simone Juin said. "Take care of yourself and the kids!"

Desil was not home. The night before, as he left for his aunt Amanthe's house, he told Clerise, "If anyone asks for me, just say I'm not here."

"What if they ask me where you are?"

"Then, say I had to go and see my father. That's all." Fortunately, Boss Dieujuste did not come to inquire about Desil.

That day, like many others who did not want to be forced to vote, Simone Juin remained inside her house, while her husband Edmond, officially not home, stayed in his room incommunicado.

Later that morning, when she saw her friend Marie-Carmelle, an excited six year-old Nicole could not wait to share the big news. "You know what! I voted today!"

Marie-Carmelle was very cool. "Me too," she said. "And I have done it twice already," she added proudly.

Nicole ran to her mother. "Mom, can I go and vote again?"

Later that month, when schools closed for the summer, Andre Juin and his family prepared to leave for a trip abroad. As in every other year, Nennenn and Parenn's house was also getting full for the summer vacation. By mid-July, Danny arrived from Port-au-Prince with his two younger Mussain cousins and their twelve-year-old niece Regine, Gisèle's daughter. Danny, who had completed his secondary education in Port-au-Prince the year before, was about to leave for Mexico, to continue his studies.

"It is very inexpensive in Spain or Mexico. You get a lot for your money there," Miss Jeanne Brijan, the book store owner, had told Mrs. Juin. The information had been welcome, since the Juins' business activities had slowed considerably. To complicate the situation, admission to the State University, the only one in the country aside from the two or three law schools in the provinces, was mainly reserved to those who had a *piston*, a recommendation from some higher up in the government.

Studies at the University had been free of charge, and admission highly competitive until the student strike of

1959. Then the government had closed all schools in the country, jailed and killed student leaders, and instituted an unofficial policy of controlled admissions at the newly named State University of Haiti so as to prevent future trouble. When Duvalier closed schools again four years later, following the failed kidnapping of his children, the campuses were quiet.

For those who did not choose to seek an official recommendation, the alternative was to take a chance at the exams, to benefit from the open admission policy of the law schools, to enroll in business school or correspondence courses from foreign schools, or to study abroad. This often took place in countries whose currencies permitted considerable stretching of the value of the Haitian gourde, which was pegged to the American dollar.

"Rosie is going to help us with Danny," Nennenn said to Clerise.

"How's she doing in Africa?"

"She loves where she is. She says that it reminds her so much of Haiti."

"It's a shame that she had to leave without coming here to say good-bye. That man Duvalier has gone after everybody. Good thing that you went to see her before she left. And now Danny is leaving too! How's Pilou?"

"He has just finished law school. He still has his job, and he's arranging his papers to go to the U.S. Gisèle is helping him get everything done."

"So, everybody is going, and leaving us all alone!"

"Well, it's hard on us; but it's for their own good. Hopefully, they will be able to come and visit… when things change," she added as an aside.

As a matter of fact, the Juins had kept in reserve, for a number of years, an old and rare bottle of rum from Jeremie that they planned to use for a celebration at the fall of Duvalier. Twice, they had almost opened it when press reports from Dominican or Cuban radio stations had announced the dictator's impending departure during political crises. However, the bottle was still hidden, along with their thwarted hopes, at the bottom of the dining room sideboard.

"I remember when Pilou wanted to enter the Military Academy," Clerise said. "Ever since he was a little boy, he was always playing soldiers. He would have been a handsome officer had things been different!"

Simone Juin chuckled. "But Edmond would not hear of it. Although he had some good friends among the officers, he had that thing about the military. He wanted his sons to be in business with him, not in the military, and nowhere mixed in politics. Well, now, here we are!"

"*Alatraka*… Oh Lord!"

"Most of Lina's children are also out of the country. I told her that the Mussain tribe was disbanding. A lot of people are leaving now. Things are becoming too dangerous. You never know what will happen from one day to the next. This year, my mom and Elia are not even coming to take the children on vacation. I wonder if anyone will go to Ducis or Camp-Perrin, the way things are. Lina sent me her two youngest and Regine.

Hopefully, they will have a good time here for the summer. "

"How is Miss Gisèle…? I mean Mrs. Roussard?"

"Still in New York, working for that international organization. She is going to send for her children soon. Regine is probably going to join her as soon as she leaves here."

"How is Mrs. Visel taking it? Regine is her baby."

"My mother is somewhat shaken by all of what is happening. She never thought that things were ever going to be that way. Before, people may have gone for a trip abroad, and then come back. Now, you don't know when you'll see them again."

"How is Matant Elia?"

"Strong as ever. But underneath, I think that she is heartbroken. She loves those children so much."

"Janine was glad to hear that Regine had arrived. They're both really growing. It's a long way from when they were little. Nearly young women now! But, I have to go. I left the baby and the *boutik* with Ania and Jesula. Nicole, let's go."

"Clerise, tell me. How are things with Desil?"

"Same way. He still stays at his aunt's."

"Are you on speaking terms?"

"Yes. He also gives me money for the house."

"Andre told us that he had never seen a man as down as Desil after that parade. Clerise, Desil is a good man. Something bad happened to him. But that's not entirely his fault. Also, he is the father of your children."

"I know that, Nennenn."

"Well, there is another thing I have to tell you. During his vacation in New York, Andre has received an offer to stay there and manage a business. He has accepted, and asked us to close his store. Edmond is going to take care of that, since what we do ourselves now is very little anyway. We'll have to let go of employees; but we'll try to keep Desil as long as possible, or at least until he finds another job. He does not know any of that yet. But my sister-in-law, Adeline, has already touched base with her cousin, the director of the bank, to see what he can do to help."

A semi-independent government body, and the only such financial institution in town, the National Bank was one of the few agencies that had managed to keep its efficiency and professional standards nearly intact. Adeline Visel's cousin, the bank director, was originally from Jeremie, a town renowned for the arrogance of its mulatto *elite*. Unlike the image of the town, the man was a *bon-vivant*, one of the guys, who made friends easily, and loved to sit for a good drink with a variety of buddies ranging from *elite* members of all colors to *Noiristes* in good standing, as well as a variety of Duvalierist officials. Married late but still youthful in appearance, he was devoted to his wife, several years his junior. Quiet, and also from Jeremie, the young woman treated her gregarious spouse with amused indulgence. Always the perfect hostess, she entertained her husband's guests and their wives, and willingly attended social functions. However, she had few friends of her own, and spent most her days keeping house, reading, and visiting often with Adeline Visel, her husband's older distant cousin, whom he considered as a big sister. Still newlyweds with no children of their own, the couple enjoyed the company of their teenage nephews and nieces from out of town during school recesses and vacations. One of their nieces was currently visiting for the summer.

"That man, the bank director, Regine says he's a pain," Janine explained. "He doesn't want to let his niece go to any function if no man of the family is present. Nennenn Simone says that he has been around, that's why he's so strict."

Clerise laughed. "Nennenn knows what she's talking about. He's a good man, though. I hear that he helps quite a few people. His niece is also a nice girl. Whenever she passes on the main street with the Mussain and Jobert girls, they always wave. And if they go in front of this house when I am on the porch, they always stop by to kiss me."

"I'm glad Nennenn is not going on vacation this year. I would not want to go."

"We already went through that," Clerise said. "I don't quite understand what is happening. You used to like Regine so much. You are nearly the same age and you grew up like sisters."

"Regine has her friends now, and I have mine," Janine answered. "It's not the same anymore."

"I'm very happy about that," Nicole said. "I don't like Regine and her friends. They're not nice."

"Regine used to be a very nice girl. Matant Elia loves her very much. What happened, Janine?" Clerise asked.

"Nothing. It's just that she's not the same when her friends are around."

As Nicole remembered, the previous summer Janine had, for the first time, refused to go to the usual countryside vacation with the Juin and Mussain children when they had arrived in town. After long and tearful pleadings, and with Desil's support, Janine had finally won over her mother's persistent and irritated objections. When Clerise apologized profusely to Nennenn and offered some plausible reason to explain the new situation, she met such rapid acceptance and sympathetic understanding that she found herself even more confused, feeling both relief and puzzled disappointment. That summer had marked the beginning of the growing estrangement between Janine and Regine.

In the past, when Gisèle had come to town for vacation with her younger siblings and her own children, she had always stopped at Clerise's home for a chat, bringing a nice gift for Janine and some trinket for Nicole. Regine did not accompany her mother for the last visit. As Janine's godmother through Elia's proxy, Gisèle had always showed great interest in her goddaughter's progress, and often discussed at length prospects and future plans with Clerise.

That summer, when Janine and her neighborhood friends would walk on the pier with Nicole and other

younger siblings tagging along, Regine would also be
there with her crowd. However, the two groups never
mixed. At the most, Janine and her former playmate
discreetly waved to each other and went their separate
ways.

Regine and her friends, a noisy bunch of young teenage boys and girls, laughed, joked, and hid their
insecurities behind the assurance of their families' social
prestige. A careless, playful, and exclusive group of
privileged youth, they sat, between their strolls, either on
the steps leading to the sea near the red tin warehouse
or on one of the two cranes that had been added nearby
across the pier.

In contrast, Janine and her girlfriends kept to
themselves and always behaved quietly and with extreme
reserve. They felt self-conscious near the *"elite"* group
and would sit as far away as possible, either on one of
the cranes if the others were on the steps, or otherwise
on one of the benches facing the sea on the plaza.

As time went by, Janine began to ignore Regine, who
always appeared busy looking at some object far away
when circumstances required them to greet each other.
Although they met at the same place almost every day
amid their respective crowds, the childhood playmates
no longer had any public personal or social contact.

One day however, the two groups briefly came
together. As many people strolled on the pier, Regine
and her friends happened to walk behind a young
woman conversing with two seemingly eligible bachelors
from out of town. A current version of Jocelyne

Nerville, with the light skin, tight clothes, and sensuous walk, the young woman also had little interest in school. The younger set particularly disliked her for her haughtiness.

Janine and her friends, who happened to be walking not far behind, noticed Regine's group giggling and pointing toward the young woman. As they moved closer, they heard the girls in front speak of *"derrière*...padding...trying to look more sexy" amid muffled laughter. Then one of Regine's friends sneaked behind the woman and lightly poked her backside with a twig, which she promptly discarded as she stepped back within her group.

Furious, the young woman turned, nearly suffocating. "How???... Miss!!... You see me quietly walking in the street, with company," she punctuated with a graceful gesture of the arm toward her escort. "And... YOU... YOU... YOU, You DARED to put your hand on my *derrière!"*

Everyone remained impassive, even six-year-old Nicole and her friend Marie-Carmelle. Eyes flashing, the young woman took a deep breath, tossed her head, and turned around, as her gentlemen friends murmured sympathetically and appeared to hide amused smiles. Once she had resumed her stroll and passed the corner of the red tin warehouse at the end of the pier, the two groups of girls had to lean on the cranes to share a good laugh. By the time the outraged party had strolled around to come into full view, the girls had gone their separate ways, looking quite composed. However, as if to compensate for a violation of some tacit boundary, the relationship between Janine and Regine grew even more distant.

"Janine, Nennenn says that she doesn't see you much," Clerise mentioned while changing the baby. On his mother's bed, Michel kicked his legs energetically, then tried to escape.

"Be quiet!" Nicole said, holding him in place.

Janine ignored her siblings, and passed a clean diaper to her mother. "That's true," she answered. "I don't like the way Regine is acting."

"I noticed some coldness from her in the past couple of days. Is something the matter?" Clerise inquired as she fastened a pin.

"Not that I know of," Janine shrugged. "Before, she barely spoke to me when we met at Nennenn's. Now, she acts almost as if I don't even exist, and we just ignore each other when we are outside."

Regine's interaction with the rest of the family also became increasingly remote, and she no longer stopped to greet Clerise when passing by her house. Complaints to Nennenn on that matter only led to perfunctory apologies. Thus, Clerise who had kept more to herself since the militia parade, no longer proudly shared with her neighbors the usual flow information about the Juin, Mussain, and Roussard children.

Desil found a new job at the beginning of August. Although unable to hire him, the bank director referred him to one of his contacts for somewhat of a supervisory maintenance position at the *Usine Sucrière*, the quasi-government sugar factory, not too far from town. "Let's not say anything to anyone about Mr. Juin's store closing," Desil said to Clerise when she had discussed with him her conversation with Simone Juin on that matter. "I don't want any more meddling and complication with Boss Dieujuste. See where that took me." Thus, Desil started his new job, using the distance involved as one more official reason to stay away from home.

The summer moved along. In the playing field in Lan Gabyon, the last rounds of the local soccer championship generated passionate discussions among fans. Clerise heard Adeline Visel tell Simone Juin, "My cousin's wife and niece asked me to convince him to stay in town until the end of the championship. But, with his vacation already scheduled from the bank, he wants to leave right now to go to Port-au-Prince for a couple of days, and then to Jeremie. There's not much I can do. He is adamant about leaving."

Another invasion of political exiles had started, this time somewhere between Jeremie and Les Cayes. "They can jump from one mountaintop to the next," people from the countryside said when they came to town. Hope sprung anew. Whispered reports pictured the young men almost as superheroes. The Tonton Macoutes grew nervous. They started patrolling the town day and night, looking grim and menacing. They put sandbags on the pier. Rumor had that they feigned illness, or ran away from the front, in fear of the rebels. Desil was forced to join the local patrols.

"Clerise," Desil said, "I have very bad news."

Not again, she thought. I don't think I can take any more! She looked at him without a word.

"Sit down. I'll get you some water." He went to the cupboard and returned with a glass. "Drink slowly," he said. "I have to go and see Mrs. Juin. There is something that she will have to tell Mrs. Visel."

"What?" she managed to croak.

"It's about the Director."

"The Bank Director?"

He shook his head affirmatively.

"What happened to him?"

"He's dead. Killed by the Tonton Macoutes and the military in Jeremie."

"How did it happen? Why?"

"They say that he and his wife had relatives among the rebels. He was arrested. He was a good man. He would not have died, if he had stayed here."

"How's his wife?"

Desil remained silent and bowed his head. "There is worse, Clerise," he managed to say after a moment. "His wife has also been killed, and their niece too. The entire families on both sides have been killed."

"Oh my God!"

Adeline Visel's mother became ill and nearly died when she learned of the murder of her relatives and childhood friends. No one was spared in the carnage in which adults and children, including grand-parents and babies, were assassinated in cold blood. As the summer ended, the Mussain girls and their niece, Regine, returned to Port-au-Prince, along with Danny. Hurricane Cleo happened next.

The weather had been inclement for a few days, with heavy rain falling steadily. That September morning, the radio advised the population to take all appropriate precautions since the approaching hurricane was forecast to be particularly violent. As usual, everybody more or less dismissed the gloomy predictions, which were traditionally made at least once a year at the end of summer, almost never to materialize. As the winds grew stronger, the rain diminished. By mid-afternoon, a few children standing on a porch near the corner of Kafou Orèl cheered every time they saw a sheet of corrugated tin, torn from a nearby roof, fly through the air. Quickly herded inside by their now-concerned parents, they soon shared the adults' sudden fear, which nearly turned to panic.

All over town, businesses closed hastily. Desil arrived as Clerise organized her household to face the crisis.

"Quick!" he said. "Let's go to Parenn Edmond's warehouse. There's no time to waste! Let's move!"

Since Hurricane Hazel in 1954, the city had not experienced a phenomenon of this magnitude. As they had done then, the Juins sought refuge in their almost empty, flat-roofed, all masonry warehouse and opened it as a shelter to the neighborhood.

By the time the Fleurantiers left their home, it was almost impossible to step outside, so great was the force of the wind. Janine and Ania had to help Desil in his struggle to keep half of the front door open long enough to allow for the evacuation of the family. The trip to the Juins' became a living nightmare, each step a small victory over death. By then, potentially lethal ragged-edged sheets of tin, torn from rooftops, flew in all directions. In the tumult of large trees falling to the ground littered with torn palm fronds, Nicole saw other trees struggling desperately against the furious assault of the wind, their limbs torn, their branches and leaves carried away in a deafening roar. Pieces of wood, yanked from the less sturdy houses, added to the chaos, amid the fury of the rain and frightful bolts of lighting.

The short trip seemed to last forever. Desil carried Nicole, and Clerise the baby. They held the children tightly as Janine, Ania, and Jesula also huddled close. They made their way carefully through open porches where they sought shelter from randomly flying debris. Finally, they arrived at the Juin's warehouse. The heavy metallic doors were shut. They banged and yelled as loudly as they could. The doors opened narrowly as three neighborhood men struggled to hold them against the wind to allow the Fleurantiers inside.

"Are you okay?" people asked.

"How's the baby?"

"How is it outside?"

The anxious faces of a small crowd of inquiring adults and children frightened the baby who started to cry. Messengers of bad news, the Fleurantiers settled and waited for the end of the storm with their companions of misfortune in common misery and fear.

Neighbors kept arriving at the warehouse, knocking frantically on the metallic doors. While the men helped pull the newcomers inside, the women tried their best to organize the children, the elderly, the three babies present, and even the two dogs that had sought refuge with their owners. An elderly neighborhood woman, almost bedridden, who had been carried to the warehouse by her son, was resting on a mattress spread on the floor. Nearby, excited children exchanged stories.

"A sheet of tin almost got my daddy in the head," a boy said, still overwhelmed by the newly discovered romance in his parents' marriage. "Then, he told my mom, 'Darling, if I had died, what would have happened to you?'"

"I left my doll with Marie-Carmelle," Nicole complained.

As time went by, people stopped arriving, and the warehouse doors remained shut. In the closed and crowded quarters, crashing noises from the outside assumed formidable proportions through the surrounding uproar. The lights went out. Panic arose. Children screamed.

"*Anmwe! Anmwe!* Help!" some of the women wailed.

People began to pray. "Hail Mary, full of grace…" someone started through a chorus of sobs. A neighborhood man sat on the floor with head in hands and began a religious hymn of penance, "Parce Domine, parce populo… o…"

Light from some kerosene lamps restored a measure of calm, while some devout church members undertook to organize a prayer session. A few of the men and women who had kept their composure during the panic, remained in the back of the warehouse. While still fierce, the storm was moving and it was possible to crack open the back door once in a while to assess the damage.

Suddenly, amid the uproar, a faint but frantic and insistent knock came from the front door. With the wind still in full force, it took an organized effort to manage a narrow opening against considerable pressure from the outside. A woman nearly stumbled in.

Soaked, her clothes torn and disheveled, her eyes bulging in terror in her ashen dark face, incoherent and near collapse, the Juins' cook was led to a chair, wrapped in a blanket, and given a drink of water to calm down. "The marketplace," she babbled, "the marketplace…" No one wanted to envision the terrifying possibility of an eventual collapse of the heavy iron-made construction, although the extent of the calamity slowly dawned. Finally able to talk, the cook told the terrified neighbors the harrowing story of her escape. "I was shopping at the marketplace. I just had an idea to leave," she said. "From across the street, I heard that big noise.

I turned my head to see what it was. It was the roof of the marketplace. It was falling on top of everyone." She fled in horror, ran through the length of First Main Street, never turned back to look, and only heard the diminishing cries of those buried alive. Everyone took turns comforting her, all individual fears and differences set aside in common misfortune.

After a few hours, the hurricane subsided. Darkness had settled, and the few hardy souls who had ventured out brought more news of the collapse of the marketplace where an estimated three hundred people had been trapped. Some rescue was underway in that neighborhood with the limited equipment available.

In the crowded Juin warehouse, the daunting task of providing food, shelter, and sanitary facilities to eighty people forced everyone to cooperate. The danger had now passed. By unspoken agreement, everything started to fall in place along social lines. Families regrouped. Clerise, Desil, and their children stayed in the back of the warehouse, except for Janine, whose assistance was requested by Nennenn toward the front.

"Desil," Clerise said while they were settling, "I know that you may be concerned about your aunt. I can handle things from now on. Feel free to go any time."

"I'll go now. But I'll be back in a while."

Desil did not return until the next day, as the militia requested his presence to go on patrol to keep watch for any potential rebel who might try to infiltrate the city under cover of the hurricane.

The next morning was the time to measure the extent of the disaster. Volunteers had worked all night to extract the dead and the wounded from the marketplace. A steady flow of victims came to town from the surrounding countryside. Soon, the hospital could no longer handle additional patients. Anyone not seriously hurt was discharged, while two or even three patients at a time shared the available beds. By midday, the stench of death pervaded the areas of the marketplace and the hospital.

All over town, people filled the streets to assess the damage and take stock of their losses. The devastation was nearly complete. Hardly any construction stood untouched, and debris, corrugated tin roof sheets, large uprooted trees, pieces of furniture, clothing items, and wet paper littered the city. The sea had advanced inland in Lan Savann, further damaging the Lycée, whose classrooms appeared completely battered through shutterless windows. Most of the two-story wooden houses lining the two Main Streets and other arteries had lost their top floors, and in some cases the wind had pushed upper stories sideways in a weird likeness of leaning towers. Scattered family papers, jewelry heirlooms, and other valuables covered the streets.

In those tragic circumstances, no looting was reported except for an occasional misappropriation of corrugated tin sheet. Despite the inaction of the public sector, ordinary citizens immediately organized in streets and neighborhoods to clear the debris and help each other salvage possessions. Soon, repairs began in the less damaged houses, with the assistance of friends and neighbors to whom hospitality was then extended. Those initiatives alleviated the initial crowding in the impromptu neighborhood emergency shelters.

"Matant Amanthe is okay," Desil said. "The neighbors are really pulling together over there. She'll be fine until her house is fixed."

"Our house is all gone!" Nicole interjected. "We can't go back there anymore." Luckily, she had recovered her doll from Marie-Carmelle. The Lifaites had lost their roof. Otherwise, their masonry house had survived. The Fleurantiers' home was in shambles. Surprisingly, some pieces of furniture, clothing, and various other household items were found scattered in the vicinity and salvaged with the help of neighbors. Upon Desil's inquiry, Louis Visel expressed his sympathy but flatly stated that, for the time being, he was not about to rebuild.

People started to leave the Juins' warehouse the first day following the hurricane, while the place continued to remain a center of neighborhood activity where food was shared, the latest news discussed, assistance for repairs planned, and resources pooled. By the end of the first week, most families had returned to their homes, including the Juins. By the end of the second week, everyone had left, except for the Fleurantiers, and another family whose home had also been completely destroyed.

With the rebels still in the mountains, Desil was forced to continue to patrol the town with the militia, now mostly clad in civilian clothes rather than uniforms. Everyday, the militiamen carried rifles and walked in formation to the pier to inspect their sandbags and make sure that all was in order. To the population's knowledge, no rebel force had yet approached the town.

Since they had not found suitable housing, Clerise and the children remained in the Juins' warehouse. The local authorities had requisitioned the space next door to store emergency food supplies that an American ship had brought, and the Tonton Macoutes had already started to sell the packages for profit. While they transferred a new shipment to the warehouse, they held at bay a small crowd of paupers who had gathered to ask for food. Among them stood an aging day laborer renowned for his skill at petty thievery and mastery at escaping pursuers by diving from the pier and swimming long distances under water. The man was also somewhat feared for his rumored supernatural abilities. His presence made the Tonton Macoutes nervous.

"Please, give me some food," the laborer said.

"Go away, thief," a Macoute barked brandishing his club. "I don't want to see you here."

The laborer moved away, but returned shortly, working his way from the edge of the crowd. The Tonton Macoute spotted him.

"I thought I had told you to go away!" he shouted while rushing toward the man and starting to hit him over the head and shoulders with his stick.

"Why are you beating me? I have done nothing!"

Other Macoutes joined the fracas, hitting the laborer with all their might from different directions. The man fell, bleeding. He got on his feet, staggered, and tried to ward blows off his face and head. By then, he could no longer speak. With his club, a Macoute delivered a mighty jab straight under the man's heart. The laborer fell, inert. *He is dead*, Clerise thought. She covered her mouth to silence her scream.

The Macoutes resumed their unloading without further attention to the man on the ground. Once more, he attempted to get up, crawled a few steps, and fell again.

"Move!" the militiamen ordered the incredulous crowd.

Clerise stepped inside her door. She knew that she could no longer stay in the warehouse.

With a dire sense of urgency, the Fleurantiers finally found a house nearby for Clerise and the children. It was smaller than the one in Pon Gonbo, both because of the current housing shortage and because Clerise could not immediately reopen the *boutik* since her inventory and furniture were gone. Thus, Ania went to work for the Juins, replacing their cook who had returned to her home in the countryside after her traumatic experience in the marketplace. Desil secured living arrangements close to his work, and continued to visit his family regularly.

The thirteen young rebels never made it to town. After a valiant battle in which most died, the last two survivors were publicly executed in front of the national cemetery in Port-au-Prince.

Back in town, Bertha Carmonot Polin organized a raucous militia parade to celebrate the victory of the government forces over the rebels. However, her marriage did not last. After their divorce, her husband, the lieutenant, married his local sweetheart. A few years later, he was executed by firing squad in Port-au-Prince, along with other military officers accused of plotting against the government during an internal power struggle.

CHAPTER 10

Decision

1969

In the following years, Clerise gradually allowed Nicole more freedom in the choice of her friends and activities. While she seldom saw Marie-Carmelle Lifaite, Nicole made other acquaintances at school and in their new neighborhood. Her best friend now lived two doors away.

Under Clerise's watchful eye, the girls kept boys at a safe distance, but they knew everybody's little secrets. Amid whispers and giggles, they told stories about who liked whom and carried secret messages between their girl friends and young male relatives to the frustration of their curious younger siblings. On that matter, Michel now about seven years old, was increasingly turning into a serious tattle-teller.

As the only one in her circle with a sister old enough to have a semiofficial boyfriend, Nicole often entertained her preadolescent peers with every detail of the courtship and subsequent developments. With eyes rolled upwards, then closed and reopened with a deep sigh, she mimicked "darling"-filled dialogues and long amorous looks. Everybody would then join in the fun, feeling all grown up and wicked.

The conversations usually took place at recess time, in Creole, and quite out of the nun's earshot in some corner of the school yard. Nicole had never felt so important in her whole life; she looked forward to instant celebrity almost every day, and the new details that she shared found a receptive audience.

Janine and her boyfriend became interested in each other at the right time for Nicole. As far as she knew, it all began the previous summer on the pier where Janine had continued to stroll with her friends, while still reluctantly taking along her younger sister. The girls had noticed a couple of young men who always arranged to walk in the opposite direction and took every opportunity to nod and smile as they came face to face. As things progressed, the two groups waved and smiled at each other, then stopped and exchanged a few pleasantries, and finally joined to stroll together. One of the young men constantly managed to walk by Janine, and soon they increasingly spoke only to each other, while everyone else pretended to ignore the situation. After much inner struggle, Nicole shared her concerns on the matter with Clerise, only to be reassured.

"Your sister is nearly seventeen. She's at the age when she can begin to think of having a boyfriend. As long as all they do is walk and talk, it's okay. But I can understand what you feel. I'll speak to Janine," Clerise said.

Her conscience clear, Nicole began to worry about Janine's possible reaction. However, her sister only teased her, and jokingly recounted the story to her amused friends. Afterwards, the young adults discussed in *jagon*, the Creole pig Latin, any subject that they wanted to keep confidential. It then became a challenge for Nicole and her buddies to decipher the coded language, in which they soon became fluent.

After a while, Janine's suitor started to visit their home, stopping for brief chats with Janine, and sometimes with Clerise. Michel immediately took to him, while Nicole, who had been friendly, continued to watch. Once, the young man even met Desil to whom he was formally introduced as a friend, and received a look of evident suspicion. Then, as the visits became longer, Janine's boyfriend was allowed to sit on the porch to talk to her early in the evening when they returned from the pier, the movies, or some other youth activity. Meanwhile Nicole played nearby with Michel, pretending to mind her own business. At first, Desil, who had grumbled about the situation, sternly kept his distance from the visitor.

"What's going on?" he asked Clerise. "What's that young man doing here all the time?"

"As you can see, he likes Janine."

"So why do you let him sit here like that? Janine is still a kid. He'd better not think he is going to come here just to get some fun!"

"I'm keeping an eye on them. As you can see, he's very nice and respectful. Better she meets him here, instead of sneaking around. Janine is getting to be a young woman now. She knows what she's doing."

Clerise's input and the young man's behavior convinced Desil not to say anything to Janine. His attitude softened gradually, although he continued to pretend to ignore what was going on. No longer requested to wear the militia's uniform and participate in its activities, except in rare occasions such as in formal parades where a display of number mattered, Desil was kept in some kind of informal reserve status. His time-consuming job at the *Centrale Dessalines*, the sugar factory where Duvalierist influence was taking hold, helped in the process. Thus, he was not required to serve at the headquarters near the pier in the former *Juvenia* club that the militia had seized. However, because of the constant political turmoil and his equivocal status, he maintained his living quarters near his work and continued his regular visits to his family.

After the hurricane and their constant trips to the pier during the past rebels' invasion, the Tonton Macoutes had moved to their new location at the old *Juvenia* club with an increased contingent of new recruits. Their nearby presence made citizens nervous and the traditional strolls on the wharf diminished to some extent. The population stayed away from the pier following the brief detention of two teenage girls who were conversing on a crane one early evening and failed to stand when the flag was lowered at the militia's headquarters.

By then, other activities had become available to city youth. Detente with the United States, following Duvalier's crucial support at the U.N. for the 1965 U.S. invasion of the Dominican Republic, slowly led to a measure of economic recovery. Thus, streets were cleaned and repaired, the municipal trucks resumed garbage pick-up, and a kiosk built atop the masonry platform in *La Place d'Armes* was adorned with pictures of Duvalier and constantly guarded by a Tonton Macoute. Restored and modernized after the previous hurricane, electricity was provided to the town twenty-four hours a day. In that context, organized sports blossomed, building on past local tradition. As the old Rex theater closed, two new and competing movie theaters opened, offering low-cost presentations to a larger clientele. Small musical groups of youths, the mini-jazz, emerged alongside the town's two established brass bands. They played at the local night club, in the newly opened restaurants and movie theaters, during the Mardi Gras period, and at various other events.

When Duvalier made peace with the Catholic Church and was allowed to select the national bishops by agreement with the Vatican, young Haitian and foreign priests enjoyed considerable freedom of movement. Through them, the international ferment of ideas of the sixties found a safe channel in town.

"... *écoute la réponse dans le vent*... the answer is blowing in the wind," Nicole sang, as she prepared to leave for her Catholic youth group meeting.

"That's a pretty song," Clerise said. "I also heard the Cathedral choir sing some nice ones in Creole. Before now, all that Creole singing would never happen. But I don't know yet what to think of it."

"Just enjoy it, mom. That's change. It's about time," Janine replied, turning to take a look in the mirror. "The priest in charge of our group wants to rename it Christian Student Youth instead of just Catholic, to make it more inclusive."

"Well, I don't know about that. But one thing I find good is the Sunday Mass at four in the afternoon. Since it's their free time and they don't have much else to do, most *timoun kay* no longer have to wake up before four in the morning to go to church on Sundays."

Nicole stopped brushing her hair. "Why do we have a maid? A lot of people that I see in the movies don't have maids."

"You're talking about people from abroad," Janine said. "They have ovens and running water inside their houses. Can you see yourself starting a charcoal fire before you go to school in the morning?"

"Nobody dreams to work as a maid or *timoun kay*, but many people need those jobs," Clerise added.

"I won't have any maid in my house when I grow up," Nicole said.

With a dismissive shrug, Janine rolled her eyes and shook her head. "Bye mom! Are you coming, Nicole?" she said, before she kissed her mother to take her leave.

"You two look very nice," Clerise smiled. She added seriously, "Come back here right after your meeting. I only let you go there because it's a Church thing. You know they are arresting communists now. So, don't stay out late."

As a gesture of goodwill to his once-again allies, Duvalier began periodic crackdowns on communists, real or suspected. Although known Haitian members of the French Communist party were part of the government's inner sanctum, the official policy had been alternately to encourage or persecute suspected or confirmed leftists, depending upon the relations with the United States. Thus, communist persecution resumed with vigor. Throughout the country, young men and women were arrested and hauled to jail, often to disappear. In Les Cayes, sweeps of suspected political dissenters occurred in coordinated operations between the military and the Tonton Macoutes who roamed the town in cars, vans, or pick-up trucks requisitioned from private citizens "for government service." Sometimes used for weeks at a time, and seldom returned to their owners, the vehicles were often found abandoned in ditches with missing or damaged parts. Although arrests of suspected opponents of the regime and exiles' relatives continued among the bourgeoisie, the middle class carried the brunt of the Macoutes' harassment.

"Have you heard?" Janine said at the dinner table. "The school teacher who had all those guys arrested, tried to kill himself. He's now in the hospital."

Clerise dropped her spoon in her soup plate and shook her head in disbelief. "When is this all going to stop! *Ala zafè!* What a mess! Is he going to live?"

"They found him just in time. He couldn't live with himself after what he did."

"He didn't do it on purpose," Desil said. "What I heard is that he invited his friend, a government attorney, to join a group of other young men who got together to discuss books they had read. The attorney took all the names and reported the guys as communists. That's why they were arrested, except for the teacher."

"I heard that the other guys were sent to Port-au-Prince. That's what the teacher couldn't live with," Janine said. "Dad, have you heard anything about that?"

"Only as much as you heard. You know I stay as far as I can from 'you know who.' I don't get into their business, and they leave me alone. I don't want to ask any question to give them an opening to drag me into anything."

"My friend next door told me that her uncle, the mechanic, is now a Tonton Macoute," Nicole joined.

After the children left the table, Desil explained. "Marcel Octavien's bodyguards kept on taking the mechanic's pick-up truck. He couldn't stand it anymore, after a while. So, he went to Octavien and told him that he wanted to become a Macoute. However, he also said that because he was so busy with his work, he couldn't come to headquarters, do regular service, or anything else of the kind. Octavien was delighted. He gave the man a pistol, and told him that all he had to do was to show up in uniform for parades and other such occasions. I heard that, the very same night, the man went to *Kay Blan*, you know… the bordello, and beat up Octavien's two bodyguards right there at their favorite hang-out. They don't come any more for his truck."

Clerise laughed. Then she paused and asked, "What about the guy who was forced to give judo lessons at the *Juvenia* barracks?"

"I understand that he's very depressed, and spends hours alone drifting in a small boat away at sea. But they keep an eye on him."

"Such a pity! He doesn't deserve that!"

"When the Macoutes arrested him and started to beat him, he really put a few of them in bad shape. They were impressed and offered him to spare his life if he would join them and train them in judo. That whole thing is hard on him."

"Such a young man! But I never could figure out where he learned all that judo?"

"Maybe around the time when those guys, who had studied abroad and returned with some judo belt, were teaching it. Since then, there has been nothing as cocky as him in town!"

Clerise laughed. "That's true. There has always been one thing or another about him over the years. But the poor kid! That must be though on him."

"I heard that one of the Macoutes tried to scare Mr. and Mrs. Juin," Desil continued.

"Yes, Janine told me that he kept buying stuff from them, always promising to pay the next time. When they refused to continue that little game, he got angry and threatened them. 'I know you have communist children,' he said. 'I'll come back for you.' Instead, Nennenn told me that Octavien who heard of what happened, briefly stopped at their house and told Parenn not to worry about anything. According to Nennenn, Octavien said that he told the Macoutes, 'Mr. and Mrs. Juin are like my mother and father. They should be treated with respect. Whoever bothers them will have to deal with me.' Can you believe that?"

"And you know why?" Desil said, "It seems that when Octavien was a mere construction worker, he used to hang around the tailor shop in Kafou Orèl where one of his friends was an apprentice. He struck a casual friendship with Pilou, who apparently had never put on airs. From what I understand, one day Pilou was sick, and Octavien went to see him at his parents' home. It was his first and only visit there, because Pilou went to Port-au-Prince a short time after that. It seems that Octavien never forgot Mrs. Juin's welcome. She made him feel at ease, 'just like everyone else,' he said."

"Well, that's the way Nennenn is."

"All bourgeois are not the same. For some like the Juins, *tout moun se moun*, everybody is somebody. That's why many people will protect them."

"And how does that Macoute figure that the children are communists!" Clerise said indignantly. "Is that because they were always taught to say 'Hi' to everyone?

It's true that some of them don't go to church. But, have they ever killed anyone? Has that man ever caught them doing anything communist?"

Desil merely shook his head. He looked at her. In her anger, she was once again the young and vibrant woman that he had discovered in the intimacy of their long-gone honeymoon. "Clerise," he said, "my wife… I love you. I want to be with you again, as your husband." He touched her arm tentatively.

Sobered, she withdrew, turned her head, and averted her eyes. "You know I can't be your wife the way I think you mean it right now. As long as we don't stay together, I can't have any more children. That's life for us!"

He got up and left.

"Crazy Man! Crazy Man!" the boys yelled in Kafou Orèl.

Michel ran inside. "Nicole, come see the crazy man!"

He had just returned from an errand with Jesula during the school lunch recess. On their way, Michel's dog, a feisty mutt, had followed them across *La Place d'Armes* where he saw fit to honor the kiosk decorated with Duvalier's pictures by lifting his back leg in a wet salute. As the Tonton Macoute on duty chased him with a volley of rocks, the dog quickly took off and wisely ignored both Jesula and Michel until they arrived a block or so away. Now, they were home.

Nicole rushed outside when she heard the commotion. The crazy man only wore only a pair of torn shorts and a live cackling featherless chicken around his neck.

Tied by the feet with only one feather left at the end of each wing, the bird desperately tried to escape. As he moved his arms frantically in an imitation of the chicken's struggle, the crazy man yelled "Quack! Quack!" from the top of his lungs while he bolted past Kafou Orèl toward the marketplace. An increasingly larger group of noisy young boys followed him for several blocks and onlookers rushed to their front porches or balconies. Suddenly, the man, an impressive figure of nearly six feet, stopped in front of the Municipal Office Building. There he stood, screaming his wrath and throwing rocks, cursing Duvalier and the Tonton Macoutes.

"Duvalier! Assassin!" he yelled. "Tonton Macoutes! Assassins! Criminals! You turned me into a murderer! You made me kill the Dominican consul! Don't you remember! Assassins! Criminals! Murderers! You turned me into one of you! Assassins!"

Afraid to be caught listening, people slowly began to leave, but actually strained to hear more as they shook their head in denial and gestured in apparent dismissal of the "crazy talk." A Tonton Macoute approached, nightstick at the ready. Promptly the crazy man fled, the chicken still around his neck. He rushed through the streets, past Kafou Orèl, all the way to the end of the pier where he stood poised for a moment, then dived into the sea. A group of Tonton Macoutes in a motorboat caught him at a considerable distance offshore and started beating him right there in the water.

Not long after, the crazy man returned to the streets and continued to curse the Tonton Macoutes in long ranting diatribes to which the population listened at a prudent distance, always ready for any needed display of disbelief should a member of the militia happen to be nearby. The mad man had become a fixture in Les Cayes where his arrival, a year earlier, had been unnoticed.

"He just appeared one day," said the brother of Nicole's best friend. "We were hanging out on the porch of the movie theater in Kafou Orèl near the shoe-shine man. There were about five or six of us. We saw a man standing in front of the law office across the street. He seemed to have been there for some advice or something. He was wearing a suit. He looked like everyone else, except he was new in town. One of the guys in our group knew him. He said 'Let's go tease that man! He's crazy.'"

"How did your friend know the man was crazy?" Nicole asked.

"His dad is friends with some big Macoutes. He knows a lot of things. Anyway, he started to call the man's name and tugged at his jacket to tease him. 'Leave me alone, little boy,' the man said. Then, he turned and left. We all went after him past the wharf and onto the beach. The guy who knew him said, 'He's going home to Gelée. That's where he lives.' The man started to walk faster. We ran after him and my friend continued to tease him. He yelled 'Crazy Man!' The man bent down and picked up a conch shell. He turned around, and threw it hard at us. The conch shell hit another guy in our group in the stomach. The guy who was hit bawled and doubled over while he held his stomach. The man said 'I'm really sorry. I was throwing that thing at that little bum over there, not at you.' After that, we stopped following him, and turned back. "

"And then, what happened?"

"I think he just went home."

"I wonder how he turned out to be as crazy as he is."

"I used to see him wearing a suit," Nicole's friend said. "It kept becoming more and more torn and dirty."

"I remember that too," Nicole added. "And that's when he started to curse the Tonton Macoutes all the time. They keep on beating and arresting him. But he doesn't stop."

"Now, he sure is totally crazy!"

"What does Janine want to do when she finishes school?" Clerise's client asked while trying on the dress that she had ordered.

"I don't know yet. Maybe teach if she can find a job, or go to the nursing school. We'll see," Clerise said.

Janine's boyfriend had encouraged her to attend the local nursing school. After he had returned to Port-au-Prince to resume his medical studies, she kept him informed of her progress in the matter, since the Canadian nuns who ran her present school were also in charge of the nursing establishment. Cautiously optimistic, Clerise also started to plan for the necessary arrangements. "You never know," she told Janine, "if everything goes well, someday the two of you may be able to work together."

That sent Nicole into a flight of romantic fantasy. She imagined her sister's wedding as she had seen in movies and in the particularly impressive ceremonies conducted in the Cathedral, which she had witnessed with her mother either from a corner of one of the lateral chapels, while they pretended to be there for other devotions, or from a bench in *La Place d'Armes* across the street.

"… and she will have that long white gown, and a veil over her face, and a train that little kids will carry. And we will all be her *filles d'honneur*, her bridesmaids, and everybody will walk from the church to the reception," Nicole said to her friends in their corner of the schoolyard. They giggled, started to walk in rows, pretending to march in a mock wedding procession.

"What's the matter with them?" Marie-Carmelle Lifaite said to a couple of other girls nearby. "What are they doing?"

Marie-Carmelle had transferred from her old school to that of the nuns. Although she and Nicole were no longer best friends, they maintained a relationship that was acrimonious at times, but generally cordial. Since she was not in Nicole's immediate circle, Marie-Carmelle made a display of annoyance at what she gathered of Nicole's talk about Janine's romance. The day after the mock wedding game, Marie-Carmelle busily contacted several girls and whispered to them while casting side glances at Nicole. So intent was she in her activities, that the teacher almost caught her a few times in the classroom. At recess, she headed straight for Nicole.

"Who do you think you are?" she asked aggressively with hands on her hips. "You keep acting up all the time! *W ap fè enteresant!* You keep trying to get attention! Telling all those stupid stories about your sister! I bet you can't tell much about your mother!"

"What's your problem, Marie-Carmelle? What's going on? Why do you put my mother in whatever business you have?"

"Keep acting like you don't understand what I'm talking about! You all are nothing! And you act so high and mighty!"

"What's the matter with you?"

"What's the matter with me? What's the matter with your mother? She thinks she's so great she can look down on people!"

The other girls had formed a circle around them. Shocked by the attack, Nicole stood dumbfounded. Marie-Carmelle went for the kill. "Your mother! She keeps saying that she was 'raised' by the Juins! What she's not telling is that she was really their little domestic! their *gadmantèg,* their chambermaid! their *restavèk!* Everyone knows that! Everyone knows too that she was a *bouzen,* a true whore on top of that! Your father picked her up from the gutter and made her respectable! Look at Janine! Does she look like you? Why don't you ask your mother who your big sister's father is? That's why your father left home. Because your mother is a *manman bouzen,* a major whore!" she concluded as she slapped her skirt and lifted a corner almost to her hip in a display of utter contempt.

"Liar!" Nicole roared. "I'm going to tell my mother about your bunch of lies, and she'll tell your mom! You're going to get it!" Enraged, she was about to lunge at Marie-Carmelle when the bell rang.

But, to Nicole, something was not right. A look at the expressions of those around her had made her doubt. As recess ended, everyone drifted away in embarrassed silence. Still fuming, but greatly disturbed, Nicole returned to class. With head high and chin up, she sought eye contact from time to time with Marie-Carmelle and sent her killer looks. After school, she found herself alone once more, as a group of girls, including her usual friends, gathered around Marie-Carmelle and purposely avoided to look in her direction. Not even her best friend attempted to join her as she left. Proudly, she walked by herself and made sure to turn from time to time to throw contemptuous looks at the other girls. When she arrived home, she found Clerise at her sewing machine.

"You're kind of early today," her mother remarked.

"I need to talk to you," Nicole answered, while distractedly giving her mother a customary greeting kiss.

Something in her tone alerted Clerise. "What's the matter? Are you okay?"

"Marie-Carmelle said to ask you who Janine's father is?" Nicole blurted. She was angry and indignant.

Clerise got up. "Jesula, come here, and stay in the front!" she called. "If anyone asks for me, say that I am busy. Nicole, come with me to the bedroom."

"Come here," she said, motioning to Nicole to sit near her on the bed. "I have something to tell you. But first, let me ask you. Who said anything about Janine?"

"Marie-Carmelle said that you were a *bouzen*, and that's why my father left home," Nicole answered with tears flowing. Suddenly she felt afraid, vulnerable. She needed to be comforted.

Clerise embraced her and wiped away the tears. "You know better than that," she said. "You know why Papa Desil does not live here anymore. Do you remember why, Nicole?"

The child shook her head affirmatively.

"What else did Marie-Carmelle tell you?"

"She said you think you are so high and mighty, and that you were only a little *restavèk* at the Juins."

"It figures, coming from Marie-Carmelle. Her mother can't forgive me for not having chosen her to be Michel's godmother. Nicole, a lot of what Marie-Carmelle is saying to you is because of that. We'll have to put a stop to it. Yes, I was a little *restavèk* at the Juins. I think you already know that. But, there's also something else that I have to tell you." Clerise lifted the child's head to look into her eyes. "Look at me, Nicole. Do you know what a *bouzen* is?"

The child shook her head "Yes."

"Do I look like a whore to you. Have you ever seen me acting like one?"

Warily, Nicole shook her head "No."

"Now, listen carefully because what I am about to say you must hear sooner or later. I was just waiting for you to get older before I told you. But, since I have to do it now, I want you to learn from it. Is that okay with you?"

Nicole nodded.

"Your father is Janine's true father, because he raised her, gave her his name, and loves her like his very own. We got married when she was almost five years old. She doesn't know any father other than Desil."

Nicole was stunned. "Who is Janine's father?"

"His name doesn't matter. It will not mean anything to you. I don't even know if the man is dead or alive, and I don't care. He did something terrible to me. Are you listening?"

Again, the child shook her head "Yes." Clerise took her hands; they were cold.

"I was a young girl, about the age Janine is now. Yes, I was a *restavèk* at the Juins, and I always behaved the right way." With an arm around Nicole's shoulder, she continued as if speaking to herself. "I remember when that young man, Paul Frimère, who now has that big store in town with his father-in-law, was trying to get fresh with me. I stopped him right away and told Mrs. Juin about him. '*Gadmantèg!* Chambermaid!' he called me. After that, Mrs. Juin started to watch me more closely. She felt she had a responsibility to my family. She realized I was getting to be a grown woman, and

was afraid that one of those young men would try to
lead me the wrong way. That made me angry, because I
knew that I had done the right thing before. So, when a
man who was leading a work crew that put asphalt on
the street started to send me messages through Elvire, a
woman who used to work for Mrs. Juin, I became
interested."

Nicole moved away and looked at her. "Was that
Janine's father?" she asked, no longer crying.

"Yes. And I will tell you what happened. It's hard for
me to do. But soon you will be a young woman, and
again, you can also learn from this." Clerise paused for a
moment, rested her chin on her fingers and gazed away
at a distance. When she continued, her voice was steady.
"Elvire arranged for this guy and I to meet for quick
talks, here and there, for a few minutes, at street corners.
Then, she started to come more and more to pick me
up to 'run errands.' Miss Laura made some comments to
Mrs. Juin about the whole thing, and Mrs. Juin told me
that Elvire was not a good example for me, because she
had a child by Mr. Mirot without being married to him.
Mrs. Juin wanted me to cut the friendship and not see
Elvire anymore except for when Elvire came to see her
grandmother Philomene, who was Mrs. Juin's cook. I
was angry at Mrs. Juin. I thought she felt the man was
too good for me. Because of that, I made sure to
continue to see him. Do you follow me?"

"Yes," Nicole said without looking at her.

"In the meantime, Elvire moved to Lan Savann. One
day, she told me to stop at her house because she had

something to show me. I was still angry at Mrs. Juin. So, I arranged with Elvire to be at her house for a quick moment while running an errand. The man was there. Elvire told me she was going next door just for a second to get the thing that she wanted to show me. As soon as she left, the man attacked me. I fought hard. He told me that if I screamed, there would be a scandal and that Mrs. Juin would send me back home. He said that if I didn't want what he was doing, I wouldn't have come there for a rendezvous. I told him I didn't know he was going to be there, and kept fighting him. But he was able to do a *kadejak* on me, to rape me. You know what that means, Nicole?"

With head bowed, Nicole nodded and started to cry again, silently.

Clerise took her in her arms. "Do you want me to stop now?"

The child shook her head, "No."

"Elvire took her time to return," Clerise continued as she let go of Nicole, "and when she came back, she helped me clean up to go back to Mrs. Juin's. 'Where have you been so long?' Mrs. Juin said. I couldn't answer. She thought I was being rude on purpose and slapped me."

"What? " Nicole jolted and looked at her mother incredulously, her face still stained with tears. "After she made that thing happen to you?"

"That was the first and only time she had slapped me. She was really getting scared for me," Clerise answered quickly. She closed her eyes, sighed, and then touched her daughter's hair. "I am responsible for what happened to me. Because I was angry and scared to be sent home, I didn't use my head, and Elvire knew it."

"What happened to you after that? What happened to the man?" Nicole asked, staring at the floor with her arms folded.

"I wanted to die at the time, but I survived. I never saw the man again. He was working for the Department of Public Works. I heard he was transferred out of town. I stopped talking to Elvire. When I found out I was pregnant, I couldn't tell anyone." Clerise paused and glanced at her daughter, who had slightly turned away. Then, she continued resolutely. "It was not until four months later, during the summer vacation, that old Mrs. Visel and Matant Elia, asked me if I was pregnant. When I told them what had happened, Mr. Juin went to see the Director of Public Works who told him the man already had a family out of town, and had asked for a transfer. Philomene quit when Mrs. Juin told her that Elvire could not come anymore to visit her in the house. Louise became the cook. Mrs. Juin also wanted to send me home, but Gisèle who was visiting pleaded for me. Mrs. Juin let me stay in her house for as long as nothing showed. Few people knew of what happened, because all Mrs. Juin said was that I was sick and had to go back home for a while. Janine was born in Fonfrède. I left her with my godmother. Then, I returned to town."

"What happened to Janine?" Nicole asked without moving.

"She stayed in Fonfrède until my aunt got sick. I used to go to see her there and bring money and clothes for her. Gisèle was supposed to be her godmother, but she could not make the trip and Matant Elia replaced her. I was so ashamed, I begged Mrs. Juin not to tell anything to anybody. The children didn't know what happened. They thought that I had a goddaughter in Fonfrède. I just fell in love with Janine and my heart broke when I had to leave her. I missed that baby so much! Then my aunt got sick. Before my aunt died, Mrs. Juin saw how sad and concerned I was. She let me bring Janine to her house, and told people that it was a little adoption of hers. She really started doting on Janine from the beginning."

With a hard edge in her voice, Nicole inquired, "How come Janine has my father's name?"

"Janine was at the Juins only for a short time before I married your father. She took to him right away. I told him what happened. I also told him that the Juins wanted to keep Janine and raise her themselves. Desil knew that I wanted to have my daughter with me, and he offered to give her his name and recognize her legally as his own child. Since that time, Janine has always been his daughter. And Desil has always acted with her as her true father.... Listen to me, my child. I made a mistake once. I paid dearly for it. But there is nothing that you, or I, or Janine, or anyone in this family should be ashamed of. This very night, I am going to see Mrs. Dieujuste."

Nicole had tears in her eyes. "May I go to sleep now?" she said.

"I'll go to see Boss Dieujuste myself," Desil told Clerise, once she informed him of the verbal assault against Nicole. The next day, the school yard was abuzz with the news of the two major spankings that Marie-Carmelle had received the night before. One was from her mother, the other from her father. Her screams had conspicuously reverberated through the neighborhood. Chastened, she approached Nicole in front of the other girls, and mumbled, "My father and my mother told me to apologize to you. I should never have used your mother's name the way I did. Mrs. Desil is a respectable woman. I am sorry."

"I hear you," Nicole said before turning away. Slowly, the other girls approached her and left Marie-Carmelle alone. She received their overtures with inner reluctance and calculated coldness. For her, things could never again be the same.

Nicole became more quiet and reserved even as the flowers reached the height of their glory in May, the Month of Mary, which began in earnest with nightly devotions at the Cathedral. For Clerise, those were part of a yearly cycle that included the Month of Saint Joseph in March, various Patron Saint and Obligation Feast days, as well as the Way of the Cross, which was conducted each Friday in increasing duration during Lent, and culminated in three days of almost uninterrupted church attendance at the end of that period. During the special "months" dedicated to various saints, churches throughout the city held nightly ceremonies with appropriate songs, prayers, and rosaries. In addition to the clergy and members of religious orders, women and a few devout men packed the churches, along with a trail of recalcitrant, rebellious, unlucky, or plainly bored children ready for mischief. Maids and *timoun kay* whose presence was not absolutely required at home to prepare supper also had to attend.

Nicole felt tired of the constant church activities, especially after the last episode with Marie-Carmelle, and she no longer enjoyed the company of her friends, their endless chats, mischievous gossip, and animated games. She was not even sure of her feelings toward her mother and Janine. Presently, she resented being dragged to church against her will and no longer anticipated to meet her friends in the relative darkness, while their mothers exchanged comments on their way home from the Month of Mary's celebrations. Sullen, she stayed close to her mother and brother as they left the church.

"When is Simone coming to town?" asked Miss Laura, who had intercepted them near the lamppost in Kafou Orèl.

"She should be coming soon. Parenn Edmond is due here in a couple of days," Clerise answered.

"They're really moving to Port-au-Prince, aren't they? Everyone is leaving town these days!" Miss Laura's tone was low and conspiratorial. Constantly throwing glances around, she appeared ready to flee on short notice. "By the way, how's Pilou?" she whispered.

"I suppose he's well." In response, Clerise's tone was also hushed.

"You haven't heard from Simone?"

"No, I haven't. Is everything all right?" Clerise asked, suddenly alarmed.

Miss Laura quickly glanced around. "Well... It's only that I heard some rumors in town. You know how people talk." Her voice remained low as she tried to maintain an appearance of casual conversation.

"What is it? What are they saying?" Clerise said in the same vein.

"It's about Pilou. People say that he came with the communists to fight the government. They say that he has been caught. I don't know if that's true, but this is what they say."

Nicole saw her mother almost reeling. "What else do they say?" Clerise asked. Her voice was low and steady.

"Clerise, brace yourself. Don't show anything. They say that Pilou has been killed. Don't do anything. Just go home. It may not even be true, but I had to tell you. Maybe Desil can check it out for you. Let me know.... Well, I have to go," Miss Laura continued loudly and with exaggerated cheerfulness. "Clerise, look at these kids. Aren't they growing? Your little girl is almost a young woman now. Good bye, children!"

Nicole remained silent. "Say good bye to Miss Laura," Clerise ordered, almost as a reflex. She remembered those sunny afternoons when she had to contend with

Pilou, the fractious and independent little boy who refused to hold her hand to walk the street. "Children, say good bye to Miss Laura," Ermance used to say before leading them to the pier. Clerise nearly winced with pain.

"Good bye, Miss Laura," the children mumbled without looking, almost an echo of the past.

"The crazy man is dead," Desil said to Clerise, as he stepped toward her.

On the porch that late afternoon, she had watched him come up the street. He looked tired, and perhaps ill. Afraid that they would be overheard, she led him inside the house and made him sit at the dining table. His lips were dry. She poured cool water from a *krich*, one of the red clay jars lined on the shelf by the windowsill. "Drink this, Desil. Tell me what happened."

"The crazy man is dead," he repeated. His hands shook as he held the glass.

"How did it happen? I heard he was arrested today because he was cursing at a Macoute."

"If I stay here, I may turn like him. Those criminals! That new colonel had ordered the soldiers to crack down on the man. Today, they beat him to death at the barracks in Lan Gabyon. They sent for the trash truck to pick up his body, and they went to dump him somewhere. Oh Clerise! I can't continue to live like this! I have to get away from these people! But I can't! I don't know what to do! I don't know where to turn!"

She held him close, stroking his hair. "Desil, it's not your fault. You are just doing what you can to protect us all." She felt an old stirring of love and tenderness.

Janine broke the spell. "Something strange happened this afternoon," she said as she stepped in the room. "When I was studying on Nennenn's balcony, I saw the trash truck going toward Lan Gabyon. It was washed clean. A while later, it returned. As I glanced at it, I saw what I think could have been someone lying in the back. I didn't see too well, because by that time it was already dusk. But, this seems kind of strange to me."

"Forget you saw it!" intervened Clerise quickly. "The crazy man is dead."

When Simone Juin returned to town, she delivered to Janine a letter from her boyfriend. Distrustful of the mail, and concerned for everyone's safety, the young man had carefully worded the message to be hand delivered. "Dearest Janine," it said "Because of my studies, I will not be able to be in town with you this summer. Perhaps, your parents will let you come and visit some of your relatives in Port-au-Prince...."

"He did not want to write much," Nennenn said, as she sat in her bedroom with Janine and Nicole. "He did not want anything to be misinterpreted, in case I was stopped on the way. Before I accepted the letter, I asked him about the content, and he showed it to me. I was very concerned because I was also carrying with me the letter that Pilou had just written to us from the U.S. We heard the rumors that he had been killed with the communists. We know that they have found anti-government leaflets here, on *La Place d'Armes*, and that they are arresting people again. All we want to do now is pack and leave for Port-au-Prince. Pilou's letter proves that he is still abroad. That's our protection."

"Is it true that a whole family was killed in Port-au-Prince a few years ago before they found out that the son was still abroad and not part of an invasion?" Janine asked.

Nennenn's jaw clenched. She took a deep breath. "From what I understand, his letter came too late to save them."

"Oh Nennenn! What could have happened to you?" Janine said. Her shoulders hunched, she clasped her hands between her knees. The letter from her boyfriend fell to the floor and Nicole moved to pick it up.

Nennenn came close and held them both. "You never can tell," she said. Letting go of Nicole, she kept an arm around Janine. "I know that it's hard for you not to see your boyfriend this summer. But, believe me, now is not a good time for students to travel. It is much safer for him to stay in Port-au-Prince than to come here."

"I understand."

"But, Janine, I also have to tell you this. Your boyfriend is a fine young man. He loves you very much. I think that at the beginning he didn't really want to make contact with Parenn and me. I can understand that somewhat. I like him for you. I hope everything will go well."

"Desil, Nennenn has an offer for me."

For the past few days, Clerise had been pensive. As Desil brought his weekly contribution to the household, his concern for her seemed greater than his own distress.

"Gisèle has found me a job in New York."

"Had you been looking for a job in New York?" he asked with surprise.

"No, not at all. I was shocked when Nennenn told me that where Gisèle works a lady needs someone to take care of her children. Nennenn said that Gisèle thought of me right away, and wanted to offer me the opportunity."

"But you have your own children to take care of," said Desil. She felt him tense and struggle to remain calm.

"I know, and that's why I didn't say anything right away. I just told Nennenn that I needed time to get back to her with an answer."

He just stood, looking at her.

"If I take the job," Clerise continued, "Nennenn says that, in two years, I can have an American visa and send for you and the kids. I have been thinking long and hard. I love my children and can't bear to be away from any of them again."

"Look..." he began.

"Please hear me out," she said. "Desil, look at you. Look at what is happening to you and to all of us. We are barely a family now, and you never know what those people may ask you to do. They can turn you into a criminal, or if you refuse to do something, they may kill you and perhaps all of us too. They can take your job away and make us starve. We have two young women growing up. We're far from being rich and have no protection. We are in their hands. There's nothing we can do. I have to take that job. It's our only way out. In two years, I'll send for you and the kids, and perhaps we'll be able to live together again. Desil, we have no other choice."

He leaned on a chair and shook his head. "Then, what are we going to do with the children?" he asked, still shocked.

"This may surprise you, but I have given it a lot of thought. The only person I would feel comfortable leaving my children with is your Aunt Amanthe. She raised you well and I know she will take good care of the kids. It's time that we make peace."

CHAPTER 11

In the USA

1977

The phone rang.

Half-awake, Rose-Marie picked up the receiver after a quick glance at the clock. Six in the morning, and on a Saturday. Who can that be? she thought.

"Hello!"

"Aunt Rosie," said Regine Roussard, Gisèle's daughter. Something in her tone jolted Rose-Marie wide awake.

"What is it, Regine?"

"Are you quite up now?"

"Yes. What's going on?"

"It's Mommy Clerise," Regine said flatly. "There is bad news."

"What happened?"

"Something dreadful happened."

"What is it?"

"We got the news last night, and mom said to wait until this morning to tell you. Mommy Clerise may have been killed by Tonton Macoutes."

"But why?" Rose-Marie asked uncomprehendingly. "Isn't Desil a Tonton Macoute?"

"This has to do with Margaret Jobert, your mom's goddaughter. She and her husband seem to have been killed too. Nicole was there also. She escaped."

"How did it happen?"

"You know how Margaret is now close to your mom, since we are all abroad and her mom is too. Her husband seemed to have been friends with some Tonton Macoutes. When he and Margaret returned to Haiti from New York, he started doing business with the Macoutes. Something must have gone wrong."

"But... what does Clerise have to do with it?"

"We got the news last night. Clerise was visiting your mom with Nicole. Margaret had a sick child and needed someone to stay with her for the night. Elia had a cold, and your mom couldn't go either because she wasn't feeling well. So she asked Clerise to do it for her, and Nicole went along."

Rose-Marie stammered. "Hold it...! So, how is my mom? And what happened to the baby and Nicole?"

"Your mom is fine. From what I think Nicole said, there was a loud knock on the door in the middle of the night. Then they heard a commotion downstairs. Next thing, a Tonton Macoute was in their room. He ordered them to get in a car with Margaret and her husband."

"What about the baby?"

"They left her in the house. Neighbors took her to Margaret's in-laws."

"Where's Nicole now?"

"In hiding. She may have already left on one of those refugee boats. Hopefully, she'll get here soon."

"How are my mom, dad, and Elia?"

"They're okay. Margaret's in-laws have made all the contacts that were needed. Everyone is protected now."

"What about Clerise's family in Les Cayes?"

"No one on the outside knows about Mommy Clerise's name in connection with what happened. When the commotion was taking place downstairs in Margaret's house, Mommy Clerise told Nicole not to say anything about Desil, not even for protection. We think she was being careful, because there are so many factions among the Tonton Macoutes. In any case, from what I heard, her family in Les Cayes is pretending that she had to return abroad quickly, and that she took Nicole along."

"How old is Nicole now?"

"Almost nineteen, I think."

"I can't believe I'm hearing this! Tell me it's a nightmare! It can't be true!"

Nearly seven years before that fateful call, Rose-Marie had gone to New York to see Clerise, who had just arrived. The moment was joyous, yet somewhat awkward. Rose-Marie felt pangs of guilt when she thought of Clerise's pain in separating from her children. In Gisèle's home in New York, no one appeared even remotely conscious of such a sacrifice.

"How are your kids?" Rose-Marie asked. "They must be quite grown now."

"Desil and his aunt are taking care of them," Clerise answered, her eyes brimming with tears.

"Rose-Marie, Aunt Simone sent you a letter," Gisèle interjected brightly.

After that, there had been no time for much personal exchange.

"Come and visit us in Washington when you can," Rose-Marie told Clerise before leaving. "Let me know when you are ready, and I'll send you a ticket."

Clerise's trip to Washington occurred nearly two years after that encounter, after she had lost her first job, her temporary visa, and her immediate hopes of attaining legal immigrant status.

"They worked me like a dog," she said. "They even made me sleep on the same couch where the dog jumped and slept. We, Haitians, are not used to that. It is disrespectful. They made me work late into the night when they gave parties, and sometimes they didn't let me have any time off for the whole week. Things got really bad when Gisèle went abroad for her job. That's when her kids told me to quit working there. I thought I was going to find another job right away, but that didn't happen. Now, I'm still looking, and I don't know how things are going to be."

"Luckily, you had a chance to go and visit Desil and the kids when you still had your visa. Too bad you don't want to try it here in Washington. But, don't worry, you'll find another job."

"I can't believe what those people did! If you had not helped me, they would have kept my passport and my bank book. I can't thank you enough for going to talk to them and get my things for me. Now, I have to find another job before I run out of money. Desil and the kids are counting on me."

On that matter, comments from her aunt Lina Mussain had kept Rose-Marie informed of Clerise's family situation. "Would you believe that they are now renting one of those two story houses on Main Street? Clerise works all the time. She has no friends and hardly buys anything for herself. But she sends boxes of things over there for her family, including that Macoute husband of hers. Now, they have watches, radios, cameras, bicycles, etc. I even heard that they have a refrigerator in that house!"

The years passed, and Gisèle returned from overseas. After a succession of short-lived jobs, Clerise finally found a position that she considered satisfactory. When not moonlighting on weekends, she spent her time in Gisèle's home, where the widowed Lina Mussain, who had grown tyrannical in the confines of her Queens apartment, held court amid the comings and goings of various Haitian acquaintances.

"Mrs. Juin wrote from Port-au-Prince," Lina told Clerise. "She tells me that your aunt Elia is very proud of you and thanks you for your gift. They are happy that you are helping me here."

Rose-Marie could not understand why Clerise spent her weekends catering to the needs of the Mussains and Roussards. Once more subservient, Clerise sat at the edge of gatherings, serving food and passing trays to guests when required. She participated marginally in conversations, except in close family circles.

"I'm all for social promotion," Lina Mussain said. "But the day she tried to call me 'Aunt Lina,' that was too much. Although one can hardly say anything now, I think she got the message and never tried it again."

"Clerise is a nice person," Gisèle added. "I love her very much. She's very devoted. But I'm sick and tired of hearing so many details about her employers' lives. That's of no interest to me whatsoever. We don't have much to say to each other. And then, people would call that prejudice."

"But that's all you do all the time with your friends. You gossip all the time," Regine replied, in her newly found militancy for social justice.

"Why don't you find something else to do on weekends?" Rose-Marie asked Clerise when they met in Washington.

"Listen Rosie, I'm a married woman. I don't want to behave in any way that would open the door to gossip. When I go to your aunt's, I'm safe. Those are the only people I really know in that town."

"Isn't that going a little too far?"

"Things will change when Desil and the kids arrive. You'll see."

With the necessary formalities finally completed, a deliriously happy Clerise prepared to leave for Haiti to obtain her permanent visa. "I'm going to see them!" she told Rose-Marie. "Rosie, can you believe, I'm going to see them? I can't wait to get the papers for everybody! I want to look nice for Desil. It has been such a long time! I also have to get something very nice for Aunt Amanthe. She did a good job with the kids. What do you think I can get her? I can't really believe I'm going to see them all!"

She left for Haiti, and returned with the permanent visa to resume her job. "I've applied for Desil and the children to come and join me. That will take about a year. Then I'll go sign their papers and get them here," she explained.

The year passed quickly while she worked with renewed enthusiasm. "Rosie, I'll see you in a while," she said before she returned to Haiti. And then... the phone rang.

* * * * *

In the refugee camp, as she leaned on the cool fence for relief from the Floridian heat, Nicole remembered. She could feel Clerise pushing her down the ditch, for her escape. Then, the machine-gun fire. The scream. Clerise! Oh Clerise, my beautiful mother! You gave your life for me... Clerise, please don't leave me... I need you. "Mother!... Mother!... MOTHER!... MOTHER!... MOTHER!... MOTHER!..." Unable to say more and crushed by her loss, the girl fell on her knees on the hot macadam covered ground, still screaming her mother's name.

She found herself being coaxed to the shade by other women, her companions of misfortune. From their side of the camp, the men gathered near the fence separating them from the women and offered advice. They passed handkerchiefs, wet with water from the fountains, to cool her face and arms. Soothing voices encouraged her to sip water and relax, while her screams turned into desperate sobs and tears.

Later, not knowing exactly how, she remembered taking a pill, which she had swallowed feeling only exhaustion and emptiness over a deep, underlying, and nameless wound. As she fell asleep, she briefly thought of her father and of her family left in Les Cayes.

She awoke somewhat dazed, finding herself in a strange place, then tears came to her eyes as she thought once more: "Mother, please don't leave me." Often, she had felt her mother at her side, giving her strength. At other times, she was overcome by depression, rage, and a deep sense of loss. Then, she started to carry on, in her mind, silent conversations with Clerise.

"Mother, I need you. We were just starting to understand each other. We had so much to do together. Did you know how much I loved you? I didn't even have a chance to tell you. Mother, can you hear me? Let me know that you forgive me for having hurt you sometimes. I didn't know you were going to leave me so early. I thought you would be with me forever, and that we would always have a chance to talk. I wasn't afraid to be myself with you. I knew you would always accept me. I'm sorry to have hurt or misunderstood you. I hope you are happy wherever you are. Please let me know that you are okay. I love you…"

"I know, *pitit mwen*, my child," she heard in her mind. "I'm okay, and I love you."

Am I going crazy? she thought.

She felt Clerise's smile. "No, you are not. Part of me will always be with you. In time, you will find peace."

EPILOGUE

Suburban USA

1994

"This time, Nicole, you are going to call her!" I said aloud to myself, as music began to play on the radio.

I cradled the phone to my chest and looked at the number on the once-crumpled piece of paper that I had just unfolded. Again, I began to feel the rage, sadness, and despair of years past. "Rose-Marie wants you to call her, when you can," my sister had said when she gave me that number, long ago.

"What for? As far as I'm concerned, she can wait until chicken grow teeth!" I spat, as I crushed the note in my hand and threw it in the thrash. Later that night, I retrieved the number and saved it in a pile of odds and ends.

On the wall facing me, my mother's picture seemed to give me a slight nod and smile of encouragement. "You look so much like your mom. You have Clerise's smile and you even speak like her," people often tell me.

Now in my thirties, I tend to agree. Sometimes, I can see in myself the dark chocolate brown of my mother's skin, the shape of her eyebrows, her almond-shaped eyes, and the fullness of her mouth. When I catch myself resting my chin on my fingers and gazing far away at a distance, I remember her in that reflective pose. Often, I chuckle hearing myself repeat some of her old sayings. "*Jou va, jou vyen*, a day goes, a day comes" she used to say, and that reminded me of what I had just heard from the conference on the radio in which Rose-Marie was a panelist.

"The only way we could get rid of the Duvaliers was when all Haitians, though unarmed, finally had enough and united in spite of all the Tonton Macoutes and their weapons," she said. "That same basis of self-determination is what brought Aristide to power. The military coup that overthrew him is indefensible; so would be the U.S. military intervention to bring him back to power. He promised that he would never return to the country on the wing of foreign troops. But now, with all the lobbyists around him, the situation is changing. We need to remind him of his pledge. We should organize."

That is when I decided to call her. As the song on the radio ended, I glanced again at the note she had sent me. Echoes of the music hung in the air. I hummed the tune and closed my eyes. Then I took a deep breath and dialed the number.

"You may not remember me. I am Nicole Fleurantier, Clerise's daughter," I said quickly when Rose-Marie came to the phone. "Is this ...?"

The response surprised me. "How could I not remember you, Nicole? I am so glad that you called! Yes, this is Rosie!"

"I heard you on the radio at that conference about the intervention," I began.

"You can't imagine how good it is to hear from you!"

"My mother told me a lot about you," I answered; and the pain surged again, still surprisingly sharp after so many years.

My hand on the receiver, I remained motionless for a while after my conversation with Nicole. Years ago, when I had attempted to reach out to Clerise's daughter, my efforts were politely rebuffed. Then, I understood and respected that Nicole wanted no further contact with any member of the Juin family or its assorted relatives. Rather than trying to rationalize or join others in their "righteous" anger at such "ingratitude," my acceptance of Nicole's decision had framed and defined my memories of Clerise.

On the phone, Nicole had appeared direct and self-assured, perhaps a bit too much for my taste. Now in my middle age, I am used to a more pleasant and considerate attitude from young Haitians, even those raised here in the United States.

"I just heard you on the radio, at that conference about the intervention. I decided to call, to tell you that I support your position. Our country is facing difficult times and we all need to come together," Nicole started.

"I agree, and I can't tell you how happy I am that you called. It means a lot to me. We don't know what is going to happen and I am very concerned."

"Like you, I am opposed to what the military has done in Haiti. But what many fail or refuse to see is that one man is not a nation. Putting him back in power is not worth the price of our sovereignty. There should be other ways to resolve the crisis. Worse

has happened elsewhere in the world without getting such a response."

"On that matter, a South African recently pointed out that, in his country, Mandela speaks as the representative of a party, and respects its guidelines during all negotiations with the power structure. For us Haitians, the danger is that we are dealing with a Messiah who speaks as the embodiment of the Nation," I commented.

As we warmed to each other in shared political understanding, the conversation later took a delicate turn. "My mother told me that you were one of the few people to whom she could really talk," Nicole mentioned.

"We certainly came a long way," I answered.

"When I asked my mom 'What makes her so special?'" Nicole continued, "she said 'Rosie has been there for me when I needed it.'"

"And she too for me." With the old pain and guilt resurfacing, I added, "I can't begin to tell you…"

Nicole's reaction was swift and unexpected. "On that matter, you can have the last word," she answered abruptly, and with what I thought to be a touch of sarcasm.

Deliberately, we moved past the awkward moment, shifted the conversation to current political concerns, and progressively resumed the initial pleasant tone. At the end, we decided to keep in touch.

I made an effort to control my anger as Rose-Marie said, "I can't begin to tell you…," when we talked about my mother. "Tell me what?" I wanted to scream. "That my mother slaved for you most of her life, and felt privileged to do so?" Then, I could almost hear Clerise's words: "We are doing it too with our own *timoun kay*…"

The radio continued to play in the background. I reached to turn down the volume, and the pounding beat of Boukman Esperyans receded somewhat. Still, I could faintly hear the group's rich melody. The Vodou-inspired *rasin* sounds, the rhythms from the roots, coursed through my blood and touched the very core of my Haitian essence; and that helped me conclude the conversation with Rose-Marie on a positive note. When I put down the receiver, I turned the volume all the way up and swayed with the music.

Later, I recalled those childhood moments in Haiti when my love for my mother was mixed with contempt. I had felt humiliated by her unending devotion to her former employers, and jealous of the protective love, admiration, and pride that she constantly expressed toward the children that she had helped raise. That, I could not accept.

I also remembered how elated I was when she had arrived in Les Cayes from abroad, seventeen years ago. Then, we had started our preparations to go to Port-au-Prince to arrange for U.S. visas for the family at the American Embassy. Still basking in the glow of our reunion, I earnestly sought my mother's company, bombarding her with questions about the life that soon would be ours. Slowly, the focus sometimes shifted to more personal exchanges when, caught off guard, I slipped from my customary aloofness on such matters.

"I can't count how many times I took children to play at the pier or the town square," my mother had mused while packing our suitcases. "But, I was never able to play there on my own. The only way to do it would have been to sneak around when I was sent on an errand and play with the other little domestic workers, the *timoun kay* of that area of town. But I was too much of a 'good' girl to do that. Looking back, I can't remember that I had a real childhood."

My anger had erupted, as I stood with an armful of clothes. "Then how can you still love those people who put you through this?" At that moment, I could not bear to use the Juins' name. "Why do you talk about them as if they were your devoted parents? Those children for whom you slaved, why are you almost in awe of them now? Haven't they done enough to you? Sometimes, I even think that you love them and their children more than you love us. It's always Rosie this, Pilou that, dear little Danny. I'm sick of it!"

Clerise ignored my outburst and continued to pack. "You can't speak like that," she answered. "My life was not different from that of any other *timoun kay*. It was even better than most. It's a way of life here. We are doing it too, with our own little domestics. The Juins raised me. I know all there is to know about them. Still, they are my people."

"Then count me off that side of your happy family!" I snapped.

"Without them, do you think I could have gone abroad to find an escape for all of us?"

"Without people like them, maybe we wouldn't have needed an escape!"

"*Pitit mwen*, my child," Clerise said, "some day you will understand."

Yes, I understand now, I thought seventeen years later. I remember your protectiveness while you watched me play with my friends when I was little, and your delight in taking us on outings to the beach in Gelée.

"I was still a little girl the first time I started to see how life really was. I know what it is to be the underdog, and what it takes to survive," Clerise had added after a pause in that conversation of years past. Then, she continued to tell me of her life as a *timoun kay*, a little domestic worker who took children out to play in Les Cayes, Haiti.

That exchange had marked a turning point in our relationship. For the first time, I saw my mother as a separate individual, as a young girl who had been forced to live on guard and make adult decisions toward an uncertain future. With grudging acceptance and restrained interest, I began to discover the real Clerise, my mother, the woman who later chose to die to save my life.

To this day, I still hold the Juins indirectly responsible for the tragedy that took her life, although I responded to Rose-Marie in the context of our national crisis. After we spoke on the phone about her radio address, my old feelings toward her family returned. Silently in my mind I reached to Clerise. "Mother, why didn't you listen to me. I didn't want to go to those people's home. You know how I felt about them. We fought enough over that. I only wanted to please you by going there. But see what happened! Oh Mother, Mother! Why couldn't you learn? Clerise, why couldn't you stop acting that way?"

Then I thought of the many times when, as a little girl, I heard my father utter the same words in anger or frustration "Clerise, when will you learn?"

My father did not dislike the Juins. He only wanted to be his own man, to set limits of privacy within his home, to assert a measure of autonomy in a society where he was forced into dependency. I realized that my mother's goals were not different. She struggled in her own way.

When Rose-Marie called some time later, I agreed to meet her in a park, on neutral ground.

Bright and breezy summer morning
Suburban USA
Playground on a hill
Two little girls playing
Squeals of delight
Swings, slides, spring horses
Monkey bars
Water fountain
Wet shirts
Fun and games… "pretending"
Picnic in the park
Bright colored ball
in basketball court
Running, jumping
Songs and laughter
Walking back home
over the bridge
Flowers in the sewer
Rock throwing in the stream
Swimming classes
Art courses
… and I thought of Clerise.

It was like a typical day in Les Cayes, warm but not hot, a time to be outdoors.

ACKNOWLEDGEMENTS

In the nearly twenty-five years and many revisions that it took to complete this book, Clerise became a familiar presence in our household. My children grew with her, from childhood and adolescence to adulthood as I worked on the novel or temporarily set it aside. While solely responsible for the contents, I thank the community of fellow writers, readers, friends, and family members for the advice and support that they generously provided, and particularly:

The Washington Independent Writers, for the resources, information, and networking opportunities provided in the early days of the project; the women of the Sherwood Writers group, for enjoyable and productive exchanges, as we shared, critiqued, and discussed our work; Ellen Roberts and Patricia Elam for their valuable advice; Diana N'Diaye and Brooke Leto, for their comments and encouragement; Richard Currey whose words of praise for the segment entitled *Haitian Memories* helped sustain a struggling author; Mary Paden, a wonderful editor; Maggie Gladson, Darah Smith, and the WALA network; Franck Laraque, and Tontongi (Eddy Toussaint) of Trilingual Press.

For giving a home to my writings about Les Cayes, I thank the publishers of *Pikliz.com*, *Haiti Observateur*, *Haiti en Marche*, *lavilledescayes.com*, and *Le Nouvelliste*; and the readers who provided information and encouragement, as well as the impetus to complete the project – you are too many to be named individually, but each one of your comments was appreciated.

I am also grateful for the support of:

Maryse, Loulouse, Marie-Lisette, my childhood buddies, who helped sharpen memories and fine-tune details in the later phase of the project;

Pouppy, my brother, the "baby" of the family, who stayed the longest in Les Cayes, and provided a wealth of background information about the later years of the story, as well as comments on the early version of the manuscript; Dominique, for those seashells from Gelée; other siblings and family members who also learned to know Clerise, offered feedback, or were available to provide any needed assistance or information; Marie-Jo, cousin and sister-friend, whose support and assistance proved invaluable in getting the project off the ground;

My children, for whom this story of Les Cayes was initially written in English: Mike and Sophia, for their creative ideas and suggestions; and Sarah, who brought interest, optimism, and multicultural insight as she read various manuscript revisions;

Teddy, my husband, friend, and first-line editor, for all the time and memories that we shared as the story took a life of its own.

Above all, I acknowledge the legacy of all the Clerises at the African core of the Haitian family tree.

SELECTED LIST OF BIBLIOGRAPHICAL SOURCES

Armand, Pierre. *L'Armée d'Haïti et les evénements de 1957*. Port-au-Prince: Les Editions Samba, 1988.

Barthelemy, Gérard. *Le pays en dehors*. Port-au-Prince: Deschamps, 1989.

Bellegarde-Smith, Patrick. *Haiti: The Breached Citadel*. San Francisco: Westview Press, 1990.

Bouchereau, Madeleine Sylvain. *Haiti et ses femmes*. Port-au-Prince: Les Presses Libres, 1957.

Charlier, Etienne. *Aperçu historique sur la formation de la nation haïtienne*. Port-au-Prince: Les Presses Libres, 1954.

Condé, Georges. *La ville des Cayes*. Port-au-Prince: Imprimeur II, 1996.

Dorsainville, J.C. *Histoire d'Haiti*. Port-au-Prince: Deschamps, 1969.

Dorsainville, Roger. *Marche arrière*. Québec: Collectif Paroles, 1986.

Ferguson, James. *Papa Doc, Baby Doc: Haiti and the Duvaliers*. Oxford: Blackwell, 1988.

Fouchard, Jean. - *Les marrons de la liberté*. Port-au-Prince: Deschamps, 1988.

———. *Les marrons du syllabaire*. Port-au-Prince: Deschamps, 1988.

Gaillard, Roger. - *Charlemagne Péralte le Caco*. Port-au-Prince: Imprimerie le Natal, 1982.

————. *La guérilla de Batraville*. Port-au-Prince: Imprimerie le Natal, 1983.

James, C.L. R. *The Black Jacobins: Toussaint L'Ouverture and the San Domingo Revolution*. New York: Vintage, 1963.

Métraux, Alfred. *Le Vaudou haïtien*. Paris: Gallimard, 1971.

Neptune Anglade, Mireille. *L'autre moitié du développement*. Port-au-Prince/Montréal: Éditions des Alizés & ERCE, 1986.

Pascal Trouillot, Ertha. *Analyse de la législation revisant le statut de la femme mariée*. Port-au-Prince: Deschamps, 1983.

Rigaud, Milo. *Secrets of Vodou*. San Francisco: City Lights, 1985.

Soukar, Michel. *Un Général parle*. Port-au-Prince: Imprimerie Le Natal, 1986.

Trouillot, Michel-Rolph. *Les racines historiques de l'État duvaliérien*. Port-au-Prince: Deschamps, 1986.

www.ingramcontent.com/pod-product-compliance
Lightning Source LLC
Chambersburg PA
CBHW071154020726
47502CB00002B/408